What Reviewers Say About Gabrielle Goldsby's Fiction

"*Such a Pretty Face* [is] a delightful read with solid storytelling and engaging characters. The reader is immediately drawn into one woman's journey of self-discovery...Mia's story...is written with deep emotion and Goldsby brings the reader into her painful transformation...deftly." – *Lambda Book Report*

In *Such a Pretty Face* "...Goldsby, skillfully mixing sharp humor and incisive insight, sorts out...emotional issues with solid plotting— and plenty of hot sex on the side." – *Q Syndicate*

"Child molestation, blazing gunplay, menacing double-crosses, ruthless cover-ups, a suspect suicide, sleazy cop corruption, and trafficking in young children—this is one gritty police procedural. Detective Foster Everett is battling alcohol and relationship demons, not getting along with her female superior, and uneasy being a dyke in a macho office. She and her supportive male partner become enmeshed in a stomach-churning case involving the filming and distribution of kiddie porn, a situation that reaches into the highest ranks of the police department—and runs right into the fabled "wall of silence" that shields law enforcement misdeeds. Goldsby's zip-quick novel is packed with a multidimensional cast of complex characters, most prominently lesbian bar bouncer Riley Meideros, an aloof woman with unexpected emotional depth for whom Foster inevitably falls. The romance element sizzles with its own tension, but the crackling appeal of this gripping mystery lies in how ably Goldsby depicts unsettling sex crimes and immoral police conduct." – *Q Syndicate*

"If you like cop stories, this one should be at the top of your 2008 reading list. It's just terrific." – *Lesbian News*

"*Wall of Silence* is a cracking goo~~d read.~~" ~~– L. Wood~~

"The novel is perfectly plotted~~…~~ ~~…~~nd consistently accurate tone, which ~~…~~ ~~…~~an mysteries." – *Midwest Book Rev*~~iew~~

By the Author

Such a Pretty Face

Wall of Silence, Second Edition

Remember Tomorrow

Visit us at www.boldstrokesbooks.com

REMEMBER
TOMORROW

by

Gabrielle Goldsby

2008

REMEMBER TOMORROW
© 2008 By Gabrielle Goldsby. All Rights Reserved.

ISBN 10: 1-60282-026-0
ISBN 13: 978-1-60282-026-5

This Trade Paperback Original Is Published By
Bold Strokes Books, Inc.
New York, USA

First Edition: August 2008

Credits
Editors: Cindy Cresap and Stacia Seaman
Production Design: Stacia Seaman
Cover Design By Sheri (graphicartist2020@hotmail.com)

Acknowledgments

My thanks and undying gratitude to the following:

Mecheal W—for being my rock when all else fails.

Linda aka Proofreader—for your boundless knowledge of the English language.

Nikki G—for your endless enthusiasm.

Cindy Cresap—for your professionalism and patience.

My fellow BSB authors—for setting the bar and continuing to raise it.

Len Barot—for your continued trust and support.

My readers—for giving me so much of your time.

My family—for being my family of birth and my family of choice.

Dedication

To the Canady, Goldsby, and Sumler families—for making me who I am.

CHAPTER ONE

"Yₒᵤ need to do something about my beard." Cees Bannigan stalked into the office of her executive producer Miranda Hamilton and shut the door.

Miranda looked up, peered around her dual monitors, and squinted at Cees's chin. "Sorry, what's this about a beard? I'm sure that little gal down in makeup can pluck those right out," Miranda said in what Cees was sure was supposed to be an understanding tone.

"Her name is Edith, and I don't need any plucking," Cees said even as her hand went to her chin for affirmation. "I'm talking about that asinine actor you hired to play my boyfriend." Cees slumped into an office chair across from Miranda.

"Vance?" Since it wasn't really a question, Cees didn't answer. Adding Vance Flowers to the show had been Miranda's idea. When the ratings jumped subsequent to his arrival, she had made huge brownie points with The Suits in New York. The problem was, as Cees often pointed out in private, Vance was a klutz and an idiot. An idiot who had to be supervised at all times. Lucky for them, Portland, Oregon, was not the hotbed of the television production industry that New York was. Subsequently, they had their pick of college students willing to be the guy's servant for class credits and a few free meals.

"I hired him to be your co-host, not your boyfriend," Miranda said.

"Then shouldn't he know how to fix things, this being a DIY show and all? By the way, my *boyfriend* would sure as hell know how to pronounce my name. If he calls me Cease one more time I'm going to pop him one."

"Come on, Cees, people must do that to you all the time. If you didn't already have a fan base, New York would have asked you to change the spelling to Case."

"And I would have asked them when hell was freezing over."

Miranda nodded her touché. "What's he done now?"

"He keeps asking me out," Cees growled, and the smile threatening the corners of Miranda's mouth disappeared.

"You mean he doesn't know you're gay? I'd have thought someone here would have mentioned something by now."

"The people that know have been with me for years. Half of them worked for my dad before I got the show. I doubt they would tell him I'm gay, but I will if no one else does."

Miranda leaned back. "Is that a good idea, Cees? Have we known him long enough to know if we can trust him?"

"I met him two months after I met you." The alert look in Miranda's eye told Cees that she wasn't the only one who remembered how angry she had become when Miranda had informed her that a new co-host had been chosen without her input. "Besides, I'm not exactly in the closet. I just don't advertise."

Miranda shook her head vigorously. "I, of all people, would never suggest that you hide who you are."

"Everyone knows you're gay, Cees. You've always been straightforward about that. We aren't asking you to keep your relationships secret. We both know what would happen if it became common knowledge. There would be constant speculation about who you were sleeping with and—"

"I'm not in a relationship, and it's my business who I sleep with."

"Well, I couldn't agree with you more since *I'm* the one you're sleeping with, but do me a favor?" Cees waited impatiently for Miranda to continue. "Let me talk to Vance first. I'll explain to him that workplace romances are now being frowned on by the higher-ups."

Cees raised her eyebrows and Miranda laughed. "All they care about are ratings, but Vance doesn't have to know that."

"All right, but if he asks me to dinner one more time…"

"Can't blame the man for having good taste. I asked you out too, remember?"

How could she forget? The restaurant had been nearly empty and the hand that had settled comfortably on her thigh during their conversation had crept a bit higher than was proper. When fingers had pressed against the seam of her khakis forcing her clitoris flat, Cees had grabbed the table edge for support. The bill had been paid quickly, and the drive to Miranda's apartment would have afforded her a speeding ticket if she had been caught. The sex was good, but the question in the back of Cees's head had been there distracting her, keeping her from losing herself in Miranda's sweet femininity.

Why was she having sex with someone she didn't love? The answer was as painful now as it had been when it first came to her. Because the woman she loved had made it quite clear that there would never be a future for them. Sleeping with Miranda allowed her to forget that fact, at least some of the time.

"You know what I mean," Cees said. "We don't know if he can keep a secret."

"So what if he can't? At this point will it really matter?" Cees folded her arms across her chest and studied Miranda. She was sure that Miranda enjoyed the sex, but there was something about her that made it very apparent that they would never have more than that. Cees, never one for uninvolved sex in the past, found that she was grateful. She wasn't available for more than that. Not yet.

"It matters. The show is geared toward—"

"I know. Single women who are first-time home owners."

What Cees didn't say was, this was nothing new; the show was geared toward women long before Miranda and the national contract that put an extra zero on the end of Cees's salary. Not that Cees cared about money. Her wardrobe for the show—fitted T-shirt, blue jeans, and boots—was pretty much her costume for life. The only changes Miranda had insisted on had to do with tailoring, fabric, and color. Although she thought the whole thing ridiculous, Cees never complained when the T-shirts changed from beefy cotton to a fine Egyptian cotton, nor did she complain when the plain white started to become pastels. She did draw the line when they tried to get her to wear pedal pushers during the pool house episode.

"Come around here. Let me show you something."

Cees reluctantly stood and walked around Miranda's desk to peer at the dual computer monitors.

"See this?" Miranda pulled up a graph. "These are your ratings when you were just a local show." Miranda pointed with a pen at the second screen. "These are the ratings of your closest competitor. Not even close. A full fifteen percent lower than yours."

Cees had heard all this before. Without those ratings she wouldn't have been picked up nationally.

"Now look here." Miranda pointed. "These are our ratings now that you're with Vance, and here are your nearest competitors." Miranda pointed to two colored lines.

"Twenty-five percent difference," Cees said.

"Yup. The show is doing great. The asinine actor is a big hit."

"I don't get it. With who? I thought you said the show appealed to single women."

"True, but you always had that fan base locally. We expected you to keep that on the national level, but we were also counting on the housewives and the thirtysomething hetero males."

"Hence the beard," Cees said with resignation.

"Wait." Miranda held up her hands. "Your sexuality is not an issue. We only asked that you be discreet. At no time have we implied a relationship between you and Vance."

"I know you haven't, but…I think people think we are. I can't figure out why."

"You're gorgeous, smart, and capable. It took the lesbian community all of two episodes to decide that if you weren't a 'sister,' you damn well should be. The straight women want to be like you, and the straight men just want you."

"What about the gay men?"

Miranda frowned as if thinking about it. "They probably actually watch the show for the DIY tips."

Cees smiled, and Miranda stood up and hooked a hand around Cees's waist to pull her closer even as she looked toward her office door to make sure that it was closed. "When will I see you again? You haven't been by to pet the kitty in almost a month." Miranda's voice was low as her lips tickled the line of Cees's jaw. "Petting the kitty" was Miranda's unoriginal term for having sex. Today it seemed even more crass than usual.

"Bastian wouldn't miss *you* if you were gone for a few weeks, as long as someone came around to feed him," Cees said, purposely misunderstanding.

Miranda laughed. "He's a Siamese. Very few of them come without attitude."

"Miranda…don't you ever wonder what it would be like to have someone other than Bastian to come home to? I mean permanently?" Miranda released Cees's waist and tucked the tendril of hair that had escaped her ponytail. Cees pushed her glasses up the bridge of her nose, a nervous habit that she wished would get edited from some of the takes, but Miranda said people loved.

"Yeah, I've thought about it. My parents would love for me to settle down and have kids. Preferably with a man, but I think they would be happy just to see me with a family of my own."

"So you have considered it?" Cees was surprised, and her

voice showed it. Why was she asking Miranda all this anyway? She knew why. The doctor's appointment this morning had filled her with joy and fear at the same time. Although she had resigned herself to a lifetime of sleeping alone, her body still yearned for the promise of several minutes of pleasure and a few moments where pain was forgotten.

Miranda kissed Cees hard on the mouth. "Of course I have, sweetie. I'm thirty-six years old. Biology forces me to consider it, but the thought doesn't linger." As if sensing the sinking feeling that her comments gave Cees, Miranda rushed to explain. "I've spent a long time getting to this position. They put me here to see what I would do with it. If the show is successful, and I know it will be, there'll be other opportunities. I couldn't ask anyone to ride that roller coaster with me right now. Maybe in a few years." Miranda brushed her lips against Cees's neck. "You should seriously think about stopping by tonight," she whispered, and Cees could hear the desire in her voice.

"I can't." The words came without thought, without hesitation, and Cees blinked after she realized she had spoken them. Why couldn't she? Why was she holding back? There was no question that Miranda wanted her, and based on the dampness of her own underwear, Cees couldn't deny being physically attracted to her as well.

"Can't, or don't want to?" The skin between the perfect brows was bunched and angry looking.

Cees stepped out of the circle of her arms. "I just...can't."

"Why not? We both enjoyed the sex last time, correct?"

Cees agreed.

"So what's the big deal? I'm not asking you to marry me, just a little lick and tickle." Miranda laughed, but Cees bit her bottom lip. *A little lick and tickle? Was that all it was to her? Of course that was all it was, and if you were honest with yourself, that's all it was to you too.*

"No, it's just that I promised Lilly we would have dinner tonight. We've both been so busy we haven't had time to catch up in a few months." *Stop being such a wimp and tell her the truth, for God's sake.*

"Call her up and tell her you're tired." Miranda's voice had taken on a seductive, wheedling tone.

"Ah no, sorry. I've already broken off too many dates with Lil." This was the truth. Lilly had started prodding at places that still ached, and it just seemed easier not to call her than to be bulldogged about why she was having sex with someone she had no future with.

"Are you sure I can't convince you?" Cees thought Miranda was going to give her a quick kiss, but the expected peck was turned into a long, crotch-pulsating kiss. Cees sighed and allowed herself to be engulfed by the heat. A night with Miranda would be delicious. She would come and she would sleep, but the next morning she would wake up hungry for something she would never have again. *Sometimes a taste is just enough to create a craving.* Cees was so tired of craving that she had decided to give up altogether. Miranda wouldn't like it. Hell, *she* didn't like it, but it would be better for everyone involved.

Cees reluctantly pushed Miranda back by the shoulders. With her eyes still closed she said, "I need to talk to you about something."

As if scripted, the phone chose that moment to ring and Miranda quickly walked around the desk and picked it up. She studied Cees's face as she said, "Miranda Hamilton's office." If there was a trace of breathlessness or arousal evident in her voice, Cees missed it entirely. Miranda listened for a moment and then sat down and began rifling in her desk drawer. "Oh, hi there. Thanks for getting back to me." She looked up at Cees, rolled her eyes, pointed at the phone, and mouthed "sorry." Cees smiled and started for the door. Just before she closed it behind her, she glanced back. Miranda was not only attractive and good in bed, she would never question Cees's inability to give her whole heart. Aside from their working together, the situation was perfect. So why was she thinking about ending it with her? The answer was as clear as the hopelessness of ever having a serious relationship with Miranda. Cees couldn't give her heart to anyone. Not now, perhaps not ever again. But just because she couldn't, didn't mean she didn't want to.

❖

There were always so many people milling around the studio at any one time that Cees simply pasted an amiable smile on her face as she passed each shadow. Part of her was glad that she hadn't had to have the first of at least two difficult conversations with Miranda. When the time came, she had no doubt that Miranda would support her decisions. She wouldn't be happy about either of them, but she would be supportive in the end. It was New York she had to worry about.

The thought had no sooner crossed her mind than two figures that she vaguely recognized as wearing suits walked past her toward Miranda's office. Miranda was good about sending out warning memos when The Suits from New York were in town so that language and attire could be modified. This was either a surprise visit, which was never a good thing, or...

"Excuse me?"

Cees mouthed "shit" and wiped the scowl from her face before turning around. Suits meant hours of fake laughing, dinner at expensive restaurants, and sometimes drinks after, when all she wanted to do was go home, put on some soft music, and sleep.

The female flashed a badge so fast that Cees wouldn't have been able to read it even if she had been close enough. She introduced herself and her partner as detectives with the Portland Police Department. "We were told we could find Cease Bannigan up here," the male detective said.

"You've found me. It's Cees. Pronounced like Casey without the *Y*." The two detectives shared a startled look. "What can I help you with?"

"Is there someplace private we can talk?"

Cees pushed her glasses up the bridge of her nose. "My office is the last one on the right."

Cees followed the broad back of the male police officer toward her office. "Have a seat." Cees sat on the edge of her desk and waited for the two officers to situate themselves on the couch. Unless she needed a nap, she rarely came into this room "What's this about, detectives?"

"Arieanna Simon."

Cees straightened, her back cracking audibly in the silent room. When was the last time she had heard that name mentioned? Over a year at least. Cees's lips parted, but no sound came out. And just like that, pain flooded her chest.

"What happened?" Cees asked.

"She's in the hospital, Ms. Bannigan."

"In the hospital?" Cees repeated automatically. She wasn't aware that the tears had begun to fall until after they were already sliding down her face. The female detective, Cees couldn't remember her name, steered her toward the couch, and her larger partner stood up to give her space. Cees sat with her hands between her legs, looking down at the floor.

"Is she all right? What happened to her?" Cees looked back and forth between the two detectives, trying to gauge the seriousness of the situation by the expressions on their faces.

"She was in a car accident. Her landlord let us into her apartment. He mentioned she lived alone and hadn't had visitors in months." Cees's mind cleared enough to recognize the question buried within his statement, but she wasn't sure how to answer him. "We found your name on her medical power of attorney."

"My name? Are you sure? I haven't spoken with Arie in well over a year." Cees remembered the shock of dialing Arie's phone number only to have found it had been disconnected with no forwarding number. She had dialed it three times, pushing each number carefully, despite the fact that Arie's number had been programmed into her speed dial. That final blow, dealt without a word, had left her curled into a fetal position.

Why would Arie give her power of attorney without mentioning it to her, and why wouldn't she change it after they split? She wasn't even sure she understood what power of attorney meant. Seventeen months ago, it might not have surprised her. She knew that Arie had listed her as beneficiary for her life insurance policy because they had filled them out together, on a Sunday morning while watching *Scooby-Doo* and sipping coffee from the same mug. But when open enrollment had come around the following year, she had changed her beneficiary back to her best friend Lilly Nguyen. "Arie was my lover, but I wasn't even sure she was still in town."

The two officers must have communicated with a look, because it was the female who spoke. "The car accident was last Wednesday. A young mother and her child stalled in the middle of Skyline road. They were just exiting their car when Ms. Simon came around the bend. She swerved to avoid them, lost control of her SUV, and flipped it."

A vision of a crumpled and bleeding Arie assailed Cees's senses. Cees dropped her head and willed herself to continue to breathe.

"Is she going to be okay? Wednesday was six days ago. Why are you just now coming to tell me this?"

"She was lucky. She slipped in and out of consciousness, but she was calling for someone when they brought her in, but the ambulance folks garbled the name. We had nothing to go on until we found the documents in her home."

"She was calling for… me?"

"We think so. We couldn't find any other references to friends in her apartment." The male officer made no effort to hide the fact that this surprised him. "Ms. Simon has no other family?"

"No. She told me her grandfather died right before she moved to Portland. We always joked about the fact that we worked so well together because we were both orphans. Wait, why are you asking me these questions and not her?"

"She's been—traumatized by the accident." The female detective's answer was hesitant. Cees recognized that hesitancy. She had hoped to never hear it again. It meant there was more that wasn't being said. That "more" was never good news. It meant that a seasoned professional was trying to spare her feelings. It meant things didn't look good. It meant, "I'm trying to spare you pain even though I'm busy." It meant, "I feel sorry for you, but my job is not to give you unfounded hope."

"Her medical power of attorney is why we're here, but we were hoping you could clear up some things that we found odd." The female cop laughed and looked at her partner. "We've been doing this so long that we see inconsistencies where none exist, but while we were trying to find Ms. Simon's family, we found a marked lack of...connections. No job, no relatives, no friends other than yourself that we could find."

"No job? For how long?"

"The last form of employment we found was when she worked with you. It took some digging, but the lawyer that drew up the power of attorney assured us that Ms. Simon has always been well off, even before her grandfather left her everything."

Cees had a theory that after the first blush of their romance had faded, Arie had begun to regret her job as the show's expert on landscape architecture. Now that theory was out the window.

"I wish I could help you, but as I said before, I didn't know about any of this until you told me." There was another long, uncomfortable moment.

"So you don't know anything about the concessions in her power of attorney?"

"Arie and I never discussed a power of attorney. We barely discussed—" Cees stopped speaking. These two weren't interested in the life she had with Arie.

"We don't mean to sound like we're grilling you over this because we aren't. It's just, she's also got some strange stipulations in it."

"Strange how?"

"If she's ever deemed unable to care for herself, her powers of attorney stipulates that she not be left on life support, which is pretty common, but what's unusual is that she also stipulates that she does *not* want to be left in your care. She is to be put in a home if she is ever deemed incapable of taking care of herself."

Snippets of what the male cop was saying filtered through Cees's conscious. *"...does not want to be left in your care. Deemed incapable of taking care."* Cees stood. Dread spread its black wings, descended, and sank its claws into her chest. Her body wavered. She had been here before. Heard similar words uttered.

Not again. She didn't think she could survive it again.

CHAPTER TWO

There were so many reasons why she shouldn't be sitting in the parking lot of Oregon Health Sciences Hospital. The least important was the fact that Arie had made it quite clear that she didn't want, didn't need, Cees in her life. Yet here she sat, watching as people entered the hospital and hoping that the end of visiting hours would forestall her from seeing Arie. Cees tightened her jaw and forced herself out of the cocoon of the truck. Normally, she couldn't wait to get out of the huge vehicle she had nicknamed the Monster for its obscenely long truck bed and its bottomless gas tank. She was used to parking at the far corner of lots so as not to block anyone. Today she was grateful; the inconvenience afforded her a little more time to ready herself for the inevitable meeting with Arie. Each step toward the hospital was punctuated by the pounding of her heart. Two double doors slid open. She blinked and walked inside.

Once, when she was young, her father had called her into the living room of an old dilapidated home to show her an ant colony that the crew had uncovered.

The two of them had watched as the worker ants mindlessly carried miniscule white eggs from one place to another. He had explained that the queen's sole job was to have babies, and the workers were to care for those eggs and to bring back food for the queen.

The automatic way that they worked with no thank-you,

no other sense of purpose, had been too much for Cees's young mind to understand. She had burst into tears, much to her father's chagrin. Hospitals always reminded her of that ant colony, and her father. The white-coated workers mindlessly, thanklessly shuttling from one place to another in an attempt to save lives.

Cees had spent a lot of time in a place like this. The scent, though not exactly the same, was similar enough to bring memories of her father's last days, his once strong body devoured by both the cancer and the cure, and finally, the blank look when the medicine that took away his pain took away everything else. She'd been there when he had taken his last breath, a surprisingly strong inhalation that was never released, or if it was, Cees didn't see it. Worst of all, she remembered the relief and joy. He was no longer in pain, no longer a prisoner of his own body. Her relief was soon overcome by a painful realization: She would never see him again. Never hold his hand, never again whisper how proud she was of him for fighting. A very selfish feeling of loneliness had remained.

Cees waited until the clerk ended her call. "Hi, my name is Cees Bannigan. I'm here to see Arieanna Simon." The words flowed like there was no obstacle, and the efficient clerk typed something into her computer and looked up at Cees. "I'll need to call her doctor."

"If visiting hours are—"

"One moment." The clerk dialed a few numbers and, speaking efficiently, explained that there was a visitor to see Arieanna Simon. She hung up the phone and told Cees that Dr. Parrantt would be up to see her momentarily.

Cees turned toward the bank of couches shoehorned into a small waiting room and wished desperately for a cup of coffee. She sat down and braced her elbows on her knees. The irony of the situation hadn't escaped her notice. Just when she felt ready to take a step forward alone, a bump appeared in the middle of the path. A spark of anger threatened, but she pushed it away. She couldn't blame Arie for this. From what the police had told her, Arie hadn't asked to see her. She had come on her own because she had no choice. She would make sure that Arie was getting the best care and then she would—what? Leave her to recover on her own?

"Ms. Bannigan?" Cees stood up, her hand going out automatically toward the man standing in front of her. He looked as if he had just awakened from a nap; his thin sweater and slacks were only slightly less rumpled than his bushy eyebrows. A white lab coat would have made Cees feel better. She had seen plenty of those in her lifetime, and they had always made her feel like there was someone with better sense than her to take care of the situation.

"The police called to tell me you were on your way."

"How is she? They told me she was in a car accident," Cees said.

Dr. Parrantt looked at Cees for a long moment over the rim of his glasses. He sighed as if tired and said, "Come with me."

"Dr. Parrantt, please, I just want to see Arie."

"You'll see her in a moment, but first I'd like to—" His words were interrupted by a young male nurse.

"Dr. Parrantt, we have a problem with—"

"Dr. Davis is in the lounge. Get him." The shocked look on the young male nurse's face was enough to tell Cees that this was not Dr. Parrantt's normal reaction. Her anxiety morphed into fear.

The doctor did not slow his pace until he opened a door marked with his name. Cees nervously took in the desk clutter and the massive number of awards and certificates on the man's wall as she closed the door behind herself.

Dr. Parrantt flipped a switch on the wall, illuminating four boxes covered with films of some sort. He went quiet for a moment and then looked back at Cees with one bushy eyebrow raised.

"Well, what do you see?" he asked.

This man must be hard on new doctors. Following his train of thought was next to impossible. Cees looked at the film smudges of white and black and then back at Dr. Parrantt.

"Am I supposed to know what this is?"

"This is a scan of Ms. Simon's brain. This is a textbook CAT of a healthy brain."

"Oh, okay." Cees stifled her impatience and obediently stared at the two pieces of film.

"You build things. Anything look incongruous to you?"

Cees looked at him again. He had either recognized her from the show, or the police had filled him in. He had given her no indication that he recognized her when they had first been introduced. Cees stepped closer and scowled at the image. "They look the same. So her brain is healthy?" Cees bit the inside of her cheek to keep herself from screaming, *Why the hell you didn't just tell me that in the first place?*

"She was brought in unconscious. When she came to, she was so disoriented that we were afraid she might have internal bleeding. We did a full physical, CAT scan, blood work. Other then a minor concussion and some other injuries caused by her seat belt and airbag, we found no serious injuries. Besides the car accident, has Ms. Simon suffered any traumatic events recently?"

"I don't…I haven't seen her in several months. We argued. Doctor, why are you asking me these questions? Why don't you ask her? She would be able to give you more accurate information than I could."

Dr. Parrantt sighed. "That's why I brought you in here. I'm afraid Ms. Simon can't give us any information. She doesn't remember anything before the accident."

Shock silenced Cees for several long moments. "That's not—uncommon, is it? You said yourself she had a concussion."

"I can't swear that the concussion isn't what's causing Ms. Simon's memory loss, but I can tell you that contrary to what popular media would have us believe, this kind of thing is very unusual."

"How unusual?"

"I've never had a case like it, and I've been practicing medicine over twenty years. I've consulted with several of my colleagues, and I'm afraid I just don't know."

"But she will get better, right? She'll remember eventually?"

"Ms. Bannigan, I wish I could give you a more concrete answer, but I can't. I don't really know what's causing this. Anything I tell you is nothing more than an educated guess."

"All right, I'll take your educated guess."

"I believe that something caused Arieanna to forget. Whether it was physical or mental or both, I can't say. She appears to be suffering from a dissociative fugue, which is why I asked about potential stressors in her life."

Cees was shaking her head. "But she must remember something. The police told me she was calling my name when they brought her in."

It was obvious to Cees that Dr. Parrantt was choosing his words carefully. "Yes, she was, but when she returned to full consciousness, she couldn't tell us who it was she'd been calling for."

Air flew from Cees's lungs. She tried to catch his eyes with her own to steady herself. "She doesn't remember who I am?"

It was the sympathetic look on the doctor's face that caused Cees's tears to well moments before he spoke the words that caused them to fall. "I don't think you understand what I've been trying to tell you. Arieanna doesn't even remember who *she* is, Ms. Bannigan."

❖

Arie's eyes weren't open, but Cees could tell by the way her chest rose and fell unevenly that she was awake.

"Arie, I could come back if you aren't up for a visitor?"

Cees pushed her glasses up on her nose and contemplated moving closer to the bed only to find herself arrested by Arie's wary doe brown eyes.

"Hi." Cees broke the silence between them first. Arie's only reply was a blink. "Are you...should I call someone?"

"No." The word sounded like paper being dragged over wood.

"Okay," Cees said, disappointed that she wouldn't have anyone with her for moral support.

"Who?" Arie had the same shy curious look she'd had in the past when meeting someone new.

A vise clamped down on Cees's throat as she struggled to introduce herself to the woman she had once loved so fervently. "My name is Cees Bannigan." *There now, that wasn't so hard, was it?* Cees thought. What *was* hard was meeting Arie's eyes. Cees had thought she had begun to forget and forgive. She was wrong.

"Now, who are you to me?" Arie rasped. The words were guttural but clear. Even though she had expected the question, Cees was still speechless.

"We used to be...lovers," Cees said and wondered how what they were could be summed up in such simple terms.

"Used to be?" Sharp eyes took in Cees's casual attire and settled on the logo at the breast of Cees's shirt. Heat settled over Cees's face as her nipples predictably hardened. Cees didn't remember Arie's gaze being so piercing.

"Yes, we...ended our relationship almost two years ago." Cees finally found a comfortable place to settle her eyes.

"Cees Bannigan?"

Cees jumped at the full use of her name. "Yes?"

"Would you mind sitting down? It's hurting my neck to look up at you."

"Oh yeah, sorry." Cees turned one way, then another until

she spotted a chair in the corner, picked it up, and moved it next to Arie's bed. She tried to meet her eyes again, but ended up looking down into her own lap. Her chest was rising and falling as if she had just run a few miles. Who was she kidding? It wasn't the chair. She had tool belts that weighed more than that chair.

"Thank you. Did they tell you that I don't—"

"Yes," Cees interrupted, not quite ready to hear Arie utter the words "I don't remember you," even though she had already said as much earlier.

"Did they tell you what happened to me?"

"I was told that you swerved to avoid hitting a stalled car and flipped your Jeep."

Arie nodded again. "The police said they couldn't find any relatives."

"You told me your parents died when you were young, and your grandfather died just before we met." Cees smiled wanly. "It was one of the things we had in common."

Arie went quiet. "Why did we—break up? What happened to us?" Arie's fine dark curls had been left to mat against her temples. Her face, though long and wan from weight loss, still managed to cause Cees's pulse to quicken.

"You said we weren't right for each other." Cees felt her back stiffen as she was forced to answer.

"And you didn't agree?"

"It was a long time ago. It doesn't matter what I thought anymore." *But it did matter, it still does.* The old hurt and anger returned, pushing any remaining vestiges of attraction from her mind. *What would have been so bad that we couldn't have worked things out?* Cees forced the question to the back of her consciousness where it had lived for nearly two years. Arie would not be able to answer anyway.

"Still, I would like to know what happened. If you don't mind."

Cees hated the way Arie hesitated when she spoke. Even

after things had started to go bad between them, there had always been a surety of purpose in Arie's voice. A certainty that she knew what she wanted.

"I don't…we fought. You told me you wanted me to leave. I haven't heard from you since."

Arie's dark eyes raked across Cees's face. Cees felt the first stirrings of real discomfort. The kind of discomfort she still felt when meeting new people, despite being on television.

Cees realized that part of the problem was that she couldn't read this Arie. Even in the early stages of their past relationship, before things went bad and Cees was forced to realize there would be no happily-ever-after for them, she had sensed that Arie was holding back. What was that saying? You never ask a question you aren't prepared to get the answer to? She hadn't forced Arie to tell her what was bothering her because she was too afraid of what the answer would be. She had been a coward and she had ended up alone anyway.

"The police tell you that you were named in my medical power of attorney?"

"Yes, they told me."

Arie opened her mouth, closed it, and then frowned. "Why would I explicitly say that you had to put me in a home?"

"I'm afraid I can't tell you that either. Arie, you have to understand. I didn't even know you had a medical power of attorney."

Arie seemed to think about that. "Maybe I knew you would come if something happened to me."

Cees turned up her lips in what she hoped would pass for a smile. "You couldn't possibly have known that."

"You're here now, aren't you?"

Cees had no answer, and Arie went on as if she hadn't expected one. *She's afraid. Arie always got methodical when she was afraid.*

"So we had a fight and that was it? It had to be something else."

"I can only tell you what I know. One minute we were fine and the next…" Cees raised her shoulders in a shrug, but never completed the gesture. "Arie, I think I know where you're going with this but…as I told Dr. Parrantt, I don't think our breakup would have been catastrophic enough to cause your amnesia. For one thing, it happened too long ago. I'm certain you moved on with your life, as I did."

Cees read disappointment in Arie's face and knew without being told that Arie had probably been hoping that Cees could give her the answers, but instead she had only created more questions.

Guilt flooded through her and almost made her tell the truth. What she hadn't told anyone was that she had seen it coming. She had felt it when Arie had begun to keep parts of herself back. She could see it in Arie's eyes when she didn't think she was being observed—a sadness that Arie would deny anytime Cees asked her about it. Those moments had been few and far between at first. The closer they became, the more they talked about starting a family and building a future together, the more Cees could see that Arie was struggling. She hadn't forced the issue because she was afraid that whatever it was would tear them apart. She'd been right. When Cees had moved her accumulation of things out of Arie's apartment, she had hoped it would be temporary—a way to give Arie time to work out whatever was bothering her. But when Arie hadn't even called to make sure she was okay, it had hurt. And now here she was, unable to confront Arie with how much she'd hurt her. What the hell was she even doing there?

Cees had been so deep in thought, she hadn't noticed the tears until they were falling down the sides of Arie's face. "Should I go get…?"

Cees instinctively reached out and took Arie's hand. Arie jumped, much the way anyone would if a stranger grabbed their hand, but she did not pull away.

Cees stroked Arie's palm, surprised at the soft skin she found there.

"What is it?" Arie's voice sounded breathless.

"Nothing."

"No, tell me?"

"Your hands are so soft." Cees realized she had been running her thumb slowly over the inside of Arie's palm and abruptly released Arie's hand. "Your hands were always work roughened. You would rub cream in them at night so that…"A shiver coursed through Cees's body at the instant memory of those hands on her skin. *Stop it. She's been hurt, and more importantly, she has made it quite clear she doesn't want you.* The last thought, more than the sight of her former lover in a hospital bed, pushed the rising tendrils of arousal to the furthest reaches of her consciousness.

The tired, agitated look on Arie's face reminded Cees that she too was exhausted. Arie watched her stand, but didn't speak. "I should let you get some rest." When Arie didn't answer, guilt made Cees rush her words. "I'll be back tomorrow after work."

After all the heartache, tears, and angry words, time had given her a respite, and now here she was visiting the one person who still had the ability to break her heart with a look. Lilly would call her all kinds of fool if she knew where she was. Cees turned to leave.

"Thank you for coming." The words were softly spoken and brought back instant recognition of soft breaths brushing across her shoulder, neck, and breast. She wanted to look back, but she didn't. The force in her chest had begun to swell, and swallowing had no effect on it as she walked down the hall. She wished she had not told Arie she would be back tomorrow, because what she wanted to do instead was curl into a ball and protect herself from the emotional punch to the soul she knew would come as soon as Arie started to remember.

❖

Arie didn't relax until the door had closed behind the stranger. "Cees Bannigan," she said aloud, but the name felt no more familiar to her lips than the one Dr. Parrantt had told her was her own. The pain in her back and neck was her first indication that she should relax, but the throb at her temple had already begun. Past experience told her the throb would grow into a pounding that would leave her so sick she couldn't think. Nurse Kerr walked in just as she reached a trembling hand to her forehead.

"Headache?" she asked in a stern voice that didn't match the concern in her eyes.

"Not yet, but it's coming," she said while thoughts and questions rushed through her head.

The nurse was about to leave, ostensibly to get medicine, but Arie stopped her with a question.

"Did you see her?"

Nurse Kerr hesitated, walked to the end table, and poured Arie a glass of water. "Yes, I saw her come in. Very pretty."

"Pretty?" Arie thought about that word. She didn't think Cees Bannigan was pretty. Pretty didn't seem to cover the way looking at Cees's face made her feel, but she couldn't think of a word that did.

"Did seeing her spark any memories?"

Arie drank from the glass before answering. "I don't think so, but when she came in, I felt…relieved."

"What do you think that meant?"

Arie frowned as she tried to identify her own emotions. "I don't think I recognized her, but she…things felt less scary after she walked in." She thought about mentioning something else, but kept that part to herself. How could she tell Nurse Kerr that although she didn't remember her own name, her body was in a state of anticipation the whole time Cees Bannigan was in the room? It felt as if an invisible string had been attached to her chest and the tugging at it didn't cease until she laid eyes on Cees. How could she tell Nurse Kerr something like that? "I don't know if she'll be back."

Deep lines appeared around Nurse Kerr's mouth, though she

didn't quite smile. "I heard her leave her cell, work, and home phone numbers at the front desk. I think she's planning on coming back tomorrow."

"I didn't ask her anything about herself," Arie said in relief.

Nurse Kerr picked up the remote and turned on the TV. "You should take advantage of not having a roommate and watch whatever TV you want." Nurse Kerr turned the channel to the local PBS network and looked at the clock. "The new shows aren't on this channel, but you might find the reruns interesting." She grinned, and Arie could picture her with grandkids, a husband, and a large family. The thought saddened her. Not because she didn't want Nurse Kerr to have those things, but because, from what she had been told, she didn't have anyone. Just this one... friend.

"Welcome to *Cees Bannigan Your Home*." The voice brought chills to her skin as she stared into the wonderful dark eyes again, this time protected by goggles. She was walking toward the camera, and Arie's heart twisted in her chest as she said the words "welcome home."

"That's her," she breathed. "She's on a TV show?"

"Yes, she's the host."

Arie turned up the TV volume. Cees Bannigan, executive producer and host of *Cees Bannigan Your Home,* was about to show her how to replace her normal light switch with a dimmer switch.

"One of my daughters loves her show. I think she's taped every one. When I tell her she was here, she'll flip. I need to get back. Do you want me to bring you anything for the headache?" Arie shook her head and leaned forward as Cees turned off the power, tested the switch, and then used an electric screwdriver to remove the light panel. The camera moved in close and showed the side of Cees's face as she appeared to concentrate on what she was doing.

"Do you think she'll let me borrow them?" Nurse Kerr was

silent so long that Arie had to turn away from the TV to make sure she hadn't left. "The tapes, I mean?"

"I don't know…"

"Look," Arie said impatiently and then curbed her tone because in the two days since she had awakened, the nurse had gone out of her way to make sure she was as comfortable as possible. "I'm sorry, I don't mean to sound curt, but…I won't be in here forever, and she's the only one that claims to know me. I'd like to remember something about her."

"Maybe you should just ask her about herself."

Heat crept up around Arie's neck as she turned back to the TV. "I will if she comes back."

"If she doesn't, I don't think a TV show is going to tell you much about her." Nurse Kerr must have felt Arie's frustration because she relented almost instantly. "I'll see what I can do, but no promises. My girl was never one to share her toys." Arie was tempted to react petulantly, but reminded herself that Nurse Kerr was not her friend. She was here to do her job. Arie didn't even remember what her job was.

"And that's it," Cees Bannigan said as she removed her eye protection and grinned into the camera, causing Arie's heart to flutter again. The smile was definitely compelling. She wasn't sure if it was familiar, but she would certainly buy Banes Brand power drills because they kept that smile on TV. She sighed, feeling odd about the thought, but unconcerned. She'd try to talk more when…if Cees Bannigan returned tomorrow. She closed her eyes and fell asleep, but not before she began to dream—remember that smile hovering over her, teasing her, whispering words that she couldn't hear and didn't need to.

The love in those eyes spoke loud enough.

CHAPTER THREE

Cees leaned against the door of her truck, with her head against the window. Stars dotted the sky like pinpricks in perfect black silk. Cees had been standing there for several minutes trying to calm the tumult of emotion that was causing her fingers to twitch despite the fact that she had them tucked into her armpits. She should have been angry—no, livid, but instead all she felt was confusion. Her cell phone vibrated, and Cees snatched it off her hip and answered it without looking at the ID screen.

"Hi, everything okay?"

Cees felt inexplicably disappointed at hearing Miranda's voice. "Yeah, fine," Cees said, although she felt anything but fine.

"What happened? I went looking for you after my call, but you were gone."

"Ah," Cees sighed. "A friend had an accident. She's in the hospital." Miranda knew about her failed relationship with Arie, but Cees didn't feel like explaining why, after everything Arie had put her through, she had visited her in the hospital. She had yet to convince herself of her motivations, so she certainly wasn't going to be able to convince anyone else. Not yet, maybe not ever.

"So, you coming by for dinner or what?"

"Dinner or what" was usually a few bites of takeout followed by sex. Cees thought about it. She even felt her pulse quicken for a second, but the urge subsided as quickly as it had occurred. "No, I think I'm going to head home and get some rest."

"I thought you said you were going out with Lilly?"

Cees sighed. The mere thought of a conversation with Lilly drained what little energy she had left. "Thanks for reminding me. I'll call her and cancel."

"Sure I can't convince you to come over?" Miranda sounded amused. No, not just amused, surprised, which annoyed Cees enough that she almost mentioned it, but decided not to. *Lilly's right. I need to stop dating people I work with.*

"Yeah, I'm positive. I'll see you tomorrow."

Cees ended the call and immediately dialed Lilly's number. After leaving a message on Lilly's voicemail, she tossed the phone into her passenger seat and clambered into the truck. Why was she feeling so damn frazzled? *Why? How about because you just had to reintroduce yourself to a woman who had free rein of your heart and your body and then decided she didn't want either?* The thought was enough to bring on the comforts of anger, and Cees spent the final ten-minute drive home gripping the steering wheel so hard that the joints of her fingers hurt.

Cees pulled slowly into her driveway and parked behind Lilly Nguyen's roadster.

Lilly was standing outside her car squinting down at the ground.

"I guess you didn't get my message. What are you looking at?" Cees walked up and stood beside her. A tiny toy soldier had been shoved headfirst between the paved driveway and the grass.

"I could have rolled over that thing and punctured a tire."

Cees stooped and picked up the soldier. "It's just plastic, Lilly. One of my neighbor's kids was probably playing over here." She managed to keep the exasperation out of her voice because she knew it would make Lilly pouty. Ever since Lilly had come into a little money and bought a small Saturn roadster, her mind had been filled with scenarios in which her car suffered some egregious injury. Cees secretly hated riding in the car about as much as she hated the big pickup that Miranda had leased for her. She had downright refused to drive it until the large *Cees Bannigan Your Home* static sign had been replaced with a more discreet CBYH.

"You're early," Cees said as she stuck the soldier in her pocket and walked toward the front door.

"Yeah, I was already in the neighborhood. Actually, I called the set looking for you, and I was told you had a friend in the hospital. Since I'm your only friend, I started looking for my BlueCross BlueShield card. Then I started to realize that I probably wasn't in that kind of hospital." She patted her nonexistent tummy and winked. "I was probably just getting a little tuck, huh?"

Cees was surprised to hear her own bark of laughter. Lilly could be pushy and overbearing, but unlike Arie, she had never failed to be there when Cees needed her. Cees unlocked her front door and walked inside her home. The smell of fresh paint assailed her nose.

"Done painting the room?"

"Yeah, I finished yesterday." Cees dropped her keys and the soldier on an end table and walked into her small, two-bedroom house. It had taken her some time to settle on this neighborhood, and though she still missed her small apartment in the Pearl District, this felt more like home. Besides, she had spent the majority of her time at Arie's place, and once she was forced to sleep in her own bed, it became evident that the apartment left no room for growth.

Lilly slumped down on the couch and winced. Cees knew the feeling. The couch was beautiful to look at, but the floor would be more comfortable on the tailbone. Cees would have never bought it.

"Why are you still keeping this thing?" Lilly asked. "Oh my

God, please tell me you didn't have sex on this uncomfortable thing and you're hanging on to it for sentimental reasons."

"Lilly, that's just ridiculous. My relationship with Arie is over. Why would I hang on to something of hers for sentimental reasons? Besides, you're the one who said we should take it, remember?"

Of course she remembered. Lilly's memory was one of the reasons she wasn't looking forward to telling her about her visit with Arie. Lilly would never forget the pain Cees went through after the breakup, even if Cees could somehow manage to.

"I said you should take it, not keep it. The fact that she never called to ask for it back tells me you did her a favor."

To Cees's relief, Lilly began thumbing through an old magazine, giving Cees time to compose herself. Lilly wasn't the ridiculous one; she was. She was holding on to the couch for exactly the reason Lilly had guessed. This couch marked a focal point in their relationship. It was one of the last times she had felt on solid ground with Arieanna Simon.

Memories came flooding back with such cruel clarity that it took her breath away.

Cees saw herself, so eager to share her secret with Arie that she had bypassed the elevator and taken the stairs.

"Hey, you won't believe what—" Cees put her hand over her mouth when she realized that Arie was on the phone. Cees dropped a large box on the bar and walked into the small kitchen to pour a glass of wine.

"I'll drive up next week, but I'm not happy about it."

Arie ended the call and stood up too quickly. Her bearing was that of someone being forced to do something distasteful.

"You okay? Where are you going next week?" Cees asked.

"Yeah, I'm fine. That was the attorney for my grandfather's estate. He's been hounding me to come up to Seattle."

"Why Seattle?"

"Because that's where I grew up. That's also where his office is, and it seems there are some documents that I have to retrieve personally."

"Seattle? The house you grew up in is only three hours away and you never mentioned it?" Cees sipped from her glass to keep the words from coming out. "He can't just mail them?"

"I've been asking him to do that for weeks. He claims whatever it is has to be given to me in person. Anyway, it's a day trip, shouldn't take too long. What's with the wine? You have a rough day?" Arie grabbed a stool and sat down at the bar, her hands folded beneath her chin and her eyes studying Cees's face in a manner that she would have found disconcerting in the early stages of their relationship.

"Your face looks flushed. You take the stairs up?" Arie asked.

"Yeah, I didn't want to wait for the elevator."

Arie gave Cees a cocky smile. "You in that much of a hurry to see me?"

Cees returned her smile. "Oh yeah, you have no idea how much I couldn't wait to see you."

"I think I know where this is headed." Arie walked around the counter and would have kissed Cees had she not been brought up short by the small droplets of spittle that hit her face as Cees burst out laughing. Arie's mouth dropped as Cees set her glass down on the counter and bent double.

"Um, ego? I have one, remember?" Cees continued to laugh, and Arie grumbled, "Had one before my lover broke into uncontrolled fits of laughter when I tried to kiss her." Arie propped her hip against the bar, sighed, took a sip of Cees's wine, and waited for her to calm down. "You finished?" she asked. "May I kiss you now?"

"Yes, please."

Arie pulled Cees against her chest and welcomed her home with her lips; first on her neck, then her temple, and finally with a salacious kiss to the lips that never failed to make Cees's clitoris pulse in anticipation.

Arie inhaled deeply and pressed her lips to Cees's neck. "How do you manage to smell so good after working all day?"

"I stop at the gym and take a shower before I come over here."

Arie's body went still. "You're kidding."

"Yeah, I am, but I could have used a cold one today," Cees said.

"Really? Do I want to know what set you off?"

"I don't know. You might find it interesting." Cees's chuckle was threatening to become something slightly more hysterical. She couldn't remember the last time she had felt so utterly happy.

Arie leaned back and scowled. "All right, what gives? You haven't stopped laughing since you walked through the door."

"Mmm, sorry. Remember the other day when I told you I bought an impulse gift for you on the Internet?"

"Yeah. Did it come?"

"Interesting question." Cees grinned. "It's in the box."

"Thank you, sweetie, but you don't need to buy me gifts. I'll look at it later…"

Cees had worked her hands under Arie's shirt and was unbuttoning Arie's pants. Arie was breathing hard from the kiss alone. "Um, you might want to look in the box first."

"What? Right now? Can't I try it on later? I promise I'll even model it for you."

Cees started to laugh again. Arie turned the box around and looked at the lid. "Sensual Seductions Incorporated? I hope this isn't tacky underwear because…" Arie scowled as Cees hung on to the edge of the bar to keep herself upright.

"I give up. I was trying to get intimate here, and all you want me to do is try on clothes."

Arie pulled the lid off the box and fished around in the fuchsia packing paper. Cees caught her breath when Arie pulled out her gift and held it aloft like a torch. They stared wide-eyed at the enormous dildo, the kitchen light glinting off the tip of its purple head. It wasn't so much that it was long, but substantial. Cees thought Arie's hand looked miniscule wrapped around its girth. Just as the thought passed through Cees's mind, the dildo began to slip from Arie's hand. Arie tried to catch it with her free hand, but the thing flopped around fishlike for several seconds before it dropped back into the box with a loud thud. Cees dissolved into more giggles and Arie took a horrified breath. "What the hell was that?"

"I think I ordered the wrong one."

"Ya think?" Arie glanced at the box again and then at Cees. "Um, I don't suppose you can send it back?"

Cees shook her head and swallowed. "Web site says no returns."

"Oh...Oh. Yeah. That makes sense."

"I messed up so many takes at work they sent me home. I kept thinking about your face when you saw that thing, and I'd start..." Cees broke off and demonstrated exactly what she had been doing so uncontrollably since the package had been delivered. "Aren't you...you promised to try it." The look on Arie's face made it impossible for Cees to suggest that Arie keep her promise and try on her gift.

Arie scowled her answer, which sent Cees into another fit of doubled-over laughter.

Arie's boot thunked to the floor, and her hands were at the fastener of her pants by the time Cees had wiped the water from her eyes. Cees was still smiling when she asked, "What are you doing?"

Arie returned the smile and lifted a brow. "I'm trying on my gift."

"You know I was just teasing you."

"Really? So you're saying you don't want me to try it on?"

Cees didn't bother answering because Arie's socks had joined her shoes. Her shirt, bra, and pants followed. Soon her underwear was being kicked off and she was standing gloriously naked before Cees. Piercings and tattoos were almost a rite of passage in the Pacific Northwest. Arie's small stud was incredibly sedate compared to some, and yet it was such a contrast in personality that the sight always sent little fingers of pleasure up and down Cees's spine.

"Does it need to be prepared?" Arie asked.

"There's some…I think we're supposed to use the cleaning stuff they sent with it…and then we wash it."

"Okay, then…" Arie looked at the box and then at Cees. They stared at each other for several seconds before Cees removed the dildo from the box, held it aloft much as Arie had, then turned on the faucet at the kitchen sink. She awkwardly placed the dildo beneath a stream of hot water, rubbing her hand along its shaft. Arie reached into the box and pulled out a harness and two small bottles, one of which had instructions for cleaning the dildo and the other proclaimed itself to be the best lube in the world. Arie placed the two bottles along with a towel on the side of the sink. "It's not going to get much cleaner." Cees turned off the water and closed her eyes. Arie pressed the length of her naked body against Cees's backside. "You always wash your sex toys in the kitchen sink, sweetheart?" Her breath teased Cees's ear canal.

"I've never had any," Cees said into the quiet.

"Never had any what?" Cees couldn't think until Arie had unbuckled her belt, unfastened her pants, and was beneath the elastic of her underwear. There would be no hiding how aroused she was. Arie had already slipped easily between the lips of her heated sex, past the swollen part of her that always demanded attention first, and into her depths with first one finger and then another. Arie was the one who moaned because Cees could not. Arie held on to Cees's hips, and within a minute had her close to orgasm. Cees expected her peak at any moment, when Arie hissed and stopped moving. Cees straightened and Arie kissed the back of her neck and removed her fingers. Cees's muscles protested, clinging to pleasure as long as they could.

"May I ask you something?"

"Anything," Cees said, breathless again.

"Did you think about the package all day? Did it turn you on to think about having it inside you?"

"No, it turned me on imaging you wearing it."

"You should have come home earlier. You're about ready to explode." They both caught a breath as Arie's thumb grazed Cees's clitoris and her fingers reentered Cees, thrusting deep.

Cees gave a whimper and grabbed Arie's wrists to keep her from pulling out again.

"Help me put the harness on," Arie demanded and forced Cees to turn around.

Cees almost lost it when she saw the heat in Arie's eyes as she picked up the harness and dildo and handed it to Cees. Cees bent down and only fumbled slightly when she put the two together. The tremor was barely noticeable as Arie's slender foot stepped into the harness and she straightened. Cees didn't look up until she had buckled the fasteners.

Arie wrapped her arms around Cees to keep her from moving away. "Tell the truth," she whispered "You like 'em big, don't you?"

Cees chuckled at the thinly guised ploy to get her to relax. "I think it would have scared me off if I had known it was going to be this big." Arie moved close, nudging her with the dildo's heaviness, cutting off Cees's chuckle as efficiently as a finger to her lips.

"And now? Does it still scare you?"

Cees swallowed. "Yeah, a little."

"We can wait and buy something else to play with." Arie's lips grazed the side of Cees's face, tickling her earlobe and making the flesh on her arm stand up.

"We could, but…it would be a shame to, uh…"

Arie grinned and Cees felt her face flush.

Arie pulled Cees's shirt over her head and stared at her breasts and stomach for so long that Cees's face heated again.

"Arie?"

"Oh, sorry. I could look at you forever."

"You don't have to apologize. I'm just glad that I still elicit that reaction from you. If we start moving for the bedroom now, we might just make it this time." Cees held out her hand and Arie took it. They made it as far as the living room before Arie made her stop.

"Hang on a sec, let's get these off now." Arie bent down, unlaced Cees's shoes quickly, and left Cees to kick them off on her own. Cees had no sooner removed her shoes than Arie was pushing her jeans down her legs. Arie stood and Cees's eye was drawn to the dildo hanging from its harness. She could tell by the rise and fall of Arie's stomach that she was also very excited. "For the record, the day you stop garnering that response is the day they put me in the ground."

Cees smiled. "We're not going to make it to the bedroom, are we?"

"Nope, can you sit on the back of the couch?" Cees complied with Arie's request despite the fact that the bedroom was less than twenty feet away. She never questioned Arie when they made love. She had learned early on that Arie's way meant pleasure.

Arie gathered Cees's small breasts in both hands and smiled. Cees loved when Arie held her breasts this way, loved how precious and cared-for it made her feel.

"I love this part of you. I love to kiss you here." Cees groaned and closed her eyes when Arie dipped her head and began kissing reverently. When Arie finally took Cees's nipple into her mouth, Cees felt as she did when she touched Arie's softness. A pull stronger than the others, and Cees threw her head back, white lights flashed before her eyes, and the breeze from the overhead fan cooled the sudden heat of her face.

Cees rested her hands on Arie's shoulders and melted into the warmth of Arie's coaxing mouth. Cees almost screamed when Arie's fingers slid along her straining thighs to the place that was even hotter than her mouth. When Arie touched the heat she found there, Cees's eyes flew open and she looked down at Arie's face, so suffused with pleasure that she tightened her grip on Arie's shoulders; their warning that Cees was close. Arie murmured her protest, but stopped.

"Too fast?" Arie asked.

"No such thing." Cees smiled and Arie kissed her again, both hands on her thighs. And then on the side of her face. Cees's breathing slowed, but the heat at her center didn't lessen. As if sensing this, Arie kissed her neck. This, Cees knew, was the land of no return for either of them. When Arie's lips kissed her shoulders and went back to her breast, Cees closed her eyes and concentrated on the feeling. Arie stopped loving her breast, and Cees reached for the back of her head to protest.

"Try not to come yet," Arie said just before she kneeled and coaxed Cees's legs over her shoulders. Cees braced herself for the first caress of Arie's tongue. She knew from experience that Arie began gently, testing, tasting, teasing her, and then she would become ruthless and insatiable, pulling every bit of moisture from Cees until both her eyes and sex were weeping with pleasure. Four times Arie pushed her to the edge of orgasm only to withdraw and start in a new direction. At some point Cees had dug her fingers into Arie's thick hair, but it was more to stabilize herself. Arie was steering.

"Arie, wait, I'm going to…" Cees didn't finish her statement because Arie was standing in front of her. Cees held Arie's hips, urging her closer, but Arie would not be hurried. She positioned the tip of the dildo at Cees's opening, moistening and teasing Cees at the same time.

Any nervousness Cees felt initially faded and pure lust took its place. Cees moaned, and Arie had the reaction she always did, a rush of breath, a stiffening of body, and a return to control. Arie placed her hands beneath Cees's butt, lifting her from the sharp edge of the couch and pulling her onto the tip of the phallus. Cees lifted her hips and pulled Arie forward. Cees gasped at the sharp sting she felt and curled her toes against it. Arie's body became rigid with the exception of her straining back muscles.

"I'm sorry. I thought you were ready." Arie's voice was raspy with her regret. "Do you want me to stop?" Arie leaned back and lifted Cees's chin until they locked eyes. "We don't have to do this."

"I want to. I've been thinking about it all day. Can you just give me a minute to get used to it?"

The worried look finally faded from Arie's face and she smiled. Cees felt herself constrict against the tip poised at her opening.

"What were you thinking, just now?" Arie asked.

"I was thinking how much I love when you smile." Cees dipped her head, feeling suddenly shy and incredibly vulnerable poised as she was with her legs wide and only Arie's hands on her backside keeping her abreast.

"May I tell you something?"

Arie's lips were so close all Cees had to do was lean forward and their mouths would be touching. She moved her hips imperceptibly and kissed the tip of the dildo instead and was rewarded with a ripple of pleasure that sent gooseflesh up her arms.

"Yes, tell me something," Cees whispered as she dropped her head to look between their bodies at Arie's small but alert breasts, the harness, and the short stub of the purple phallus.

"I almost came when I saw what you had bought."

"Really?" Cees looked into Arie's solemn eyes.

"Why?"

"I don't know. I just kept thinking I wanted to wear it and I wanted to give you an orgasm."

"You've never failed to give me an orgasm. You don't need that."

It was Arie's turn to look vulnerable. "I guess the thought of it just turned me on."

"You are so innocent sometimes, you know that?" Cees said and Arie moved imperceptibly closer, the tip of the dildo nudging her still wet folds farther apart. Cees stiffened again and Arie kissed her.

"You're so tense, sweetheart. I need you to relax so that I don't hurt you."

"It's okay, you won't hurt me," Cees said, but Arie was already moving. Small, imperceptible thrusts that weren't meant to go deeper than the outer opening. Cees lifted her head, and Arie kissed her with a surprising amount of tenderness that sent a boomerang of arousal that caused her to inhale and hitch her legs higher. As if expecting the move, Arie moved closer, and the phallus slid an inch or so deeper inside Cees. Before she could stiffen, Arie had pulled it back out. This time when Cees gasped it was in pleasure and then disappointment. She found herself lifting for the invasion, waiting for it, and exalting in the pleasure that followed the receding sting. Arie was breathing as hard as she was. Cees could feel the muscles in Arie's shoulders tremble as she lifted her higher and closer to her. Neither of them made any attempt to break the kiss.

Arie's tongue toyed with the tip of Cees's tongue as she pulled the phallus back until only the tip lay poised at Cees's opening. She waited, stock still, until Cees desperately latched on to Arie's shoulder and pulled herself forward, gasping at the sound of their bodies coming together so suddenly and explosively.

"Cees, be careful." Arie's voice was tense with effort, and Cees had the sudden realization that she was holding herself back. Cees grabbed her ass and, using her calves, pulled Arie closer. To her surprise, Arie moaned. "Cees, let yourself get used to it first. I don't want you regretting this tomorrow."

"I won't, I promise," Cees said and dropped her forehead against Arie's shoulder. She smelled the wonderfully heady scent of them making love and inhaled deeply. Her body tightening around the gentle invasion. Arie's stomach shuddered in response. "You felt that?" Cees asked, and Arie nodded. Of its own accord, it seemed the dildo slipped deeper, separating her farther, and Arie's stomach was resting against hers. No longer afraid that Arie would walk away, Cees wrapped her arms around Arie's shoulders. "It feels good," she said and bucked her hips.

Arie slipped her hands beneath Cees's butt, holding her close. "Let me know if it's uncomfortable."

A spasm of pleasure shifted through Cees, and with Arie's support, she started moving against it, pleasuring herself against the unyielding apparatus. Arie's breathing was becoming labored, and Cees wondered if it was from the effort of holding her or if it was because she was aroused.

"Please, Arie, it won't hurt." As if she had been waiting for permission, Arie began to move, and the friction sent shock waves reverberating up Cees's back. Arie used her upper body to tilt Cees back slightly and her hands to bring Cees's ass to an angle. Arie looked at her for a long moment before kissing her with a passion that could have ended things before Cees was ready. Their bodies rocked rhythmically, Cees sighing with each long thrust. Her mistake was in opening her eyes to make sure Arie was enjoying herself. The pure, unadulterated lust she saw there was the beginning of the end. Arie must have felt it or seen it too because the muscles beneath Cees's arms tensed suddenly and Arie was driving into her, taking full advantage of the few seconds where Cees felt anything and everything as the most exquisite pleasure. All thrusts were exquisite, all retreats were agonizing promises to be followed up by a friction so intense that Cees knew her cries of pleasure had become a long, soft wail. Arie's kiss was passionate and rough. All Cees heard was the sound of their bodies coming together in a fury of orgasm. Cees had to turn her head away when her orgasm slammed through her, shocking her into an uncharacteristic silence that seemed to slow down her world. Arie slammed into her one last time and unbelievably, her orgasm seemed to heighten and arch, and she cried out. Arie seemed to arch into her, releasing her butt and wrapping her arms around her back, holding her close.

"Oh my God. That was…."

"Intense?"

"Yes. Very."

"I'm going to take it out, okay?"

Cees nodded and braced herself for what she thought would be an uncomfortable withdrawal but wasn't. Cees tried to stand so that she could help Arie unbuckle the harness, but her legs were so weak that she would have dropped to the floor if Arie had not caught her.

There was a tense, almost angry look on Arie's face.

"What's wrong?" Cees was almost too afraid to ask. Maybe the impulse buy hadn't been such a good idea.

"Nothing." Arie helped her down from the back of the couch.

"Then why the scowl?"

"I just wish we had made it to the bedroom is all."

Cees laughed, relieved that she now understood. "Arie, you can't plan for everything. Sometimes life throws you a curveball."

Arie raised a brow.

"Okay, sometimes the curveball comes in the form of a big-ass dildo."

Arie sighed. "You sure you're all right?" She put her hand on Cees's hip and pulled her close. Their hips fit together almost perfectly.

Cees's lips tingled. "I'll be all right in about two minutes."

Arie's gasp was so soft that had Cees not been staring at her lips, had she not seen them part, not watched the tip of her tongue moisten them, she wouldn't have heard it.

"What happens in two minutes?"

"That's about how long it will take us to finish this

conversation, get into the bedroom, and for me to devour you till you make me stop. How does that sound?"

"That sounds like a fantastic plan. It would sound even more fantastic if I didn't have to wake up at five in the morning just to make sure I get to Seattle by ten."

"Who says you're going to sleep at all?" Cees asked quite seriously.

❖

"Hey, what's wrong?" Lilly's touch pulled Cees back from her painful memories. Despite being as close as sisters, the Nguyen family didn't show affection by touching. The last time Lilly had touched her with such kindness, they had been standing in front of Cees's father's grave. She blinked and then blinked again because there was water in her eyes, and her normally carefree friend was gnawing at her lower lip and close to tears as well.

"Everything's fine, Lil. I was just remembering something that made me sad."

Lilly stood up quickly. "You scared the shit out of me. I thought you got bad news about getting pregnant." Lilly walked out of the room, and Cees heard her open the refrigerator. A few seconds later Cees heard the sound of a bottle cap hitting the floor, followed by the sound of Lilly scraping it up and tossing it into the trash. She reappeared, pressing the bottle to her forehead.

"Sorry," Cees said, and she did feel bad. She had put Lilly through hell over the last few years and her friend had stood by her side, being there for her through everything.

"So, tell me what she said." It took Cees a moment to realize what Lilly was referring to.

"It was just a consultation. I have to go in for a physical." Cees stopped speaking and stood up.

"Why are you so quiet? I thought you'd be happier. You getting cold feet?"

Cees turned around and frowned at Lilly.

"Lilly, I've never been so sure of anything in my life. I've always wanted a family, and I won't let my job or…or anything else change that."

"I know, but why do you have to have kids now? Why not wait a few more years? Who knows? You might meet someone and start the family together." Lilly looked so doubtful that Cees didn't know whether to burst into tears or laugh out loud. "Hey, I have an idea. Remember when we were kids and you used to play with those…" Lilly frowned.

"Dolls?"

"Yeah, dolls. You played with those baby dolls and stuff. Always dressing them up and changing their—" Lilly's mouth turned down in distaste.

"Diapers?"

"I know what they're called, you ass. Look, Cees, I'm not saying you shouldn't do it. I'm just saying maybe you should get a doll, or better yet, rent a kid first. You know, try before you buy."

"Rent one?" Cees couldn't keep the grin off her face. She had been stumbling into this kind of discussion with Lilly for over twenty years, and yet she was still bewildered at the turns her friend's mind could take. "Lilly, you can't just rent a kid."

"Yeah, you can. Hang on." Lilly riffled in her enormous purse and pulled out a flyer. "See? This paper says that Oregon has hundreds of kids in foster care. An enormous amount of them are from racially diverse ethnic groups. You could take in a foster kid, and if you don't like it, well, no harm, no foul."

Cees started. "Lilly, we're talking about a child. You can't just…you can't just insert yourself into their lives and then disappear."

"People do it all the time."

"Yeah, I know, but it doesn't make it right."

"It's better than having a kid and figuring out after the fact that you're bad at it."

"Is that what this is about?" Cees asked softly. "Do you think I'm going to be bad at it?"

The question brought Lilly up short. "Of course I don't think that. You'd be a fantastic mother. You'll probably love washing out dirty diapers."

"They have disposable now."

"Yeah, whatever. That's not my point. You're happy now. Why bring in this uncertainty?"

"It's not an uncertainty for me. I want children, Lilly. I want to pass on some of the things that my dad taught me to my own sons. I want to hand his antique tool collections down to my daughters. I want them to have this house if they want it. I don't get why you're so bothered by this."

"Suit yourself, but Momma said childbirth felt like pulling your bottom lip over your head. She doesn't recommend it. She said I should get a Chihuahua and dress it up instead." Cees would have laughed if Lilly hadn't looked so offended.

"Aren't you afraid of raising kids alone?"

Cees sobered, sensing the very real concern behind Lilly's question. "I won't lie. I'm scared, but my dad and your mom did great with us. They were single parents."

"It wasn't on purpose, Cees. They just did the best they could with what they had."

"And that's what I'll do too. If I had a choice, I wouldn't be doing this on my own either, Lil."

Lilly's face hardened. Cees didn't need to ask who she was thinking of, and she kicked herself mentally for having brought up Arie, however inadvertently. It would have been so easy for Cees to overlook the obvious opening to bring up her visit with Arie. Cees could only imagine the fireworks if Lilly and Arie should ever end up in the same room again. Lilly, at barely five feet, would probably hold her own against Arie's five-feet-eight, but Cees would just rather not think about the outcome if she didn't have to.

"I saw her today."

"I know. I was listening. The next step is the physical, right?"

"I'm not talking about the fertility doctor, and my consultation was yesterday. I'm talking about Arie. I saw her."

As expected, Lilly didn't take the news sitting down. She leapt up from the hard couch like a jack sprung from its box. Cees expected the long string of obscenities that Lilly was usually good for, but her friend surprised her and walked back into the kitchen. Cees heard her open the refrigerator door and then she reappeared carrying two more Heinekens and a bottle opener. Cees was shaking her head, but Lilly set the two bottles next to the still half-full one she had grabbed earlier and popped the top on each.

Cees watched as she dumped half the contents of one into her mouth and swallowed it in three careful gulps. Again, Cees waited for the cursing, but none came. "You not going to say anything?" she asked finally.

"Why should I? You're the one with a death wish."

"A death wish?" Cees laughed. "You're threatening me with bodily harm because I saw my ex?"

"No, I'm not the one that's going to hurt you. She is."

"Lil, she was in the hospital. She was hurt. She doesn't have anyone."

"Her decision, not yours. She made it clear that she could take care of herself. So let her."

Cees's hand went to the heart-shaped locket hidden beneath her T-shirt. At one time the locket held two tiny photos: one of her as a baby and one of her mother, taken a year before an undiagnosed heart condition took her life. Now the locket held photos of both her parents.

"If it were me lying in that hospital bed, I'd want someone to look in on me."

"Somebody would. Me, my mother, my family." Lilly spoke so fiercely that some of her Heineken sloshed onto the couch and rolled tearlike to the floor.

Lilly and her family had been there when Cees's father died, and they had been there to celebrate when Cees got the show and when *Cees Bannigan Your Home* went national. They had accepted her as family. And despite the fact that they didn't understand why Cees would decide to raise a baby without a man, she knew they would be there for her and her child.

"She has a problem."

"She had one long before she ended up in the hospital."

Cees laughed. Lilly, like any true friend, was still filled with righteous indignation that anyone could dump Cees.

"So what did the bitch say?" Lilly asked and took a swig of her beer, her mouth already tight.

"She didn't say much because—"

"Because there's nothing she could say. Did you tell her off like I said you should if she ever came skulking around again?"

"Um, no. She's not in any shape to handle that kind of drama."

"So why did you go see her, then?" Lilly's patented scowl appeared, and Cees's heart sank. Lilly wouldn't be letting this one go anytime soon. "Who told you she was in the hospital?"

"The police came to the set."

"The police? What happened to her? Someone bash her ass?" Lilly's mother, Momma Nguyen, was always afraid that Cees would get gay-bashed. Despite the fact that Cees's job as a TV host made it hard for her to be out. Although Cees didn't exactly hide the fact that she was a lesbian, lack of any meaningful relationships in her future made it easy to stay closeted.

"You really should stop reading those articles your mother cuts out. Portland's a lot smaller and a lot more tolerant than she thinks."

"Momma says that's what people thought years ago until the skinheads bought a freeway."

"They didn't buy..." Cees shook her head, refusing to be pulled back into the old argument.

"So what did she say when you saw her?" Lilly was in her small-dog mode again, and Cees knew she wouldn't let up until she had the whole story.

"She didn't say much. She doesn't remember anything. The doctor—"

Lilly was up again. This time she was stalking. "You mean the bitch has the nerve to forget that you and she were together? Well, ain't that convenient? What hospital is she in? I'll remind her."

"Listen, Lilly, it's not just our relationship. She didn't even remember her own name. They had to tell her. She has amnesia."

Lilly stopped mid-stalk and turned her scowl on Cees. "Have you lost your mind? Amnesia? That's bullshit. She tell you that?"

"No, her doctor did. That's why I went to go see her." Cees let the little lie come out because now that Lilly knew, she felt a little embarrassed. She hadn't known about Arie's amnesia until Dr. Parrantt had told her at the hospital.

"Well, I could have told you she wasn't right in the head when she left you. But I still don't get why the police came to you."

"She, um, must have forgotten to remove me as beneficiary on her insurance forms." Cees frowned. She'd never had any inkling that Arie was well off. They rarely ate out, and when they did, they tended to fight over the check until they agreed to split it. It made sense that Arie had been so unconcerned about finding another job; she hadn't needed one financially. But the Arie Cees knew only stayed still when she slept. It made no sense to her that she would be unemployed for so long.

"Oh, that's just great. They trying to accuse you of attempted murder? You didn't talk to them, did you?" Lilly whipped out her cell, hit a button, and put the phone to her ear.

"Talk to them about what? Who are you calling?"

"Momma. My cousin Yon just passed the bar."

"Lilly. Don't." Cees put her hand over Lilly's, forcing her to close the phone.

"She had a car accident while trying to avoid hitting a mother and child stranded in the middle of the road. They contacted me because I was listed on her paperwork and she has no other family."

"Oh," Lilly said and grudgingly dropped her phone back in her purse. Before she could zip it closed, the rap song "Mama Said Knock You Out" blared.

She glared at Cees as she began rooting around in the bottom of the purse. "Why'd you buy Momma a phone with Caller ID?" Cees shrugged and tried not to look guilty. Why had she bought her that phone?

"Yeah?" Lilly barked her standard greeting. "Nah, I thought Cees needed cousin Yon's number. Nah, nah, she all right. I thought she was gonna be on trial for murder because she was the sole beneficiary on an insurance policy. You know how they always come after you for that on truTV." Cees reached for one of Lilly's beers and took a swig as an explosion of rapid-fire Vietnamese emanated from the cell phone. Lilly answered back, and Cees took another long pull from the beer when she heard Arieanna's name mentioned.

"Okay, okay," Lilly said before hanging up without saying good-bye. "Momma said to tell that skank bitch to stay away from her girl."

Cees covered her mouth to keep from spitting out her beer. "She did not say that."

"She sort of did."

Lilly's bottom lip was stuck out, and Cees entertained the thought of hugging her before judgment prevailed. "I love the way you two try to protect me."

"Somebody needs to. So what was it like? Seeing her again?"

The change in conversation confused Cees for a moment and then she realized that Lilly was referring to Arie.

"She's confused, in pain. The doctor says she's been having nightmares and migraines."

"But otherwise she's gonna be fine?" Lilly probed.

"Yeah, her doctor thinks so."

"Good, then you don't need to keep seeing her."

Cees felt something tighten in her chest. "Lilly, she doesn't remember who she is. She only knows her name because they told her. She's alone."

"Again, her choice, not yours." Lilly pointed this out gently, but it still hurt Cees to hear it. In the weeks after their separation, Lilly had asked if she thought Arie was seeing someone else. Cees had racked her brain and came to the conclusion that there had been no one. It was another dagger to the heart to realize that Arie had simply decided she didn't want a life with her.

Momma's ring tone blared again, and Lilly stood to answer it. Cees wondered if Lilly's choice of ring tone was a conscious one since she seemed to brace herself every time she answered the phone.

"Okay, okay." Lilly clapped the phone closed. "Momma said dinner's ready and she wants you to come." Cees knew she would get a grilling about staying away from bad girls like Arieanna. Momma Nguyen treated Lilly and her like they were still fourteen and sixteen instead of thirty and thirty-two. As much as she loved the Nguyen family, Cees didn't think she was up to a lecture tonight. Surprisingly, Lilly's had been mild compared to what she'd expected.

"I think I'm going to stay in tonight. Maybe have a glass of wine while I still can." Cees smiled as she remembered the monumental decision she still had to make. Arieanna's sudden reappearance into her life couldn't have happened at a worse time.

Lilly gave a disgusted grunt and stood up. "Promise me

you'll stay away from her. I know you want to help her. It's in your nature to help, but…I don't think I can stand seeing you like that again."

Cees smiled. "That was a long time ago, Lilly. What we had, what Arie and I had, is over. Like you said, she made sure of that."

Lilly stared at Cees for a long time and then she did something surprising: she hugged Cees hard. "Momma said you're like a dumb abused puppy. You just keep loving and loving no matter how many times someone kicks you in the chest."

Cees pulled away from Lilly and laughed. "She didn't say that."

Lilly stood up to leave. "Yeah, Cees. She did."

CHAPTER FOUR

The absolute darkness was interrupted by the sound of someone crying. The sobs of the brokenhearted could never be mistaken for physical pain. Arieanna reached toward the sound, but something stopped her. Offering comfort would only make things worse in the long run.

"Why are you doing this, Arieanna?" The question was a sledgehammer to her brain. She pressed her hands against the side of her head, and a wave of nausea swept over her. She knew the voice; she knew it as well as she knew her own.

"Please don't do this." Arie wrenched herself from her nightmare and cried out.

A night nurse must have been walking by her room because she was at her side almost immediately. "Ms. Simon, are you all right?" Arie reached out and grasped the hand on her arm tightly as she tried to catch her breath. The nurse reached across her with her free hand and pressed the button for the small lamp next to Arie's bed. "Okay, sweetie, let me look. You need to calm down. Do you understand?"

Tears spilled down the sides of Arie's face as she thought of the voice and remembered the look in Cees Bannigan's eyes when she'd seen her. She had found the recognition she was seeking, as well as some unexpected emotions—pain and fear. She was certain of one thing. She had done something so awful that those eyes, those beautiful eyes, had been crying. She hadn't seen her face, but the sound of Cees Bannigan weeping was as familiar as her own body. It was more than memory, it was knowledge. Another wave of nausea hit, and this time resulted in her retching into the basin that was put in front of her. Tears of frustration slid down Arie's face. Was that why Cees seemed so vague about her whereabouts? Had they argued? Had she perhaps done something to hurt her? No. Arieanna pushed the thought away as quickly as it had come. She didn't need memory to know she wasn't a violent person. She would not have hurt her physically. Not ever. No.

"Better?" the nurse asked.

"Of course not, I don't know who I am," Arie snapped. "Oh God, I'm so sorry. I...thank you."

The nurse smiled, and Arie realized that she was young, perhaps a few years younger than herself. According to the driver's license found tucked in her sock, she was thirty-two.

"Nightmare, huh?"

"Yes."

"Do you remember it?"

Arie stiffened, recognized that the nurse was only doing her job, and forced herself to relax.

"No," she said, and although it was a lie, it did make her to feel better not to have to relive the dream.

"All right, keep your call button close."

Arie watched until the nurse left the room. Her eyes went to the television. She picked up the remote and was disappointed when she found the local broadcasting station had gone off the air. She hoped Nurse Kerr would be able to get the recorded shows for her because she wanted to find out if watching them brought back memories. So far, Cees Bannigan was the only one who knew her and the only person or thing that seemed to jog memories in her, though they didn't seem like good ones.

The fear of more nightmares kept her awake long after she should have fallen asleep again. Something Dr. Parrantt said to her kept floating in the back of her mind. *The brain is a funny piece of equipment,* he'd said. *Sometimes it will act as a protector if it feels we need it.* He'd left soon after that, but what he said lingered with her. It scared her that her doctor had been either unwilling or unable to give her a better idea of when she would start to remember.

Arie ran her hand through her hair. She hadn't forgotten the way her hair felt, nor was her own body unfamiliar. But it was familiar in that way that an old childhood toy was familiar. As if it belonged to her—only, a long time ago. Detached. She fell on the word and almost smiled in triumph when she found it. That's how she felt.

The nightmares were the only thing she could be sure of, and the fear of them had been making it hard for her to sleep. She was happy for the lack of a roommate, even temporarily. Being alone meant she could watch TV despite the late hour. She searched the channels as she had searched Cees Bannigan's face for something she recognized.

The fear and confusion were still there, still hovering in the back of her mind, but she didn't feel so alone. She had been disappointed to learn she had no family, but not surprised. She felt as if she would remember a family, and that they would at least have missed her if they hadn't heard from her in a week. She frowned. Cees Bannigan said they had argued, that she had decided they weren't right for each other and had ended it. Arie sensed there had been more to it than that. She had been hoping the police would find someone who knew her, and they had. She hadn't been prepared for her reaction when Cees walked through the door. Arie felt both shy and unable to remove her gaze from Cees's face. She thought she was familiar, but she didn't know why. She was unprepared for the pain. No, it had been stronger than that. It was as if something had been pulled forcefully from her when she looked at Cees.

"What did I do to you?" Arie said aloud. The fear was skulking back. She could feel it creeping up around her chest, paralyzing her vocal cords. She closed her eyes and tried to force herself to remember, as she had numerous times since she had awakened in the hospital. When no memories came, she tried to remember the way Cees looked that morning. To her relief, Cees's face came to her as clearly as if she had been standing in front of her bed at that very moment. Arie's limbs relaxed as she focused her mind on Cees, hoping the memory of their one meeting would keep the nightmares and the painful headaches that followed at bay.

I am not alone. I am not alone. She repeated the mantra in her head until there was only Cees's face, only her smile, and the oblivion of sleep.

❖

When Cees didn't come the following morning, Arie reminded herself that she hosted a television show and was probably busy. Still, she found herself glancing at the clock often. Visiting hours came and went. When Nurse Kerr arrived to check on her before her shift ended, Arie was watching a sitcom, but the only laughter in the room was from the TV.

"I asked my daughter about the shows. She said she would let you borrow them."

"Never mind," Arie said shortly.

"Maybe she just got busy at work."

"Maybe."

"She left her number at the nurse's station. I could call her to remind her that—"

"Visiting hours are over, aren't they?"

"I could leave word to make an exception for you."

Arie shrugged and turned to the TV. "She knows I'm here. I'm thinking most people don't forget they have a friend in the hospital. But then again, I guess most people don't forget their friends, and I seem to have managed that."

Nurse Kerr paused for a moment, glanced at Arie, and then

left. Arie closed her eyes. She had been rude for no reason. No, she knew the reason. She was scared at the possibility of being so alone, but more than anything, she was sad and disappointed that Cees Bannigan had not come to see her. If the nightmares had any truth to them, their relationship had not been a good one. So she understood why Cees had decided not to come, but the disappointment was acute. The need to see her was almost stifling in its persistence. She wasn't sure why or how, but she knew she had hurt Cees Bannigan, and in doing so she had lost a part of herself.

What was wrong with her? Cees Bannigan owed her nothing. Hell, the nurse owed her nothing more than she would offer any other patient in the hospital. Nurse Kerr had stopped to check on her out of kindness, and she had reacted like a petulant child. Now she was angry because a woman she didn't remember hadn't come to visit her. *What kind of person am I?*

❖

"And cut. Hold steady, Cees." Cees obediently stood still while her director, Jan Kutchings, checked lighting. She had been distracted and grumpy all day, both of which were showing in her performance, though Jan had been kind enough to overlook it.

"We're done." Cees pulled off her protective goggles and started to walk toward the door of the set. She was going to head home and grab a cup of tea, but Miranda was waiting for her when she got up to her office.

"I watched the screen repair scene." Cees sighed and plopped down on the couch next to her. "Is there something wrong?" Miranda expressed the concern that had obviously been on Jan's mind but that he hadn't been comfortable enough to express.

"I'm fine. Just distracted."

"I could tell. You didn't look like you were having fun out there at all."

Miranda was right. Guilt over not having visited Arie the

day before was making her distracted and short-tempered. She had intended on driving to the hospital, had been sitting in the Monster with the engine grumbling and her hands ten and two when an ache started in the center of her chest and swelled to full-blown searing pain. She had told herself that Arie wouldn't care. Hell, Arie didn't even remember her, why would she care? But deep down Cees knew that wasn't true. She had bumbled into the situation because in the back of her mind she had hoped there would be an explanation for what happened to them, something final enough that saying she had moved on was no longer just lip service. But Arie couldn't even tell her what she had been doing the last year, let alone what happened to their relationship.

"That's what I said when you replaced that toilet." Miranda shuddered. "Imagine someone actually doing that themselves?"

Cees smiled. "That's what you have me for."

Instead of returning her smile, Miranda looked at her steadily. "And do I...have you, I mean?"

Cees felt her smile fade, and she looked down at her hands. What was she doing? First she pushed Miranda away, and now she said something like that.

"Miranda, I..."

"Cees, it's okay. It's just that, when I was in here the other day, I got the distinct impression you were trying to break things off with me, and I have to admit I was a bit disappointed."

Cees searched Miranda's face. She did look disappointed. Cees was tempted to reach out to her, tell her it was PMS and everything would be fine. They had given each other pleasure, comfort, and companionship. Sex with Miranda was good, but was it enough?

"You've met someone else, haven't you?" Miranda asked. "She willing to settle down and have a family with you?"

Sadness swept over Cees. It would have been easy to let Miranda think there was someone else, but she couldn't lie about something like that. "It's more complicated than that."

"Don't tell me you're getting involved with someone who doesn't want the same thing you do?"

"No, it's not that. I'm not really sure what she wants, and it's not exactly a relationship."

"But you want it to be?"

Cees sighed. "No. I think I'd like… I think I need to be on my own for a while."

Miranda continued to search Cees's face. "But there is someone else. I can't imagine you being this distracted because of a decision not to have sex with me anymore. Mind you, I plan on wearing some tight and revealing sweaters here and there in an effort to change your mind."

Cees laughed and gave Miranda's shoulder a light push. "I'll look forward to it."

"So, you going to tell me about her? I have to admit I'm feeling damn jealous but fairly adult about the whole thing, so if you need someone to talk to, I'm here."

"There really isn't anything to tell…she's someone from my past."

"Unfinished business?"

"Cliché, huh?"

Miranda stood up and stretched. Cees's eyes traveled up her thin body, taking in her khakis and button-down shirt, and almost willed the small tingle of desire to return. When it didn't, she had to bite down her own disappointment. Miranda had a small smile on her face, and Cees almost blushed. It was as if Miranda had read her mind and forgave her for finding her wanting.

"Sweetie, we all have our unfinished business. Some of it is worth pursing, and some of it…" Miranda shrugged, her eyes clouding and clearing so quickly that Cees wondered if she had imagined it. She realized that she and Miranda had worked together for eight months and had been sleeping together for half that, yet she really knew nothing about her. All she had to do was kiss Miranda, tell her that she was right, and things would be as they had been. Cees wouldn't though part of her wanted too, because like Lilly said, she deserved more. She deserved stability, she deserved to be loved.

"I came in here to tell you I need to go to New York for a few days," Miranda said.

"Need me to feed Bastian?"

Miranda grinned. "I wasn't sure you would still be willing."

Cees was surprised. "We're friends. Why wouldn't I be?" Miranda shrugged and Cees hurried her words to get past the awkwardness that had fallen between them. "What are you going to New York for?"

"The bigwigs are giving me an audience for your cabin miniseries idea."

Cees stood up. "You're kidding. They liked it? That's fantastic. Why didn't you tell me?" She had first approached Miranda with the idea months ago. Miranda had told her no promises, but she had promised to broach the subject if she ever had the opportunity. The idea had been for a small workspace in a backyard that could be used for writing or painting. Miranda's obvious skepticism convinced Cees it was a bad idea, so she had let it go.

"Don't get your hopes up, okay?"

"I won't. When do you leave?"

"Tomorrow. Here, let me get you a key for my place." Miranda reached in her bag and pulled a key off her ring. "I bet you thought things would never get serious between us, and here I am handing over my key."

"That's because we aren't sleeping together anymore." Cees took the key and almost bit her bottom lip at having said it out loud.

Miranda seemed unperturbed. "You say that now, but I think you're going to miss me and come crawling back." She winked. "I'm gonna make you pay when you do."

❖

After Miranda's departure, Cees spent several minutes shuffling papers, checking e-mail, and cleaning the inside of her desk drawer. Finally, she leaned back in her chair and stared up at the peeling ceiling.

The thought of Arie alone and scared in the hospital made Cees shake her head. She had no misconceptions about why she had broken her promise. Self-preservation was a powerful thing. Cees stood and reached for her leather messenger bag. Any anger she thought she would feel at seeing Arieanna again had disappeared when she saw her lying in the hospital bed. All she could think about was protecting her, being with her. Memories of the pain hadn't returned until she had tried to sleep that night. The anger showed up the next morning during the carpet repair scene. And now here she was, two days later, sitting at her desk and kicking herself because she wanted to see Arie. No, she would go home, maybe call Lilly to see if she wanted to get a late dinner, maybe drink a beer or two to help her sleep, and that would be that.

Cees rested her head against the seat as the Monster warmed up. The sky was turning a deep purple, and she wondered if Arie could see it from where she lay in the hospital. She wondered if she was lonely or scared. *Damn it.* Cees hit the steering wheel with the palm of her hand at the thought of Arie ever being scared of anything. Maybe she would call the hospital tomorrow and check on her progress. She wouldn't be at all surprised if they told her that Arie had regained her memory and was doing fine.

Cees had almost convinced herself that she was doing the right thing—for herself—but the memory of how Arie had looked at her when she came into the room reminded her of what it felt like to be needed. Arie's eyes seemed to plead with her, begging for some assurance from Cees that she belonged somewhere and to someone. Everything in her wanted to gather Arie close and tell her that she belonged with her and that she didn't have to be afraid. *Even after the devastation of our failed relationship, how could I still feel so strongly for her?*

The light turned red and the monster settled to a heavy, sighing stop.

"Everyone eventually comes to their fork," Cees's father was fond of saying when Cees was struggling with a difficult decision. "The road you choose is the road you gotta travel. There is no right or wrong."

The light turned green, and Cees found herself getting onto the freeway. The monster was taking her toward the hospital—toward Arie, toward probable pain, toward possibilities.

CHAPTER FIVE

Cees told herself that visiting hours were over and that she should not feel guilty about pointing the monster toward home. So why was she standing in front of the hospital wishing she smoked so that she could bum a cigarette off one the blue-clad doctors or nurses furtively stealing a puff in the shadow of the building? They, of all people, should know better. But then she, of all people, should know better too. Lung cancer had leached into her father's tall muscular frame and eaten at him until he had looked twice his age. He started smoking on his sixteenth birthday and stopped five weeks before his fiftieth, the day he was diagnosed and a year before he died.

Cees crossed her arms in front of her to keep the shiver that went through her body from starting again. His death had left her feeling lonely in a crowded room, until Arie had come into her life. A nurse with a familiar-looking scowl walked through the sliding glass doors of the hospital and looked right at Cees. At first Cees hoped she would keep walking, and she did, right toward Cees. "Visiting hours are over," she said gruffly.

"I know. I had to work late."

"Did you work late yesterday too?"

"Yeah, something like that."

"She was very upset."

Cees swallowed. She had been telling herself that Arie didn't remember her and that it wouldn't matter if she visited or not. But she knew she had been fooling herself because as much as Arie had tried to hide it, there had been fear and hope in her face when Cees had walked in. Arie had searched her face as if looking for salvation. Despite her fear and remembered pain, Cees would have given anything to ease the desperation on Arie's face. Cees told herself she would have felt the same for anyone.

"You're the only tether she has right now." The lack of accusation in the nurse's tone forced Cees to drop her head.

"She and I, we had, have a past. Things didn't end well. It's hard for me—" Cees stopped speaking when she realized how selfish she sounded. She looked up at the nurse and then at the building. "What time should I be here in the morning?" Cees asked.

"She might not want to see you."

Cees looked at the building and back at her truck. "What time?"

"If you come before seven o'clock, you can talk to her after she eats dinner."

"I'll be here." Cees started to walk away, but the nurse stopped her.

"I can let you see her for a few minutes now, if you want. You can at least tell her you'll be here tomorrow so she can stop fretting."

"Really?" Cees couldn't help the smile that came to her face.

"Yeah, but make sure no one sees you when you leave." Cees agreed and told herself that her heart was pounding hard because she had to walk twice as fast as usual to keep up. It was still pounding when they came to the door leading to Arie's room.

Cees looked at the door and remembered her father's words. "Everyone eventually comes to their fork." She knew what her father meant by those words. Everyone had a road to travel. She just wished her journey was a little less painful. Unlike Arie, Cees remembered with crystalline clarity the moments before her life veered off track.

❖

Cees had been waiting for Arie for hours. Arie hadn't bothered to say good-bye that morning, nor had she bothered to call. Saturdays had always been their time to lie in bed, to make love until someone's stomach protested the lack of food. And then they would gorge themselves on Wheat Thins, Laughing Cow cheese, and grapes, before making love again. Ever since Arie had gone to Seattle, things had been steadily declining between them. Except for one almost desperate night of making love, Arie hadn't made any effort to initiate sex, even though Cees could feel that Arie's desire for her had not lessened. Cees could see it in Arie's eyes every time she removed her clothing or walked from a shower. Arie had never been good at hiding her desire. Cees just couldn't figure out why she suddenly felt she needed to. A hopeless feeling shrouded Cees.

The front door opened and closed before Cees realized that a key had been inserted in the lock. She walked out into the living room. Arie was bent over removing her boots, carelessly dripping water on the floor. This was another one of those new things that Cees had noticed and didn't like. Arie just seemed not to care anymore—about her home, about finding another job, about her relationship with Cees. Unfortunately, Cees thought she knew why, and it broke her heart to think they couldn't work things out.

"Arieanna?" When Cees spoke her name, Arie stopped struggling with her boot lace, one foot still crossed at her knee. A flash of pain ran across her face so deeply that Cees caught her breath and rushed to her. Arieanna held her hand out, and Cees stopped, but not before she saw it—love. Arieanna still loved her, but she was hiding it. Which she did expertly right before she looked down at her boots and began to unlace them with slow determination.

"Where've you been, Arie?"

"Out. You should try it. Every time I come home, you're here."

"Were you out looking for a job?" Cees asked softly and then kicked herself for dropping right into the question. She had been racking her brain trying to figure out what had gone wrong with their relationship. One thought was that Arie blamed her for not having found another job. The other was too hard to contemplate right now. To think that the thing they both claimed to want so desperately was now tearing them apart.

Arie attempted to move past her, but Cees reached out and grabbed her. Arie had obviously made no effort to keep herself from being drenched. Water dripped from her long dark hair. Her lean but strong body had started to look frail. Cees hadn't seen Arie eat anything of substance in weeks. Early in their relationship, Arie had confided that if she wasn't diligent about eating, her body would waste to nothing. It was obvious she wasn't being careful now.

Arie started to tremble.

"Tell me what's hurting you. Why are you pulling away from me? Did I do something wrong? Is it the job situation? I can talk to them. I can get your job back—"

A guttural noise emanated from the back of Arie's throat. Cees would have pounded at her back, if not for the smile. No, it wasn't a smile, it was a snarl. Cees's heart sank. She didn't know this person, and she was starting to think that there was nothing she could do to help her.

"Job? Cees, I don't need a job. My parents didn't leave me broke." Cees blinked and let go of Arie's arm. Confusion turned to hurt, but only after Arie's words screwed themselves into her heart. The point had been that Cees's father, the focus of her life until she had met Arie, had left his daughter penniless. His illness and subsequent hiding of it had been one of the first serious things that she had confided to Arie. To have her throw it back at her now…

"Why are you doing this? Tell me what I did."

"Did? You didn't do anything. I don't know what you're talking about."

Arie started to walk away. The screw had finally buried its head just below the surface of Cees's heart. "If you want me to leave, just say so. You don't need to insult my father or me. Just say it." Arie turned around and glared at her. The anger was palpable, causing Cees to take a step back. "Arie, what... Don't—" Cees was shaking her head, but Arie continued undeterred.

"I want you to get your stuff and leave," Arie said, and from the look on her face, Cees expected the words to be angry and biting. They weren't. They were soft, almost as if it hurt Arie to say them. But the words couldn't have hurt Arie half as much to say as they did for Cees to hear.

Cees shook her head. This made no sense. It was as if Arie was a different person. Could a person change that fast? It had been two weeks—no, three, since she first noticed the coldness.

"Cees, did you hear what I said? You wanted me to tell you, now I'm telling you. I think you should leave."

"Are you breaking up with me, Arieanna? Is that what this is all about, or are you just trying to tell me you need space?"

Arie opened her mouth and closed it. The wobble of her chin was enough of an opening for Cees. Disregarding Arie's soaked clothing, she pulled her close.

"Just tell me," she said into Arie's neck.

She felt Arie trying to push her away, but she held on tight. "Tell me what I can do to help you. I'll do anything you want. Just tell me how I can fix this."

"You can't fix everything." Arie's voice sounded garbled.

"Let me try." Cees pulled back and saw that Arie was crying. Her own eyes welled instantly. "Tell me what you need and I swear I'll move mountains to get it for you."

"I need...you to leave."

"For how long?" Cees said, the tears flowing hard now.

"I don't know."

Cees's mind swarmed with confusion and pain, but she

forced words out of her swollen throat. "Are you telling me this is it?"

Arie's eyes seemed to scrape over her face. "You deserve—" She stopped speaking and looked off to her left. "We're not right for each other. It's over between us."

Cees felt as if she had just been gut punched. She looked around for her keys and started rushing toward the door.

"Cees." The cry sounded as if it were ripped from Arie, and Cees stopped, eyes closed, hand on the doorknob. *Please*, she mouthed, hating herself for knowing that all Arie had to say was that she didn't mean it and Cees would be hers.

"What about your stuff?" Arie asked, but the agony in her voice was too much, and Cees turned the knob and ran out of the apartment before something else could be used to hurt her. "Cees," Arie's voice sounded strangled. "Cees, wait." But Cees hadn't waited, and for a while her anger had been enough to sustain her.

She and Lilly would return to get her stuff when Arie's car wasn't parked in the lot. They would steal the couch in a fit of immaturity. Unbeknownst to Lilly, and despite the tears and heartache, Cees had placed two calls to Arie. One saying that she loved her; one saying that she understood and would never call again, but if Arie ever needed her, she would be there.

That last phone call hurt the most. Both went unanswered.

"Well, you going in, or not?"

"Yeah, thanks." Cees took a deep breath and stepped inside.

Arie didn't look away from the TV for so long that Cees thought she was ignoring her on purpose. Cees leaned against the door frame and studied Arie's profile. Her thick dark hair had been cut short and lay against her temples in soft wisps. Cees tightened her fingers into fists behind her back in an effort to stop the wistful memory of what those curls felt like. The small swell of Arie's chest rose and fell in a sigh, and Cees looked up at the TV. Cees caught the inhalation before it could embarrass her, but only just. Blood raced to her face, leaving her light-headed and giddy. Arie was watching her show. Seemingly so involved in it, she hadn't noticed Cees standing there. Cees felt guilty at having caught Arie unawares. She cleared her throat softly to let Arie know she was there. "That stuff will rot your brain, you know."

"I assumed you were one of the nurses." Arie's voice was emotionless and distant, a total contrast to the hurt in her brown eyes. Cees felt summarily chastised without any accusations being voiced.

They looked at each other for a long moment. Words of apology and explanation came to Cees's mind but never reached her lips. Cees withstood Arie's gaze until the sadness receded as if Arie heard, or at least understood, how sorry she was. Cees looked away first.

"That's one of my favorite episodes. It looks so easy up there." Cees cocked her chin toward the TV. "But I actually had to do like seven or eight takes to get it right."

Cees felt Arie's gaze on her face, and she wondered what she thought of the small lines at her forehead that Edith expertly covered with makeup before she filmed. Cees didn't need to look in the mirror to know that the stress lines were visible at the sides of her mouth and that her hair was windblown. She was not the perfectly casual woman as seen on TV. She felt stiff and uncomfortable, and would no doubt have a bruise on her shoulder from leaning against the door frame. Yet she couldn't bring herself to straighten because that would mean she would have to walk inside the room.

"Why are you here?" Arie finally asked. A better question would probably be why was she still staring at the TV when the show had gone to commercial? Cees straightened and looked at Arie.

"I told you I'd be back."

"You told me you'd be back yesterday."

"I'm sorry. Look, I know you don't remember, but…it's complicated." Why was she having trouble looking directly at Arie?

"Complicated? I don't know what happened to us, what debt you think you owe me, but consider it paid in full." Arie's voice sounded muffled, and when she finally looked at her Cees felt pinned by the intensity of her gaze.

"What are you saying? You don't want me to visit you?" Cees couldn't decide whether she was surprised or relieved by the idea.

"I'm saying I'll be fine. You don't need to feel obligated to come here. I'm tired. I think visiting hours are over with anyway."

"You're lying," Cees said as she pushed herself forward and toward Arie's bed. "You're lying," she repeated, dumbstruck by her realization.

"You need to leave." Arie's voice was calm but firm.

Cees sat down in a chair and looked at her.

"Did you hear me? I want you to—"

Cees continue to stare. Whether Arie intended to say "leave" or "go to hell," the words never came. Cees stared until Arie closed her mouth and looked away.

"Do you know you look off to the left when you lie?" Cees asked. "You looked off to the left when you told me to leave, when you broke things off with me, and you're doing the same thing now."

"I'm not lying. I want you to leave. I'll call the nurse if I have to."

"You don't have to do that. All you have to do is look me in the eye and tell me you want me to leave."

Arie said nothing, glaring at the TV instead of at Cees. Cees snatched the remote up from the bed and turned the television off. She set the remote on the bed and leaned forward, her hand palm up as if inviting Arie to take it. Arie's eyes looked glassy and Cees noticed that her fingers had curled into white-knuckled fists. Cees quickly sat back and removed her hands from Arie's bed. The joy at her discovery receded. "I'm sorry. I didn't mean to scare you. I just...I just realized something, and I guess I got overzealous. Do you really want me to leave? I didn't mean to scare you. Please look at me." Arie's eyes didn't stray from the TV, but the loosening of her fists gave Cees hope. "The last time we were together, you said some pretty hurtful things. I was afraid that if I continued to come here, you would say them again."

"What did I say that hurt you?" Arie asked.

"You told me to leave." Cees forced a smile in the hopes that Arie wouldn't guess how devastated that request had left her.

Arie's inhalation was audible, and Cees was unable to stop a tear that appeared and dropped before she could will it away. Cees laughed and brushed roughly at her check and then wiped her hands on her pants.

"I'm sorry," Arie said.

Despite the fact that Cees knew she didn't remember all of what had been said, had no inkling of the pain Cees had gone through, a weight lifted from Cees's chest. She placed her hand on the bed again. This time, Arie reached for it.

"Tell me what I did wrong. Let me fix this." The voice resonated with pain and confusion. Arie fought against hearing it, but couldn't escape. The voice was spoken in a tone so low that Arie couldn't make out everything, but she didn't need to understand all the words to know they were spoken in distress. When the voice lightened, it should have brought relief, but didn't. She could still hear the confusion. The pain was no longer as obvious, but it was there, hovering just below the surface. She will get over me. I know she will. It's better this way.

"Hi, it's me," the voice said. "I just wanted to tell you that..." She paused, and Arie struggled to hear what she said next. "I'm sorry for...well...you know. And if you want it back...it *was a dumb move and...if you ever want to talk...no pressure... I'll still..."*

Arie cried out, and the voice went away. She was relieved until another voice bloomed in her head. This one didn't make her cry; it made her angry. She was glad of the anger. Anger she could deal with.

"Stay out of my business," she heard herself say.

"Then handle it better. Don't just make her wonder what she did wrong."

"I told her it wasn't her fault. She didn't do anything."

"Yeah, she told me you said that right before you sent her packing. You really have no fucking clue, do you? You're killing her. You went from loving her to kicking her out of your house. How the hell is she supposed to move on if she's still in love with you?"

"Arieanna, it's me—Cees. You're having a nightmare. Can you open your eyes?"

Arie gasped, reached out, and caught hold of something warm—yielding.

"Arie." The voice was close to her ear, confused, sleep-clouded. She trembled. Sweat dripped down her temple. She remembered the hospital and that Arie was her name, and she remembered the voice crying. She closed her eyes, and flashes of light kept pace with the pounding in her head. She dug her fingertips into her temple and pressed.

"God, it hurts." The pain was too familiar. She had hauled herself from the nightmare by grabbing on to someone and pulling herself from the dream. "It hurts," she whispered, hoping the nurse or whoever it was would just give her something to make the pain go away.

"Should I call someone?" Arie winced and turned away from the voice, then realized that it wasn't more of the nightmare. Cees had finally come to see her, and then she remembered how she had acted like a spoiled child. She tried to open her eyes to see, but tears blurred them.

"Cees?" she whispered.

"I'm here. Tell me what you need. How can I fix this?" The words sounded so helpless and scared. The nightmare, the voice, the one that had hurt so much to hear had been Cees's. Arie pushed the memory of the voice away, pushed it so far away that even the pain from the migraine couldn't reach it.

"I thought you left me."

"I fell asleep in the chair. Arie, I need to get a nurse for you," Cees said softly near her ear. "They don't know I'm still in here. If they make me leave, I'll come back tomorrow, okay? I promise I'll come back, but I need them to get you something."

"Don't leave."

"If they let me, I'll come back in. Otherwise I'll be here after work, okay?"

"It's just a migraine." Arie tried to open her eyes. All she could see was Cees's outline hovering over her. Cees's left hand was holding hers while her right was stroking the side of her face. Arie leaned into it and closed her eyes.

"It seems bad." Perhaps it was the hour, perhaps she was imagining the depth of concern in Cees's voice. But hearing it, knowing it was there felt better than any medication she could take.

"I've gotten them since I woke up. The stuff they'll give me makes me sleep."

"I'd rather you slept than hurt."

"Okay," Arie relented. Not because the pounding in her head had gotten so bad that she actually needed the medicine, but because she needed time to explore her thoughts on Cees.

"They aren't going to like the fact that I was in here after hours, but I'll be back tomorrow." Cees repeated the promise, but Arie couldn't answer, caught off guard by a wave of nausea so intense she was seconds from asking Cees to help her to the restroom so that she could vomit. Arie felt Cees's fingertips on her temple and then her breath fanning her damp brow. She thought for a moment that Cees was going to kiss her, and she felt herself tense.

"Okay?" Cees asked again.

"Yes," Arie said softly, and the shadowy figure hesitated and then was gone. The door opened and Arie hoped that Cees would turn around and look at her. Arie caught a glimpse of disheveled hair, jeans, a polo shirt tucked neatly into belted jeans before the closing door blocked her view. Arie lay blinking at the darkness, the hammering in her chest outpacing the one in her head.

❖

"Hey, you sure you're up to doing this right now? You look a little out of it."

If the question had been asked by anyone other than Philly Panadara, Cees would have made light of her sleepless night. But Philly wasn't just her construction lead, he had been her father's crew leader. Cees had known him all her life. Philly would know a brush-off when he heard it.

"I've was at the hospital visiting a sick friend yesterday, and I'm afraid I didn't sleep much last night."

"I can see that. Looks like Edith had to use a pot of makeup on the luggage under your eyes alone." Philly sighed and leaned back in his chair, exposing his rounded belly and the straining buttons on the front of his plaid shirt. "You know I think of you as family. Your dad would want me to make sure you were okay, so if there is anything I can do for you, anything at all, you let me know. That goes for your friends too."

The sincerity in Philly's voice made Cees want to crawl into his lap and cry like she had when she was six and had been scolded by her father for wandering too far out of sight on a job site.

"That really means the world to me, Philly." Cees looked down at the table until she was convinced that her eyes wouldn't fill and then back at Philly. "Work is the only thing that is keeping me sane right now, but I'll let you know if I need to hash it out with someone. You mentioned something about changing the doors?"

"Yeah, I was saying if we used one glass door instead of double, we don't have to worry about blocking this egress. We would also get the added benefit of more sunlight in the master bedroom."

Philly pointed to a spot on the blueprints. Cees nodded and tried to focus her eyes where his finger rested on the paper. She told herself to concentrate on what Philly was saying, but her vision had blurred with more unshed tears. Philly's baritone faded into the background as once again, against her will, she remembered.

❖

Light, nickel-plated and cool, settled cautiously on the ravaged bed covers. The scent of their lovemaking hung in the air and on her lips. If she had cared to guess, Cees would have placed the time close to noon on Sunday. From the moment Arie's fingers had slipped into her body to the moment her muscles had reluctantly released them, she had stopped questioning time or date. Cees lifted Arie's hand, and almost as if she had been asked, Arie spread her fingers so that Cees might slide her own between them. Cees held their entwined hands aloft, staring at the contrast, loving the way her larger, lighter one fit just over Arie's smaller, darker hand. She straightened her fingers, and Arie did the same. Cees's were longer, but not by much.

"How come you never get as pale as I do?" Cees's voice was still thick from their lovemaking and soft from the secret desire not to disturb the air around them.

"My mother's parents came here from Brazil. I must have inherited my skin tone from her," Arie said, turning her palm toward Cees's and lowering their hands onto the bed.

"I should have been able to guess that." Cees pulled their clasped hands up between her breasts so that she could continue to look at them. She liked the way their fingers folded together. A puzzle completed.

"Why would you have been able to guess something like that?"

"Because you even sound like you have the remnants of some sort of an accent." She could have gone on; she could have mentioned how Arie's skin had that luxurious copper tone that didn't require lying out in the sun. Although Arie and she shared a similar hairstyle—the classic ponytail, Arie's hair was thick and the darkest Cees had ever seen. Anytime Cees fantasized making love with Arie, it started with digging her fingers into Arie's hair.

Arie laughed. "My mother's parents—whom I never knew, by the way—were from Brazil, not me."

Cees wanted to leap into that opening, wanted to know everything about Arie's parents and grandparents. Starting with the question of why Arie never spoke of them, but she knew from past attempts that she had to tread carefully.

"And where are you from? I don't think you ever told me," she asked and immediately regretted it. Arie's languid muscles stiffened, and Cees closed her eyes. Why did she have to insist on knowing everything now? What difference did it make if Arieanna was reticent to talk about her family? Arie was here with her now. Why couldn't that be enough? It wasn't as if she had any family to speak of either. *Yes, but you've told her everything there is to know about your father. Just like Lilly said, family is everything, and if she won't talk about hers...*

"I was raised in Seattle." Arie spoke as if the words were being pried from her with a crowbar.

"I figured as much after you told me your grandfather's lawyers were there." Cees sat up on one elbow and frowned down at Arie. It wasn't just the slight lilt of an accent that confused her. "Arie, why don't you ever talk about your parents or your grandfather?"

"There's nothing to talk about. I didn't know either of them. My father died just before I was born, and my mother died in a car accident soon after. I spent most of my school years in boarding schools in Europe. My grandfather was too busy to deal with a kid. We don't all have happy childhoods, Cees. Mine was better than most. I had a roof over my head and clothes on my back. I had what I needed." Arie spoke as if she were trying to convince herself as well as Cees.

"Sweetheart, I am so sorry." Cees rolled over until she was on top of Arie.

"I don't want to go down there tomorrow. I felt bad when he died, but he kept himself separate from me all my life. When I was a kid, the only way I could make myself feel better about him avoiding me was by convincing myself that something made him scared to love me. For a long time I thought there was something wrong with me that made it hard to love me."

"I love you." Cees held Arie's face in her hands until the distant look dissipated. "I love you, and I always *always* will. You believe me, don't you?"

"Yes, I believe you." It wasn't the smile or the kiss Cees had hoped for, but it was better than the anxiety.

"Maybe you should call the lawyers back. Tell them you'll need to come down next weekend so I can go with you."

"No, I should go, get it over with. Do we have to talk about this now? I just want us to be happy together. Who cares about yesterday or tomorrow? I just want now."

If Arie's obvious panic wasn't alarming enough, the look in her eyes frightened Cees into action. "Shh, baby, we don't have to talk about it," she said and she pushed the doubts, both Lilly's and her own, from her mind. The only thing that mattered was that they loved each other, that they would have a lifetime of living in each other's arms.

Cees kissed Arie softly. There was something about being kissed with little to no pressure that drove Arie nuts. It was as if she felt that Cees was teasing her. Arie's hand went to the back of Cees's neck, forcing Cees to increase the pressure.

Cees intended to move slowly, to soothe away the fear she had unwittingly caused. But the feel of Arie's satin skin beneath her and the way Arie's thighs fell apart when Cees settled on top of her caused her to forget her good intentions.

Cees moaned and arched into the vee created by Arie's legs. They stared at each other for a long moment, and almost as if choreographed, Arie turned her head and Cees feasted on the pulse at Arie's neck. Arie pulled Cees closer, her hips rotating in the slow circles that meant she was already close. Cees moved so quickly that Arie barely had time to utter a moan of protest before Cees buried her nose and then her tongue in a sea of moisture, happily drowning herself in Arie.

Arie sank her fingers into Cees's hair, her work-shortened nails scraping at Cees's scalp. Cees edged her shoulders between Arie's legs, spreading her wide and then imprisoning Arie's clitoris with her love-swollen lips so her tongue could begin its slow torture.

Arie's harsh breathing was now a cry, and Cees yearned to hear it peak and go just beyond real control, but she dreaded it too because it would mean she would have to stop, and eventually the taste and the smell of the woman beneath her faded.

The next time, no matter how soon, was never soon enough. Arie was calling Cees's name now, which meant she was too close to stop. Cees opened her eyes to see Arie's bronzed, lean body arching off the bed. The pose was almost artistic. Her back was arched and every muscle was tense and perfectly still, then a loud gasp escaped Arie as the orgasm struck. Cees continued to hold Arie in her mouth until she felt her body become boneless.

Finally, Cees rested her face on Arie's hip and closed her eyes, unwilling to lose the connection just yet. Much to her own surprise, she felt too shy to look at Arie for fear she would see how much these moments meant to Cees.

She felt Arie's hand beneath her armpit seconds before she found herself flat on her back, looking up into Arie's black olive–colored eyes.

"I—" Cees said and stopped because she didn't know what she was going to say. "You don't have to—" she said, but cut herself off as Arie glared at her. Was she angry? Why? "Arie, did I do something—"

Arie cut her off with a kiss so full of passion that heat flushed through her. Arie was the first to pull away, but she was breathing hard, and for the time being, the tension was gone.

"A lifetime wouldn't be long enough for me to get enough of you, would it?" Cees asked.

Arie's eyes clouded. She looked like she wanted to say something, but Cees couldn't resist the temptation of Arie's parted lips and kissed her. This time she wasn't gentle, and the increase in Arie's heartbeat told her she didn't want her to be. Cees's hand was covering Arie's breast, and she was already thinking about Arie's lips when she felt strong, work-roughened hands on her ass. Even though she had watched Arie methodically rub hand cream into them nightly, she could not prevent the calluses from scraping gently at Cees's bottom. Cees deepened the kiss, no longer trying to drive Arie crazy and temporarily forgetting her plan of action. Arie had spread her legs and pushed the down comforter off both of them so that the sun was hitting Cees's rear. The strong palms pulled at her ass until she felt the hard steel of Arie's belly button ring. That had been a shock the first time they had made love. Arie seemed too serious to have walked into a piercing studio to get her navel pierced. She had claimed it was a youthful indiscretion, but Cees figured it had been much more than that. Cees moaned, attempting to move away from the stud.

"Does it hurt?" Arie asked.

Cees shook her head. "No, I'm afraid I'll hurt you."

"I'll let you know if it starts to hurt." Arie's hands were firm on her ass, and Cees's head sank into the pillow. She was breathing hard, probably directly in Arie's ear. The hands on her ass were urging her to move. Her clitoris had swollen, parting her lips and giving the stud easy access. Arie's fingers were more forceful now, and at some point she had parted Cees's legs.

"Move your knees up to my side," she whispered, and without thinking, without concern, Cees did. The position left her open and exposed. When the tips of two of Arie's fingers entered her, Cees moaned and pressed down on the navel ring.

"Ah, not yet," Arie said and arched away from her.

Cees shivered but obediently stopped seeking her release. Arie squeezed her ass, and Cees lifted her head but kept her eyes closed for fear Arie would drive her over the edge. She knew what she would see, what she had seen in the eight months they had been dating—passion, lust, and even love, the last of which Arie had yet to utter, but Cees saw it.

"Cees?"

"I can't hold it off."

"I know, sweetheart. Neither of us are very good at that," Arie said, and Cees opened her eyes to gaze into Arie's sexy, knowing smile. It was enough to push her toward the first of many crests. Arie was right—as much as Cees loved the orgasm, as much as she loved the increase in movement, the release, she hated the end. She hated the slow death and the feel of Arie leaving her body because that would mean that Arie would start to remember whatever it was that left her tense and slightly unreachable.

Cees moaned: a slow, pleading sound that was as much a refusal to come as a wish that she could. Arie drove into her, hands and her wrist slapping into Cees's ass, and then Cees no longer even wished to hold it off. She arched into the ring and turned her head away from Arie's ear in case she couldn't curb the scream that was threatening the back of her throat. Arie's stomach was slippery with her desire, and she was sure it would be more so now her orgasm was long, drawn out, almost painfully slow. She writhed defenseless against it, eyes squeezed shut so tightly that a tear of protest crept out and still Arie thrust and she writhed uncontrollably.

Cees was still breathing hard when her muscles stopped trying to squeeze the circulation from Arie's fingers. She was too weak to protest when Arie eased from her and urged her onto her stomach. Arie ran her fingertips along her back, easing her into a drowsy half-slumber interrupted by shivering reminders of pleasure that faded too quickly.

❖

"Earth to Cees Bannigan." Laughter knocked Cees from her thoughts, and her face flushed with heat at being caught fantasizing about the past. "The Brazilian?"

"What about her?"

Philly, frowned. "Floors are a her? I always thought floors and walls were a him. Curtains and frilly things are her." Cees punched him.

"Ouch." He rubbed at his shoulder and mock glared at her. "Well, you're the one not paying attention," Philly said, but the grumble was good-natured even though the punch had probably hurt.

"Do you want to put the Brazilian wood in here?"

"You don't think the house is too rustic for Brazilian wood?" Cees said just as Miranda walked into the room.

"Can I speak to you in my office when you're done here, Cees?"

Cees looked up, taking in the neatly pressed khakis and the tucked long-sleeved shirt. Cees knew without smelling it what perfume she would be wearing today, knew from experience what the body beneath the crisp, no-nonsense business casual attire felt like. But there was no arousal, not like the memory of those few moments with Arie the night before that already seemed like years ago.

"Sure, of course." She stood up to follow Miranda out the door.

In the four months Cees and Miranda had been lovers, there were whole hours when Arieanna Simon had not crossed her mind, whole nights when she had not awakened reaching for Arie. She told herself she was moving on just like Lilly had said she ought to, but Lilly would never have understood the emotions that rioted in her every time she awakened in Miranda's bed.

"Cees?" Philly sounded exasperated. "So no Brazilian?"

"Yeah, let's go with the Brazilian," Cees said and smiled, but she could tell by the way Philly returned her smile that it hadn't been all that convincing.

CHAPTER SIX

The phone trembled against her temple as she dialed the number to the hospital. "Hi, this is Cees Bannigan. I'm calling to check on Arieanna Simon."

"Ms. Simon is doing very well today. She got her exercise, and she even ate her lunch. We all got an earful about your unauthorized sleepover."

"Sorry." Cees bit her bottom lip.

"S'okay. Wasn't my shift." The voice was young, carefree, and hadn't gained the weariness that Nurse Kerr's had.

"She having any headaches today?"

"No, none. Like I said, she seems to be fine. She's in the best mood I've seen her in, so she must be feeling better. Why don't I connect you with Dr. Parrantt? He can answer all of your questions." It took a few moments for Dr. Parrantt to answer the phone. Despite the nurse's assurances, Cees still felt a bit fearful while waiting for him.

"Ms. Bannigan, I hear you caused a bit of excitement last night."

"I'm sorry about that. I only came in for a few moments and then I fell asleep in a chair."

"No harm done. The rules are archaic. If the nurses don't mind, no one else should either."

"I…she had a migraine."

"Yes, I'm sorry I didn't mention that when we spoke before."

Cees swallowed. "So she's had others?"

"Yes, this was the third."

"She looked so out of it."

"There's no way to know when the migraines will hit, but I can tell you that stress exacerbates them. She just needs time to heal. In fact, that's one of the things I wanted to talk to you about. I think she would do better if you took her home."

"Home? But she doesn't remember yet. You can't just send her home...can you?"

"Ms. Bannigan, I understand how stressful a situation like this can be. Ms. Simon is healing physically. I recommend she start psychotherapy as soon as possible, but being in familiar surroundings might help in the interim."

"When will you release her?"

"In a few days. We'll watch her to make sure there's no relapsing." As if sensing her apprehension, the doctor asked cautiously, "Is there someone else we should call?" There it was. Her exit, her way out of the problem of Arieanna Simon.

"No, just me." Cees pressed her fingers to her forehead. "Can she...I mean, do I need to get someone to stay with her?"

"Her migraines are very painful. However, she can stay a few hours by herself."

Cees sensed the caution in his voice. "But not all day?"

"I wouldn't recommend she stay alone for long periods of time unless absolutely necessary. The first time she had a migraine, she suffered a short blackout. If she's standing she could hurt herself."

Cees said good-bye to Dr. Parrantt and hung up the phone. How in the hell was she going to make sure that Arie had round-the-clock care? She only hesitated a split second before pressing redial. "Hi, may I have Arieanna Simon's room, please?" The phone was picked up after the first ring. Cees's heart rate increased upon hearing Arie's voice, and slowed when she noticed the sadness in it.

"Arie, it's Cees Bannigan."

"Hi."

Cees smiled, thinking that Arie sounded young and shy. "Um, I'm just calling to see how you're feeling today."

"I'm okay." Cees thought Arie sounded as tired as she felt.

"They made me leave, or I would have come back to check on you." Cees could have kicked herself for her need to explain. The ensuing silence told her that Arie was probably as uncomfortable as she was. "Did you have any more nightmares after left?"

"No, I couldn't get back to sleep."

Join the club, Cees thought. "I'm not surprised. You looked horrified when you woke up."

"It wasn't as bad as it looked."

"So you remember it?"

Arie hesitated before answering, "No, not really. That's why I'm assuming it wasn't that bad. I think I would have remembered a really bad one."

Cees frowned at nothing. "It was bad enough to cause a migraine."

"Dr. Parrantt says migraines can be caused by anything from stress to allergies."

"Great, for all we know, I'm the reason you had the migraine." Cees's bid for levity went unanswered as the phone grew quiet again. "Okay, well I should probably let you go."

. "I wanted to, thank you, I…" Arie seemed to want to say something else, and Cees felt resentful that she was not alone in her office. "Thanks for, you know, staying."

"This is the first time I've been thanked for falling asleep on a woman." Cees stiffened, realizing too late that she had carelessly broached the subject of sexuality. Her heart stuttered at the silence, but when Arie laughed, Cees devoured the sound like food to a famine victim. *It's been so damn long since I've heard that sound.* Cees was still smiling as she listened to Arie's chuckle when Miranda walked in.

"I just called to tell you that I have a late meeting," Cees said reluctantly. "But I'll be there around 6:30. If you need anything, have someone call me and I'll pick it up on the way."

Cees thought about shooting Miranda a look to get her out of her office so she could continue her call with Arie in private. "I'll see you soon, okay?" Cees told herself that she had imagined the sound of regret in Arie's voice when she said good-bye. She resented having Miranda sitting across from her because she might have kept Arie on the phone longer, perhaps even asked her what was on her mind and why she had sounded so forlorn when she had first answered the phone.

"I feel cheated. I don't think I ever got that tone when we spoke by phone."

"What tone? I don't know what you're talking about."

"I'll see you soon," Miranda said in a deep, almost seductive voice. She was grinning, but Cees thought she saw hurt in her eyes. It disappeared so fast that Cees couldn't be sure it was ever really there. "Is that why you turned me down for dinner?"

"I don't know what you're talking about. Did you come in here to accuse me of something?"

"Whoa, don't get all snappy, I was only kidding." Miranda opened her folder, her voice curt and formal. "Sorry for sticking my nose where it doesn't belong."

"Miranda, I didn't mean anything by that. That was my friend, the one I told you was in the hospital? Actually, she was more than a friend. Things ended badly between us and we never had closure."

"You still care about her?"

"More than I should," Cees admitted reluctantly. "But the truth is, she isn't the reason I broke things off with you."

Miranda studied Cees's face. "Damn, I was kind of hoping I had just been dumped for a better catch. Now you're telling me I was just plain dumped."

"Dumped is a pretty strong word." Cees almost added "for what we had" but realized how cruel that would have sounded. Miranda's pride might be a little injured now, but she'd find someone else to salve her wounds. Cees was sure that when all was said and done, they would continue to be friends.

Miranda's smile lacked depth. "I know, I just thought you could use a laugh."

"I could. Thanks."

"So does she want you back?"

"Miranda, if you don't mind, I'd rather not rehash this. I'm still pretty sensitive about the whole thing. I just want to make sure she's going to be okay so that we both can get back to our own lives."

"What's keeping you from doing that? I mean, who's to say you have to be the one to look after her?"

"She doesn't have any family, and so far, I'm the only friend that's shown up to the hospital."

"I don't get it. What's in it for you? It sounds like she hurt you pretty badly. Why even put yourself through this?"

It was a valid point, one that Cees had asked herself as recently as a few hours ago, but the honest confusion on Miranda's face made Cees sad. It seemed to solidify the fact that they were two very different people and that she had been wasting her time in the hopes that she would grow to feel for Miranda as she had for Arie.

"Because I don't really have anyone either."

"Would she do the same thing for you?"

"I'd hope so, but I don't know. It doesn't really matter. I'm not doing this in the hopes that she would reciprocate. I'm doing it because it's the right thing to do. How hard is it to be there for someone?"

Miranda raised a brow as if to say "you tell me." Cees shook her head and Miranda opened her file and pulled out some documents she wanted Cees to look over. Cees nodded at what she hoped to be the appropriate times, but her mind was on Miranda's question. There was a time when she would have given an unequivocal yes to the question would Arie have been there for her. Whether or not their relationship had lasted. Now she wasn't sure. Now she wondered if she had ever known the real Arie at all.

❖

Arie told herself she was sitting near the window for the view and not because she was watching for Cees. She didn't know what kind of car Cees drove, and even if she did, it was too dark outside her window to recognize the people entering and leaving the hospital.

Arie had spent nearly an hour looking at her face in the small mirror she had been given, but her hands had been more interesting to her. She'd kept remembering how good it had felt to have Cees's fingers laced with her own, how the feel of Cees's hands on her had calmed the pain and turmoil in her head. She knew enough to know that she had caused the haunted look on Cees's face, and she sensed that the smile, the one she saw in the opening credits, was a little less vibrant because of something she did.

Arie's subconscious had just began tormenting her with doubts about the probability of Cees's not showing up, when she came bursting through the door of the hospital room looking harried and clutching three magnificent yellow flowers. She stopped abruptly, her eyes on the neatly made hospital bed. Arie saw a flash of disappointment cross Cees's face.

"You brought me flowers," Arieanna said. Cees's head swung toward her so quickly that Arieanna believed she heard an audible crack.

"I thought you had gone."

"Where would I go?"

"Home to your place?"

"I just got tired of being in that bed all the time." Arie stood up and both Cees's hands went out as if she wanted to help her, but she didn't move.

"Should you be doing that? Should I help you?"

Arie felt confused and shy as she looked at the outstretched hands, the one holding the flowers and the empty one. The back of her head complained, but not by much. Her back and hips were screaming, but the look of utter relief on Cees's face when she stood within inches of her was worth the pain.

"I'm taller than you are," Arie said. From that damn bed she had been unable to gauge Cees's height. She'd taken for granted that Cees would be taller than she was, but then, if not for her driver's license, she wouldn't even know her own height was five-foot-nine.

Cees smiled when she said, "Only by an inch or two. I could still carry you if I needed to."

Arie watched her mouth say those words, but she felt as if they were something else. Something that made her pulse race and her face feel flush. She swallowed and wondered if she should ask Cees to help her back to her seat.

"I like flowers, don't I?"

Cees looked down at the flowers in her hand as if she had forgotten them. She thrust out her hand and Arie reached out to take the flowers. Layered petals formed an orb so perfect that Arie was afraid she would destroy them by taking them.

Arie's fingertips grazed the edge of Cees's skin, and she noticed how much paler Cees's skin looked against her own. She liked it. She also liked the way Cees's long fingers held on to the flowers. When Cees finally released the flowers and put both hands behind her back, Arie immediately buried her nose in the blooms, the perfect pillow.

"You love flowers," Cees said.

"But especially these, right?"

"Right."

"I can see why. Look at how full these are." Arie put the flowers to her nose, closed her eyes, and inhaled. "Oh, God, that's…" Arie struggled for the right word to use, but her tongue refused to find it.

"Ambrosia," Cees said in a soft voice.

For some reason, Arie felt she had been given another clue to her former self. Was that what she used to say when she held these particular flowers? Did Cees bring them to her often? Why would she?

Arie opened her eyes and saw confusion and fear written clearly on Cees's face. The weeping voice from her dream came slinking to the surface. Arie looked away. "I should put these in something."

"That water glass should do," Cees said and quickly disappeared into the bathroom. It was a few long moments before Arie heard the water running, and soon after, Cees came out with the flowers placed in the glass.

"Peonies," Arie said.

"You're starting to remember!" Cees had a delighted look on her face.

Arie wanted to keep that look of pure joy on Cees's face, but she didn't want to mislead her. "Am I, or is that common knowledge?"

Just as she suspected, some of the excitement left Cees's eyes as she looked down at the flowers and then back up at Arie. "They're not that common. It took me forever to find a place that sold them. I had never even heard of them before I met you."

"Really? But you have a gardening portion on your show."

"We bring in experts to help us develop things like that."

Something pulled at the back of Arie's memory, but when she tried to focus in on it, it disappeared. Cees shifted from one foot to the other, breaking the spell.

"Oh, why don't we sit down? I had them bring in a second chair so we could sit together." Cees didn't offer to help her this time, but Arie noticed that she let her walk toward the two chairs sitting next to the window. Cees didn't sit down until Arie had.

From the sigh Cees let out, Arie realized that she wasn't the only one grateful to be off her feet.

"You look exhausted. Maybe you should head home." Cees did look like she could use some sleep, but Arie knew she hadn't quite kept the disappointment from her voice.

"I'd like to sit for a few, if you don't mind. Visiting hours are over at seven, and I've already been warned that there'll be no repeats of last night. How's your head?"

Arie blushed as she remembered the sound of Cees's voice. The feeling of her hand on her head and the softly whispered words of comfort. "It's fine."

"Dr. Parrantt said that the migraines can cause blackouts. He said you should make sure to sit down if you should ever get another one."

"He told me that too."

As if recognizing that Arie was looking for some way to change the subject, Cees asked, "Did he also tell you that you can go home soon?"

"Yeah, he said in a few days."

"Are you looking forward to it?"

The question should have been an easy one to answer. The sobs from her dreams came flooding back. Arie couldn't swear to it, but she was almost certain that they had been a memory— a memory in which she had done or said something that had broken Cees's heart. Dr. Parrantt had reluctantly admitted that there might be some parts of her memory that never returned. She hoped the memory of hurting Cees was one of the spotty parts. Cees had shown nothing but gentle concern for her since she had awakened. "I don't know if I am or not. I *will* be glad to have my freedom. I don't get the impression that I'm used to sitting around much."

Cees laughed. "No, you were never one to sit still for long. In fact, I'm surprised you haven't gone stir-crazy, not being able to get your hands in some dirt."

"I was a landscape architect."

"You remember that?"

"The police told me." Arie hated the way the hope ebbed from Cees's face. "Is that how we met?"

It was twenty seconds, maybe longer before Cees answered. "Yes."

"Did I work on your show?"

"Briefly." This time her answer came quicker.

"Why briefly?"

Cees stood up so quickly that her chair made a shrill scream against the linoleum. Startled by the sound, Arie turned just in time to catch the distraught look on Cees's face before she hid it. "You thought it best that we not work together if we were going to be serious about our relationship."

"Things were very serious between us, weren't they?" Arie didn't expect Cees to look so startled and vulnerable, nor did she expect the longing it caused in her. Turning back to the window was the only way she knew to break the spell. Arie focused on the plain, boring rows of flowers in the hospital parking lot. Cees's hand rested briefly on her shoulder and was gone before she could comment. She closed her eyes and imagined turning around and falling into Cees's arms. It was a surprising thought, but not an unpleasant one. When the long silence forced her to turn around, she found Cees sitting with her elbows propped on her knees. Her eyes were so intense that Arie should have been uncomfortable, but wasn't.

"Tell me about your day."

It didn't escape Arie's attention that Cees hadn't answered her question about the seriousness of their relationship. "Why would you want to hear about my day? I lie in that bed. Stumble down that hall once or twice a day. Nothing much to tell." Arie hooked a thumb at the blackened TV screen. "That looks like it might be fun."

Cees smiled. "It is fun, but mostly it's a lot of work. You'll remember how much soon enough," she said with confidence. "Why don't you start with before you stumbled down the hall? I heard you ate a good-size lunch without being forced?"

Arie felt awkward telling Cees the mundane details of her limited life, but she did, and soon the awkwardness faded. Arie liked the way Cees leaned forward when she talked. Liked the way she asked questions and frowned when something concerned her.

The constant discomfit and fear that went along with having no memory was muted when Cees was present, a fact that scared Arie because she wasn't sure how long Cees would be willing to let her interrupt her life. Dr. Parrantt had said she would be allowed to go home soon. Home meant an unfamiliar place without Cees Bannigan.

Arie pushed the thought away and answered Cees's question. She wouldn't think about going home now. For now, she would gather as many of Cees's smiles as she could. When the lights went out and the world outside her hospital room quieted, she would use the memory of that smile to help her forget that she was supposed to be afraid.

Construction forced pedestrians and bicyclists to share the road with rush-hour buses, cars, and Cees's large pickup truck. Cees vacillated between fuming and being grateful that it was Friday. The fuming stemmed from the fact that thanks to the traffic, she would be lucky to have thirty minutes with Arie tonight. She was grateful because tomorrow was Saturday and she would be able to spend a few hours playing cards or reading as they had done last weekend.

Lilly was right. She had allowed herself to get too close. Cees pulled into the parking spot that she now thought of as her own and jumped out of the car. Lilly hadn't asked her about Arie, so it had been easier for her to gloss over the fact that she was visiting her daily. It was very much like Lilly just to assume that Cees had done what she suggested.

Cees slowed her trot to a steady walk. She entered the hospital, waved to the front desk, and made her way to Arie's room. Cees was surprised to find Dr. Parrantt in Arie's room when she arrived. Arie was sitting in the chair near the window with a cup grasped between her hands and a frown on her face.

"Everything okay?" Cees asked. To her pleasure, Arie's frown disappeared and Dr. Parrantt looked relieved.

"Ms. Bannigan, if you would—"

Dr. Parrantt was interrupted as Arie stood up and walked toward Cees. Her movements, though still stiff, were slightly more natural looking. The jeans that Cees had purchased for her were fitting better. She still looked too thin, but she looked good. Damn good.

Arie stopped in front of Cees, and they looked at each other and then down. There was always this moment when she came to visit. She never knew whether she was supposed to just walk in and sit down or if she was supposed to hug Arie or do what she wanted—to brush her lips across those full lips. They had progressed to neither, so Cees usually contented herself with walking into the room and claiming the seat that had been brought in especially for her visits.

"I'm sorry I'm so late. Traffic was a mess."

"I thought maybe you couldn't make it tonight."

Cees searched Arie's eyes, wishing they were alone yet glad they weren't. "I told you I would call if I couldn't make it." Cees wondered why she sounded like she was pleading for something from Arie.

"I know. I always worry, though. I think the worst until you get here." The admission was so sweet that Cees's palms itched to reach for her hand. Movement behind Arie distracted Cees long enough to realize that she had forgotten Dr. Parrantt was still in the room.

"Ms. Bannigan," Dr. Parrantt said hesitantly. "I was just telling Ms. Simon, she's physically on the mend. Staying in this room isn't going to help her regain her memory any sooner. What could help is if she returned to more natural surroundings."

Cees looked from Arie to Dr. Parrantt and back again. "Well, that's great news, isn't it?" If it was so great, why did Cees feel like the bottom of her stomach had been ripped out? How could she possibly think that she could let Arie back into her life only to let her turn around and leave again? How could she forget how much it hurt the first time?

"I was trying to explain when you walked in." Dr. Parrantt's voice was soft, apologetic. "Ms. Simon can't be left alone for long periods of time, but she insists on going home alone."

"You don't have to go home. You can stay with me as long as you want. I'll make arrangements to have someone sit with you while I'm at work." The words sprang naturally from Cees's lips. She and Arie blinked at each other.

Arie spoke first. "I don't want to take advantage of you."

"I know you don't, and you aren't."

"I can hire someone to check on me."

The fact that Arie was so tentative reminded her that this was not the same woman she had known. Maybe she should just walk away. From what the police said, Arie had plenty of money to hire the best care available. Did Cees really want to deal with the twin problems of Lilly and her inability to keep her own heart for herself?

"You could do that, or you could stay with me." Cees looked at Dr. Parrantt. "Would that be all right? My place is more comfortable, and I'm more familiar than anyone she would hire."

Dr. Parrantt cleared his throat. "Anything would be better than having her stay alone at this point. Please come by my office before you leave tonight." He voiced his next words to Arie. "Regardless of what you decide, I'd like you to stay here tonight. I'd like to see you biweekly for the next few months, and when you're up to it, there are some avenues of psychotherapy we can explore. I'll leave you two to discuss your options."

Dr. Parrantt left the room and Arie went back to her seat and looked out the window. Cees watched her for a long moment before joining her. She tried to remember why she had been so sure that ushering Arie out of her life was a good idea moments before she had insisted that she stay with her. She wished she could just take a step back to…

"Arie, I just realized you might not want to stay with me. I'm so sorry if I made an assumption. I thought you were just afraid of imposing."

"No, I mean yes, I want to stay with you."

"But?"

"It terrifies me."

"I terrify you? Why?"

"Not you specifically. The idea of going home with you."

"Do you know what's causing you to feel this way? Is it something I've done?"

Arie shook her head but wouldn't meet Cees's gaze.

"Okay." Cees blew out a breath and stood up. "I suppose someone at the front desk can give us recommendations on home healthcare providers."

"That's not what I want, either."

"Arie, would you just help me out here? I'm trying to do the right thing by you, and right now I'm a little confused as to what that is."

When Arie finally did look at Cees, she wished she hadn't. Arie hadn't fabricated the depths of her fear. The fact that she was terrified was evident in her face. All of her previous frustration drained from Cees. She sat down and reached for Arie's hand. Arie took it without hesitation.

"Tell me what would make you most comfortable. If you want to stay at your place, I'll come there to visit you after work, just like I come here. If you want to stay with me, that's more than okay too. I'll do whatever you want. All you have to do is tell me what that is and I'll make it happen."

"I don't want you to go away," Arie said, and this time, she didn't look left or right. She met Cees's eyes with an honesty that both thrilled and frightened the hell out of Cees.

"I'm not going anywhere until you ask me to go." Arie tightened her grip and looked out the window. Cees closed her eyes briefly and then pretended to gaze out the window as well. Instead she saw an unclear reflection of Arie and herself in the tinted glass. Cees wondered how long it would take for the feeling of being raw and exposed to pass.

CHAPTER SEVEN

Arie looked up just before Cees entered the room. She felt the same confusion and insecurity she had felt when she'd fist regained consciousness, but it was coupled with excitement and anticipation.

"You look nice," Cees said.

Arie wanted to return the compliment but wasn't sure how to do it in a natural way.

"Thank you," she said, looking down at the jeans Cees had purchased for her.

"Sorry if they're a little big. You've lost some weight since I bought jeans for you last."

"They're very comfortable. You think I lost weight in here? I feel like they keep forcing me to eat when I'm not hungry."

Cees smiled, and the worried look she didn't seem capable of hiding disappeared momentarily. Cees pushed her glasses up on the bridge of her nose, and Arie fought the urge to grab her hand. "Maybe, but you've always had trouble keeping your body weight consistent. This all of it?" Cees reached out to take the two bags Arie was holding. Her voice was gruff, which was totally at odds with the vulnerability that seemed to become more pronounced by the moment.

"Yeah, I don't have much. Only the stuff you picked up for me." Arie saw Cees look at the soft brown teddy bear peeking out of one of the bags. Arie remembered the way Cees had shoved it into her hands on one of her visits and how much the small gift had thrilled her.

"We can stop by your place to pick up more of your clothes."

"That's fine, but it can wait until tomorrow if it needs to." Arie would have told Cees the truth, that for reasons she didn't really understand, she was reluctant to go to her own apartment, but Cees had looked distracted from the moment she had walked into the room, and Arie didn't want to burden her further.

She's probably tired. You aren't her whole world. She has a job, a life, real friends. She's probably wondering how she ended up with an invalid to take care of. Arie's thoughts were interrupted by an orderly with a wheelchair. She was wheeled to the front desk, where she signed whatever they put in front of her, then allowed herself to be wheeled out of the hospital. At the curb she watched as Cees jogged out to get her car. She was grateful not to have to keep up with Cees's quick strides.

The clothes Cees wore on the TV show were of a much tighter-fitting ilk than the jeans and T-shirt she seemed to choose on her own, and the glasses were different. Arie liked how comfortable Cees always looked. Her dark blond hair was in a French twist at the back of her head, and she wore no makeup or jewelry. Arie wondered if she liked to wear makeup or jewelry. The thought of jewelry caused Arie to remember the ring that she was told had been removed from her navel. She shuddered. What had possessed her to do something like that anyway?

Arie got up from the chair as Cees pulled a large blue truck to a stop in front of her. Arie said a distracted "thank you" to the orderly who wheeled the chair away.

"Sorry, they wouldn't let me leave it here while you checked out. Something about it being a hazard," Cees said when she appeared at her side.

"That's not what I pictured you driving." Cees unlocked and

opened the truck door. Arie looked up into the cabin and back at Cees. "You like 'em big, don't you?"

Cees's lips parted slightly, but she didn't answer. Thinking perhaps Cees had missed what she said, Arie repeated herself. Finally, Arie pointed up into the truck, and Cees gazed into the cavernous cab of the truck. Arie frowned. Cees was starting to concern her. Maybe this had been a mistake. "The truck? It's kind of big for you, isn't it?"

Cees looked relieved and then blushed. She seemed to be having a hard time meeting Arie's eyes. "It was leased for me. I'm told it's good publicity to have people see me tooling around town in it. I didn't have much choice in the matter. Is it too high? I forgot to ask how you were feeling." Cees had a strained look on her face, and Arie rushed to assure her that she was fine despite the fact that she had been struggling to catch her breath during the walk.

Cees put the bags she'd carried for Arie into the truck and took the one Arie had carried. Then, with a soft inhalation, Arie launched herself up and into the passenger's seat. Cees stood holding the door. "Put your seat belt on," she said softly and waited until Arie did so. Arie caught her eye, trying to determine if she was having second thoughts. What she saw there confused her more than anything. She recognized her own mixture of surprise and excitement. But Arie read fear in Cees's eyes and that confused her. What could Cees Bannigan possibly have to fear from her?

❖

Cees pointed out the bridges crisscrossing the city and told the story behind each of them. Arie murmured appreciation in the appropriate places, but her mind and stomach were roiling. She didn't remember this city; she couldn't find her own home if she had to, and she didn't know the woman next to her either. Arie stole a glance at Cees's profile. They had been lovers; this she didn't doubt. But Cees either didn't know or was being purposely evasive in giving the reason they had broken things off, and that made Arie feel uncomfortable. Cees said they had argued, but she knew instinctively that it had been much more than just an argument. Arie had pushed the thought away as too distressing... no, not distressing, just another obviously important detail that she had forgotten.

"Headache?" The question was asked so softly that Arie almost missed it. If the faint throb threatened to become the stabbing pain of a migraine, she would 'fess up. For now, there seemed no point in worrying Cees unduly.

"I'm fine." Arie sneaked a peek at Cees's profile, again noticing the way her hair curled beneath the arms of her glasses and the way her mouth was full and her skin hinted with the lightest tint of darkness. Arie felt a tickle at her lips. She put her fingers to them and wondered if it were a memory or an overactive imagination.

Cees glanced at her and frowned. "If you want, we can go to your apartment tomorrow and just head to my house now if you're tired." Arie looked straight ahead. She was tired. It had been an emotionally exhausting day.

"I'd like to see where I lived," she said, and within a few moments they were pulling into the circular drive of the waterfront apartment complex. "I live here?" Arie ducked her head to look at the high-rise. "For how long?"

"You'd just moved to Portland when we met, so less than four years. You have your keys?" Arie turned to get one of the bags she had been sent home with. Pain shot up her spine and swept around to her rib cage. Air hissed from between her teeth like a deflating balloon as pain racked her body.

"What is it?" Concern colored Cees's voice.

"Turned wrong, bruised ribs from my seat belt. The pain's already fading. Just give me a minute." Arie prayed the pain would go away even as she enjoyed the feel of Cees's comforting hand at the small of her back. In a few moments her breathing had returned to normal.

"Okay?" Cees asked.

"I forget I'm still healing until I do something like that."

"Yeah, well, stop forgetting. You scared me." Cees reached behind the passenger seat, pulled the bag up, and set it between them so that Arie could root around in its contents for her key ring. She pulled it out and held it up. At least nine keys hung from the ring. "I don't know which one opens the door."

Cees took the ring from her and held up a small gray fob. "This one lets you in the front door of the complex." She held up a key. "This one is to your apartment."

Arie looked from the key to Cees. Finally, she couldn't keep herself from asking a question that would lead her closer to the one she wanted to ask but didn't know how. "Did you live here, too?" Arie tried to keep the question light, as if forgetting the person you used to live with not quite two years ago was common enough.

"No, I was just here an awful lot." Arie watched the smile disappear. "It's been a long time since I've been here." Arie filed the information, acutely aware that Cees had turned away from her before she could read anything in her expression.

She didn't say anything as Cees opened the door for her, and she stepped out of the truck, her emotions fluxing from anxiety to outright fear in the space of seconds. It felt as if Cees was holding back information that wasn't hers to keep. Arie was quiet as Cees waved the security fob in front of the panel to release the door, and she remained pensive as they rode the gold-mirrored elevator up to an apartment she didn't remember. Cees walked into the apartment and waited for her to follow. Arie noticed the scent first. The hospital smelled like an old building and cleaning supplies. Muted, but there. This place smelled of cleaning supplies, but lemon scented.

"I'm a neat freak?" she asked through clenched jaws.

Cees looked from the pristine living room to Arie. "No more so than I am. What's wrong? You look angry."

Arie shook her head, took two swift steps into the room, and realized that Cees was right, she was angry. "So this is my apartment? Kind of nice for a gardener, huh?"

"Landscape architect," Cees corrected gently, although the frown told Arie that she could no longer act as if she wasn't angry. "Arie, please tell me what's wrong. Is your head hurting? Maybe we should have gotten your prescriptions filled first."

"I'm fine. Let's just get my stuff and go."

"Is it that you would rather stay?"

"I can't stay by myself, remember?" Arie's voice was cold, biting. Arie realized that she was lashing out at the one person who was helping her without motive. From the look on Cees's face, the lash had struck home.

"Tell me why you're so angry."

Arie closed her eyes. When she opened them again, Cees was standing right there, and she felt a sob stick in her throat. "I don't know why."

She let Cees pull her into a hug. Though she didn't remember having this kind of contact with Cees in the past, it felt right. And she hurt because she didn't remember the countless other times she was sure this woman had held her. A muscle in Cees's back rippled beneath her hand. Cees held her firmly but gently as Arie released her frustration at not remembering. She didn't know how long they stayed that way, but by the time she pulled away, the feel of Cees had been imprinted on her senses. She couldn't imagine how she could have ever forgotten that—how could something so important be forgotten in an instant? She lifted her head and looked into Cees's eyes. Tears had made crescents on her cheeks beneath the glasses and pooled there before seeping down along her jaw. Arie cupped her cheek. Cees's full lips parted and Arie's eyes sought, focused, and were drawn to them. She realized she was going to kiss her just before Cees stepped back.

"We should—" She didn't finish her statement. She just walked out of the living room and into another room, the bedroom Arie realized, as she followed her slowly. Cees stood in the middle of the room with her head down. Arie took in the queen-sized bed and sparse furnishings and wondered what Cees saw that she didn't. No, not what she saw, what she remembered.

"Cees?" She turned around, and Arie realized that Cees had begun to cry even more and that this was not in response to her own tears.

"Can we just get some clothes and get out of here?"

Arie hesitated and began opening drawers. She pulled out shirts, underwear, and socks as if shopping for someone other than herself. Something was hurting Cees. Being *here* was hurting Cees, and Arie couldn't remember why.

Cees's neighborhood was dark and quiet when they pulled into the driveway. It was too dark to see the exact color of the house, but Arie could make out light siding and a shingled roof that cut a dark triangle against the gray sky. One of the two windows that bracketed the door glowed, giving the home a one-eyed pirate look. Arie's palms itched as she looked at the nondescript and slightly unkempt front yard. She trembled when the car door was opened and Cees stepped back to let her get out.

"Cold?"

"A little," Arie said, though it wasn't that cold.

"Let's get inside, then. I bought this house last year, so I'll have to show you where everything is."

"It wouldn't have mattered if I had been here before now, would it?"

Arie was shocked by how bitter she sounded. She meant to apologize instantly, but the hurt look on Cees's face froze the words on her tongue. "I don't know why I just snapped like that."

Arie crossed her arms in front of her chest. A familiar throb began at the base of her skull.

"Don't apologize. The reason Dr. Parrantt asked me to come see him last night was to tell me that mood swings, amongst other things, can be par for the course with a case like yours. I'll grab the bags. Let's get inside. It's freezing out here."

She's trying to sound carefree, which means she's anything but. Arie sighed and eased out of the truck to follow Cees up the walkway to her front door. A light came on as they stepped on the porch just as it had when they had driven into the driveway. Arie squinted. She had hoped that the headache would just stay at a low roar, but the light and the chill seemed to be exacerbating the situation. Cees mumbled something under her breath as she fumbled with her front door keys.

There was a time when I would have held her close to me to keep her warm while she opened the door. Whatever made me push her out of my life had to be very bad. Arie started at the unbidden thought. She took in Cees's frame and wondered what she looked like without clothes. Heat settled on her face and warmed her body. It wasn't an uncomfortable feeling, just without basis, without anything to back it up, and it scared her. Would Cees expect things from her? The thought sent a shiver through her body. Of course she wouldn't. They weren't lovers anymore.

"Jeez, I could have picked the damn lock faster than that." Cees opened the door and switched on another light in the entryway.

Arie stepped in, temporarily forgetting her nervousness at her first glance at the inside of Cees's house. She had expected a larger home, but she was pleased that Cees seemed to have found one that fit her personality. The small entry led immediately to the living room and dining room. One door was closed, but two others were open, and Arie could clearly see a bedroom with a queen-sized bed. Arie set down her bag and walked into the living room. She trailed her hand over the black leather couch and noted the faint scent of cinnamon. She had noticed the fragrance on Cees when she had visited, and now she spotted the culprit—scented candles in glass apothecary jars lined the coffee table.

"It's small, but it's just me." Cees sounded almost apologetic as she explained. "Two bedrooms and two baths. Your bathroom's out here." Arie flushed as Cees pushed the door open. She could see the large claw tub stuffed into the small room. A pedestal sink made the space seem less cramped. Just as she had imagined, candles were spaced out on a shelf above the tub. Arie had a vision of Cees sitting in the tub with bubbles failing to hide her important parts.

"You look flushed. Are you getting tired? Here, let's get you some towels and I'll show you where you'll be sleeping." Cees opened a door and began handing Arie large sand-colored bath sheets. Arie took them, grateful that Cees was either unaware or ignoring the fact that she hadn't spoken since they'd walked into the house. Arie was feeling overwhelmed by this new place and by the fact that she and Cees were alone together. No nurses to interrupt, no voices just outside the door. She felt hyperaware of everything Cees did. Cees must have finally noticed that Arie was too quiet. "Tell me what's wrong."

"Do you… Is that where you're going to sleep?" Arie wasn't aware of what she was going to say before she said it.

Cees turned to look at the door Arie was looking toward and back at Arie. "Yes, I was in the process of redecorating that room, so it's not exactly ready for guests. Why do you ask?"

A bell sounded from the back of the house, startling them both. "I'm not expecting anyone," Cees said as she walked to the door. Arie watched her peek through the peephole. Almost instantly, her head jerked back as if she had been slapped.

"Shit." The word was a drawn-out whisper, a combination of "be quiet" and "what the hell am I going to do." Before Arie could ask her what was wrong, someone began pounding at the door.

"Cees, I know you're in there. The monster is out front, and

all the lights are on in there. I can't find my key. It's cold out here."
The voice sounded annoyed, but not as annoyed as Arie would
be if she had been standing out there in the cold while someone
peeked at her through a peephole. Cees stepped away from the
door and looked back at Arie, a harried look of annoyance on her
face.

"Is someone in there with you? Cees Bannigan, you got
somebody in there?" The doorbell rang again, but this time it was
followed by the distinct sound of a purse being unzipped.

"Shit, shit, shit. Why did I give her a key?" Cees
whispered.

"I don't know," Arie whispered back. "You want me to go
into the bedroom?"

Cees looked surprised, but then she looked as if she were
considering the offer. "No, of course not. I'm not scared of her."
But Arie sensed there was more to it than Cees had time to say. She
might not be scared, but she was definitely not looking forward to
talking with this individual. A shunned lover, perhaps?

"Should you let her in if she already has a key?" Arie thought
Cees looked resigned as she opened the door.

"You should have called before coming over, Lilly," Cees
said to the crouched form in her entryway.

Arie had to crane her neck to get her first look at this Lilly. A
dark curtain of bone-straight black hair hid her face from Arie as
she fumbled inside an impossibly large purse. Even squatting as
she was, Arie could tell she was small and would come no higher
than her shoulder, if that. She was wearing tight black leather
pants and a matching leather bralike top. The bra was covered by
a voluminous white shirt that Arie imagined was absolutely no
obstacle to the biting chill in the air.

"'Bout damn time. It's cold out there," she groused as she
stood up and teetered past Cees on ridiculously tall heels. Heels
or no, she couldn't be more than five-foot-two, Arie decided.
Her makeup accentuated her almond-shaped eyes and her hair
glistened with a sheen that Arie would have thought impossible if

she wasn't seeing it for herself. The woman could have worn a lot less suggestive clothing and still exuded sex appeal. Arie looked down at her jeans. Despite the fact that Cees was similarly clad, she still felt frumpy.

"You should have worn a coat, Lilly," Cees said while watching the newcomer with the caution of a person about to handle something volatile.

"I didn't have one that went with the outfit." Lilly was still rooting around in her purse as she walked in. "I know for sure I put that key in here." Lilly turned to Cees. "Anyway, I think you should get smashed while you still can. They have this new club called the Velvet Rabbit and…" Lilly trailed off as the curtain that had apparently let her walk into the room without noticing Arie lifted.

There was a long, shocked pause, and then a strangled, "Oh—no you didn't." Lilly dropped her bag and began tottering toward Arie at an alarming speed. Arie looked for a place to put the towels in case she had to defend herself, but Lilly stopped just short of ramming her head into her chest.

"What is she doing here, Cees Bannigan?" Her accent had thickened, and Cees's last name sounded like bunion instead of Bannigan in her anger. Definitely a lover. Arie clenched her jaw and refused to step away from the furious figure in front of her.

"Lilly, Arie doesn't remember anything about our past."

"Oh, so you thought you'd start over fresh?"

"Lilly, please, let's not do this now."

"You know what, Cees?" Lilly held up her hands. "Let's not do this at all." She finally turned away from Arie; her long black hair seemed to reach out and slap Cees across her face the way her hand probably wanted to. What was going on here? Did she actually know this Lilly? She had to have known her to make her hate her so.

Lilly yanked up her open purse, barely managing to keep from spilling its contents, and hobbled back out into the freezing cold, taking short little choppy steps that made the extent of her anger even more clear. Cees looked from Arie to the back of her furious friend.

"I'll be right back. I need to go talk to her before she drives off angry."

Arie nodded and Cees pulled the door closed behind her, leaving Arie standing in an unfamiliar house, clutching bath towels while the ex-lover she couldn't remember ran after someone else.

CHAPTER EIGHT

Cees pulled the front door shut and jogged across the grass toward Lilly's ridiculous little Saturn. She caught up with Lilly because she was still fumbling in her luggage-sized purse for her keys.

Before she could say anything, Lilly turned around. The motion light illuminated Lilly's face with an icy light. Damn it, she was wearing her battle face. The one she wore on the playground, the dance floor, and according to rumor, in the bedroom. Cees searched her mind for the best thing to say to defuse the situation.

Lilly, as usual, knew just what to say. "You are so damn stupid. I thought hetero women were stupid for chasing after men who don't want them, but you're stupid too."

Cees winced. The accent was par for the course with Lilly's anger; so were the insults.

"It isn't what you think." Cees tried to keep her voice modulated in the hopes that Lilly would do the same.

"It isn't? Really? Let me see. The person who stepped on you and then kicked you out the door with the trash is now standing in your house in front of your bedroom with some clean sheets in her hand."

"Those weren't sheets. They were towels. I was planning on letting her have my room and I was going to sleep in the... You know what, Lilly? I don't have to explain myself to you. You are not my mother." The words were automatic. A response launched on the pressure that she'd felt since walking out of the hospital with Arie.

"No, I'm not your mother, but I was there for the weeks and months you wandered around trying to figure out what you did wrong and how you could fix it. I was there when you finally started getting your damn pride back, and I was there when you finally got angry and bitchy. And I've been here as you tried to put the pieces together by sleeping with someone who means nothing to you."

"That's not true. I care about Miranda."

"Really? Enough to let her hurt you?" She glanced toward the house. "Twice?"

Cees wanted to deny that Arie still had the power to hurt her. She wanted to, but she was afraid that it might be a lie. Lilly ferreted out lies as easily as her mother. "She needs my help, Lilly."

"Who's gonna help you?" Lilly pointed at her chest so hard that if she had made contact, one of her long nails would have done damage.

"No one will need to help me. It's just until she gets better and—"

"And decides she doesn't want you again?"

English might not have been Lilly's first language, but she was deadly with it. Cees resisted the urge to turn away from her friend. In all the years they had known each other, they'd had five real fights. Oddly, the first had been over a boy. The last—before this one—had been over Arieanna.

"I'm not trying to get her to want me. I loved her once. I loved her with everything I had, but she didn't love me back. Now she's hurt and she's alone. I can't just—" Cees gestured with her hands, at a loss for words, because in all honesty, she didn't know why she felt she had to be the one to help Arie.

Lilly's anger and the fact that she still had to look down at her made Cees remember how they had met. She'd had the misguided idea the small stranger needed help when she was bullied in the school yard. Boy, had she been wrong. Lilly fought like a cat threatening to scratch the eyeballs out of anyone who came near her. Cees would have smiled at the memory if the cat wasn't standing in front of her now, back hunched, hair electric.

"Don't come crying to me when she hurts you."

"I won't come crying to you because I won't get hurt. She's just a friend."

Lilly smacked her lips and started chewing viciously on a piece of gum that must have been tucked into the side of her jaw the whole time. Her claim to fame at Providence Elementary School was being the girl who had chewed the same piece of gum for two weeks before her mother found out about it and made her spit it out.

"You need to look up the definition of 'friend' in the dictionary. Heartache isn't normally involved. I need to get going. I'm not paying the cover at the club." Lilly must have realized then that she hadn't locked her car because she opened the door and got inside, still fumbling around in her purse for her keys.

Cees caught the driver side door before Lilly could slam it and tweaked the set of keys hanging from the ignition. Instead of a thank-you, Lilly slammed her purse into the passenger seat.

"Call me tomorrow and let me know how it went, okay? I'll even listen if you want to tell me about some guy you met."

"No, you call me when she's out of your life for good." Lilly started the car, so Cees had to practically lean in through the window to hear the second part of her statement. "Oh, and by the way? I'm telling Momma," Lilly yelled.

Cees would have laughed if she didn't think Lilly was serious. "You don't have to do that. I was planning on calling her tomorrow to tell her anyway."

Lilly must have spotted the lie coming because she just

smiled. "You can step away from my car now or you can hop away later."

Cees backed away quickly and Lilly yanked her door shut and gunned out of the driveway without so much as a proper look behind her. Cees winced as the Saturn's tires peeled off down the street. The cold and the thought of a conversation with Momma Nguyen about Arie caused her to shiver. Back in the house she was relieved to see that Arie was not standing in the hall peeking out the window as she would have been.

The bedroom door was open, though there was no light on inside. Cees hesitated and looked inside. Arie was curled into a tight ball on the bed. Cees reached in to shut the door, but just as she did Arie's face distorted and she placed a hand over her forehead. She had mistaken Arie for half asleep. She was wide-awake and tense with pain.

"Arie, what's wrong?" Cees walked into the room.

"My head."

"Where's your bag? Did they send anything with you?"

"Took it already."

"Okay. What can I do?" Arie didn't say anything and Cees walked into the room and touched her back. The muscles there were so tense they trembled. Cees felt her throat close as she tried to imagine what kind of pain would cause Arie to be almost rigid from it. *Don't scare her by getting upset.*

"How long before the meds kick in?" Cees asked, her voice devoid of emotion.

"Don't know, maybe fifteen minutes. They'll make me nauseous before they make me feel better."

"Can I help you get under the covers?" Cees asked.

Arie didn't speak for so long Cees almost repeated herself.

"I don't want to move."

Cees sat down next to her on the bed, careful not to shift it too much. Her hand went to Arie's back again, and since Arie didn't protest, she let it stay.

"Did my argument with Lilly cause this?" she asked in a near whisper. A small movement from Arie told Cees that Arie wanted to protest, but couldn't.

"Hang on a second." Cees stood up, cut the light out in the living room, and pulled off her shoes.

When Cees sat back down on the bed, Arie mumbled a barely discernable "thanks."

"Did your headache just start?"

"When we left the hospital.

"Why didn't you tell me when I asked you if your head was hurting?"

"Thought it was just nerves."

Cees, too, had had a bit of a headache upon exiting the hospital. The feeling of helplessness and fear was familiar. She had tried to forget it, but here it was again. The palms of Cees's hands itched. She wanted to fix this. She wanted to fix Arie's pain so she could go back to her own apartment and Cees could somehow move on with her life. Not move on in the way Lilly thought she should. Cees had admitted to herself long ago that she would never fully get over Arie. She had simply gotten better at hiding her loss. The fact that Arie hurt now tore her apart. She began to rub Arie's back. It didn't take long before Cees felt some of the tension ease from the tight back muscles. "Is this okay?" she asked, careful to keep her voice soft so as not to inflict more pain.

"Yes, please."

Cees smiled, relieved that she could help in some way. At least for now. The thought, negative and remote, had nothing to do with Arie and everything to do with her father's slow, agonizing death from cancer. Even with the attentive support of the Nguyen family, she had still felt lonely. Until she met Arie.

Arie's back slowly began to relax, and impulsively, Cees whispered, "Can you turn all the way onto your stomach?"

Arie immediately began the slow process of uncurling

herself from her pain. Cees crawled onto the bed with her knees on either side of Arie's hips and put her hands in Arie's short brown hair, the shock of feeling it again not as profound as she thought it would be. She kept her fingers gentle and worked her way through the soft, thick hair and up to Arie's temple.

"Don't lift up, just relax," she said. Cees spent several long minutes working the stress from Arie's scalp before she worked her way to her tense neck muscles.

"Cees, you don't have to do this." Arie's voice was muffled by the pillow. It sounded as if she had just awakened from a night of lovemaking.

Cees pushed the spark of arousal to the far recess of her mind. "I know I don't, but I feel so helpless when I see a problem that I can't fix."

"I bet you don't have many of those," Arie said, sounding drowsy and relaxed.

Cees's thoughts went to the day her father told her he wasn't going to get any better. "Try to get some sleep," Cees said as her fingers settled on Arie's trapezius muscles and rubbed, soothing gently until sleep released Arie from the pain.

❖

The voice from her dream was back; so was the darkness. There was no weeping this time. This time the quiet was interrupted by one word. "Yes." Arie felt herself reach for that voice. Her fingers touched it, grazed it, found the spot, and curled around it, pulling it close. This time the "yes" was desperate, pleading, and, yes, weeping, but not sad or desolate. This voice was joyful and so very familiar.

Arie opened her eyes and would have sat up had her short-term memory not kicked in, reminding her of the splitting headache she'd had and at the same time, Cees's panacea for it. Arie mentally took stock of herself the way she had when she had awakened in the hospital alone in the dark and in pain. She had told herself to move her toes and waited the agonizing split second it took her drugged brain to recognize the command. Assured that she hadn't lost the use of her feet and hands, she lay quietly, listening to the sounds of this new place and the pleasant scent of laundry soap and cinnamon candles.

A soft sigh to her right caused Arie to turn her head quickly without thought of the possibility of pain. Her eyes landed on Cees's relaxed face. She must have fallen asleep next to her. Arie could just make out the small dimple in Cees's chin. She had the absurd thought to place a finger there but decided against it. At one time, Cees had been her lover. *My lover*. Arie tested the words though she made no sound. She wasn't sure if she should feel distress or joy. Truthfully, she felt neither. She was simply curious.

Cees's lips parted and moved as if she were dreaming, and Arie remembered part of hers. Yes, of course. The voice. It had been Cees; she was sure of it. Was it a dream or a memory? Had they been making love? Was she remembering? Arie squeezed her thighs tight against a slow throbbing that had begun there. She openly stared at Cees's mouth. How many times had she kissed those lips? How many times had that simple word urged her on? "Yes" meant "please continue," didn't it? In such a breathless tone it could mean nothing else. Arie closed her eyes so that she wasn't looking at Cees, but she didn't need to look at her to remember what she looked like. Her short-term memory was in peak condition—she could remember everything about her, from the way her lower lip was drooping slightly to the way her dusky lashes rested against her cheek. She carefully turned on her side despite the fact that her mind was telling her to go back to sleep. What if Cees woke up and caught her staring?

She couldn't seem to stop. She had noticed that her body seemed drawn to Cees no matter where she was in the room. When she wasn't in the room, Arie felt as if she was in a constant state of waiting until she appeared. She wondered if Cees felt the same way about her, before quickly scuttling away from the thought.

Aside from the moment when Arie thought Cees was going to kiss her in the waterfront apartment, Arie had sensed no attraction or any other feelings from Cees other than a desire to help. Still, Arie wasn't sure, but she didn't think Cees went around kissing just anyone.

Something bad had happened to them almost two years ago. She knew that much. Whatever it was had left her living in that stale, cold apartment while Cees lived in this home alone. Arie was starting to realize that if her memories ever returned, not all of them would be pleasant.

Whether or not her mind was letting her remember the relationship, she had felt angry when Cees had gone after Lilly. And Lilly, well, there was no doubt that there was a lot of anger in her eyes when she looked at Arieanna. Arie's surprise at the situation changed to anger as soon as Cees had walked out the door. Her emotions had gone from relief that Lilly was gone, to anger that she had spoken to Cees as she had, and finally to complete and utter jealousy that Cees had gone after her. The headache followed on the heels of the deluge of emotions, and Cees's touch had chased away the pain. This time Arie sighed. She was relying on Cees too much. She meant what she'd said last night. She didn't want to disturb Cees's life any more than she already had, but she was happy and grateful when Cees had ignored her protest and insisted she come home with her. She enjoyed being around Cees. She wasn't ready for that to end, not yet.

Cees moved, she whispered a word, a half word in her sleep. It reminded Arie of the dream, and her face flamed. Now fully on her side, she watched for another uttered phrase, but a slow frown had started to crease Cees's brow, and Arie ached to smooth it away. Cees's lips were no longer parted and were tense. Arie wanted to soothe out the furrow, but she was afraid she'd wake her. She tried closing her eyes against temptation, but she could still see Cees behind her closed lids and when she opened them again, Cees was closer.

It seemed natural to kiss the furrowed brow, she hardly had to move at all, and when her hand went out to stroke Cees's chin, that seemed natural too. Cees tilted her head back, and as if in a dream, Arie kissed her. The moment their lips melded, Arie felt her body take over; she didn't need to remember. She just knew. Her hips scooted forward toward Cees though she didn't pull her close. The kiss was soft but searing. Cees's lips parted and Arie hesitated, sensed what she was supposed to do, but almost fainted from the sheer pleasure of finding the tip of Cees's tongue with her own. She deepened the kiss ever so slightly, thinking it couldn't get any better than it already was. Cees made a small sound in the back of her throat, a small yes. Arie urged her to lie flat on her back and pulled herself fully on top of Cees.

Arie could tell that Cees was fully awake because she was pulling her close, her hips grinding, pressing up into Arie's hips. Arie dug her hands into Cees's hair and held her head while she kissed her hard. Arie felt herself falling into Cees; her body taunted her with dark memories of remembered pleasure that was still too far out of reach. *Please let this be happening. Please don't let this be a dream*, Arie thought as she ran her hands down Cees's sides while her hips kept a rhythm she couldn't have slowed if she tried. Arie broke the kiss, but her hands had crept beneath Cees's pants and were now cupping her buttocks, urging her on, encouraging the rhythm that was both giving them pleasure and driving them crazy.

Abruptly, the warm body beneath her stopped moving, the hands that had been gripping her ass now held her hips hostage. Fear or something close to it ripped through her body as she realized she didn't know what to do next. Cees's heart was beating so hard Arie could feel it through her shirt. Cees needed something, and Arie wanted to give her exactly what she needed. At one time she knew what Cees liked; she was sure of that, but now… Arie jumped at the sound of Cees's voice. "We have to stop now," Cees said, but her voice told a different story, a story that Arie knew she had heard before, only she couldn't remember the beginning, middle, or end.

Arie felt the same sense of hopelessness she had felt when she first awakened in the hospital. She loosened her grip on the front of Cees's shirt and let her body relax in defeat. When Cees gathered her into a gentle, nonsexual embrace, she told herself that it was for the best, this was what she could handle. Regardless of whether or not she could remember their relationship, she knew there was something more to their estrangement than a simple argument.

That something felt as tangible as a brick wall, but she couldn't see it. Arie closed her eyes and stilled her body willing herself into the oblivion of sleep where she would hopefully find the thing she wanted most, but didn't remember at all.

CHAPTER NINE

Five a.m. came too quickly for Cees, and the fact that she had to try to sleep with the memories of Arie lying on top of her again made the night sheer hell.

The scent of eggs and coffee made her finally sit up. Cees remembered the careful way Arie moved sometimes and the way she had laid on top of her last night, injuries be damned. Cees flushed from equal parts embarrassment and renewed arousal. She had told herself she would be content with just holding Arie; the feel of her skin beneath her fingertips. But the slight hitch in Arie's breathing told Cees what Arie wanted, even more than a gently pleading hand moving her own into the right place would have. Cees had stayed in bed with Arie for as long as her willpower would let her before escaping to the other bedroom.

Over the last year and a half she had forgotten about this particular effect that Arieanna had on her—this constant state of waiting to be touched by her. Cees thought about going out front to say good morning and instead went into the bathroom. She washed quickly, pausing briefly at her stomach. One day, hopefully soon, it wouldn't be so flat. Miranda wouldn't notice the weight gain at first, especially now that they weren't sleeping together, but she wouldn't be able to hide from the camera. There would come a day when she would get that talking-to about keeping her weight within the five-pound guidelines as stipulated by her contract.

Cees turned off the water and grabbed a stale-smelling towel from the rack. She needed to go out front or risk being late for work. She found Arie in the kitchen dressed in jeans and a T-shirt, her feet bare. Cees was able to watch her for a moment noticing that she was moving fine, no residual effects from last night.

"Morning," she said softly. Arie jumped before turning around. Cees noticed that her jeans were hanging low on her hips and the fitted Prana shirt didn't fit as well as it would have in the past. It was no surprise that Arie had lost weight while in the hospital, but the fact that she looked so frail made Cees feel protective.

"Morning." Arie took a step toward her, looked uncertain, and stopped. Cees couldn't blame her. What the hell had happened? How had they gone from still trying to get to know each other to her forgetting that this Arie would be frightened of her passion?

"I need to explain. About what happened last night."

"Don't say you're sorry," Arie said, and Cees saw a strange look cross her face as she turned back to the stove.

"I wasn't going to." Cees could tell by the look on Arie's face that she didn't believe her.

"I like to cook, don't I?"

"Yes, you remember that?"

"Some things I remember and some things I don't," Arie said as she moved the pan from the stove and began looking through the cabinets.

"Next one over," Cees offered.

Arie thanked her without looking back. Cees watched her T-shirt rise as she reached for the plates, briefly revealing her back. Cees's hands itched to touch the skin there.

"It's like I know how to do things," Arie was saying, "but I don't remember what you like, so I'm not sure if…if I'm doing it right. It's just a dark void."

When it finally occurred to Cees what Arie was saying, she yearned to fix the tension clearly written on Arie's face.

"Arie, you did fine. Better than I did."

"I don't remember ever making love with you." The words came out in a rush.

Of course she wouldn't remember making love to her. Why would she forget almost everything about their relationship and yet hold on to that one piece of information? Cees tried to think rationally, but her chest felt like someone had slammed a plank against it.

"I know. I should have remembered that last night. But I wasn't thinking right," Cees said.

"Neither was I at first, and then I needed—"

"Instructions?" Cees asked and smiled in case Arie thought she was insulting her.

Arie smiled back. "Yeah. Instructions would have been good."

Cees took the plates from her, letting her eyes linger on Arie's. "You don't need instructions."

Arie looked surprised and then embarrassed, and Cees realized she should probably change the subject real fast before Arie ran screaming into the early morning darkness. "How do you feel about coming to work with me today?" she asked.

"Is that okay? Do you have to ask anyone?"

Cees smiled, almost told her that she would be welcomed on the set like a long-lost sibling, and decided against it. "It'll be fine. I'm the talent, remember? I can bring anyone I want." Not exactly true, but showing off in front of one's girlfriend was allowed. *Girlfriend. Girlfriend? No, no, Cees Bannigan. Do not go there.* But even though she told herself that, smiled, and ate what Arie cooked, later, she wouldn't be able to remember what words were spoken or what the food tasted like.

What she *could* remember was the way Arie's eyes held hers. The way those same eyes focused on her hands while she cut into her food, followed the food to her mouth, and lingered on her lips when she drank from her water glass. Arie was the one who didn't remember how to make love; she was the innocent. But Cees was the one who couldn't meet those candidly curious eyes. She was the one who was afraid that Arie would see the truth, that she still wanted Arieanna Simon to distraction.

❖

Cees knew she was prattling when she started explaining the history of the steel bridge to Arie. Information she hadn't even realized she had retained until she heard herself spewing out the dates the bridge had been built and the number of men who had worked on it. The drive to the studio took fifteen minutes, but Arie said very little, telegraphing her nervousness with her monosyllabic answers and the tense way she sat. They turned into a gate and a security guard stepped out to check Cees's badge despite the fact that the gate was already sliding back. "Hey, Barron, Arieanna here is visiting the set today." The security guard squatted and peered into the truck. Recognition followed by a grin spread across Barron's face as he caught site of Arie.

"Arieanna Simon! I remember you. It's good to see you again. Hang on, I'll get you a visitor's badge." He ran into the guard post and was back with a clipboard and the badge. Cees signed Arie in and took the badge from the board.

"How's everything at home?" Cees asked in the hopes of dissuading Barron from asking Arie where she had been.

"Good, first one is going to UCSB next year, and the second will be going in two years. Hopefully on a lacrosse scholarship, but if not, I'll find a way." Barron grinned. The astronomical costs associated with having two children in college at the same time did not blight his pride in his children. Cees grinned back. Someday she hoped to have those concerns.

"Thank you." The voice was soft and shy, and Cees turned

to see Arie offering Barron a tentative smile. Barron looked surprised, but he smiled back and waved at her as he walked back into the guard post.

Cees parked the monster in its normal spot and turned the truck off. "Let's get inside. I'll show you where everything is before I have to get to work." Cees led her into the building and up to her office. Thankfully, they didn't see anyone who would have remembered Arie from her short stint with the show.

Cees enjoyed showing Arie her office and the lounge with its two TVs that showed the active filming out on one and normal satellite broadcast on the other. "If you get tired of watching up front, you can go to my office or here." Arie had her hands shoved in the pockets of her jacket. "So this is the set. We're doing a bathroom remodel. All of our projects are geared toward the single woman." Cees pointed to the large tub and the sink with no faucet as well as the floors with no heat.

"I guess she's a single rich woman," Arie said. Relief and the fact that Arie had managed to mirror one of the few criticisms of her show, that many single woman couldn't afford or had no time for the projects they suggested, struck Cees as funny. Arie started to laugh as well. "I don't even know why I just said that."

"What's all that ruckus about?" The voice was loud and more bark than bite. Cees knew it, but Arie didn't. The look of consternation on her face turned to fear as Philly Panadara came barreling around the corner, took one look at Arie, and picked up his speed.

Cees knew what would happen and intervened before she had to call off today's shoot in order to take Arie back to the hospital. She stepped in front of Arie and put her hands out to stop Philly's forward momentum. "Hang on, hang on, big guy. As much as we all love your bear hugs, Arie just got out of the hospital. One of those wouldn't do us much good in keeping her out of there for a few more days."

Philly's big face cracked into a smile. "Aww, come on. I

never hurt y'all." Cees smiled. He was right; he never had. But recipients of his hugs were usually picked up and held in a tight clasp against his chest. Cees wasn't sure how Arie would feel about being held like that by a stranger.

"Arieanna, where you been? Love the way you kept in touch. Cees here used to keep us up to speed, but that well dried up." When his expression changed, Cees hoped Arie didn't notice. It wouldn't have taken a rocket scientist to notice that Cees had been going through the motions of working after Arie broke things off. She had smiled too little, begged off too many after-work gatherings, had retreated to her rarely used office too many times.

"Uh, *Philly*, Arie's been—"

"I'm sorry I didn't keep in touch, Philly."

Cees glanced at Arie from the corner of her eye. It was a lot to explain, and if Arie didn't want people to know she didn't remember them, she would comply with that.

"I thought you looked a little pale and skinny. Both of you need to come over for some of Heidi's cooking." Heidi was Philly's partner of fourteen years, and Cees had had many a meal with the couple when her father was at his worst. In fact, if not for them and the Nguyen family, Cees would have gladly survived on dehydrated noodles.

"We'll come by soon. I promise." Realizing she had just made plans for Arie, as if they were a couple and without asking her first, she turned to Arie to make sure. If Philly noticed that Arie was more reserved than he remembered, he didn't let on.

Cees heard voices, recognizing them as Vance, her untalented co-host, and Thomas. She turned to warn Arie that although she had been long gone when Vance started, Thomas would expect her to remember him. Her phone rang and a quick glance at the screen told her it was Momma Nguyen. Cees frowned. Momma Nguyen only called her at work if something was wrong. She was notorious for calling at all hours of the night and morning and was fond of telling anyone who would listen that her children caused her lost sleep, so it was her right to wake them up. She included Cees in that statement.

"Arie, I need to take this. That's Thomas Youngblood coming. You worked together. He took over when you left. He'll be happy to see you. The guy with the curly hair and the green eyes is Vance Flowers. You don't know him and you don't want to."

"Okay."

Cees stepped away from Arie, feeling bad for leaving her to fend for herself. She answered the phone, making sure to watch Arie. If she sensed that she was getting too uncomfortable, she would hang up and deal with the ramifications later.

"Momma Nguyen?" Cees said.

"What you do to my baby?" Cees winced. Momma Nguyen preferred to get right to the point. She never said hello or good-bye. She just launched right into the conversation, and when her point was made she hung up.

"What did Lilly say?" Cees asked cautiously, feeling a pool of dread forming in her stomach as she watched her beard appear around the corner. She was too far away to see his eyes, but she knew they lit up when they saw Arie. Her jaw clenched.

"She said you let that skank shack up with you."

"Momma, Lilly has no right to talk about Arieanna like that. She barely even knows her."

"Why can't you just play the field like Lilly? Want me to tell her to show you how?" Cees threw all her annoyance into a scowl that she directed at Vance as he approached Arie, walking for all the world like he had stashed several tools in the front of his pants. Cees had seen the strut on two other occasions, and each time it had made her laugh. This time it made her want to kick him in his tool stash, three, maybe four times.

"You sleep with her?"

The question caught Cees by surprise, and she turned away

from the scene briefly to get her thoughts together. "Momma, I can't talk to you about my sex life."

"Why not? Lilly does."

"Lilly needs to learn what's appropriate and what isn't. That's why she's on my sh…on my bad list now."

"You leave my baby alone. She's just scared for you. You're kind of stupid about love."

"I am not. I wish you would stop saying that." Cees looked back to see Vance leaning closer to Arie. She started walking toward the two when a shocked look came over his face. Thomas laughed and said something that didn't relieve the situation, but he allowed Thomas to pull him away from Arie.

"You okay?" Cees mouthed. Arie held up her hand and shrugged, but there was something in the way she did it that reminded Cees of a time when Arie wasn't scared and confused and would often take it upon herself to pull some kind of a trick on Cees. Yelling followed by making up in the form of lovemaking was the rule on those occasions. The teasing smile on Arie's face reminded Cees of those wonderful days, and it hurt like hell. Cees turned her back on that smile and sighed.

"No, I have not had sex with her!" she hissed into the phone.

"Oh." The line grew quiet. "Well, my flower is still upset."

"Look, Momma, Lilly is my friend, but I'm an adult. I don't have to go to her for approval on everything I do."

"So you hurt Lilly to shack up with someone who hurt you?"

When she put it like that, it did sound kind of different.

"Momma, Arie used to be my lover. Now she needs my help."

"You love Lilly."

"Yes, but Lilly isn't my *lover*."

"I know. I'm not the stupid one. I mean you love her too."

Cees closed her eyes. "What I'm trying to say is that Arie

wasn't just my friend. I wanted to spend the rest of my life with her."

"Don't forget about Lilly. She's already been there for half."

Like always, Momma's point struck center. "How mad is she?"

"Pretty mad. Scared you're going to get hurt like last time."

Cees turned and watched Arie walk through the set looking at the fixtures, turning on the cold water at the sink and smiling when nothing came out. She wanted to tell Momma that she was scared too. But she couldn't, because that would just get another stupid label.

Arie moved differently now, cautious and slow, but when she reached out to touch something it was as if she did so with reverence. Cees had noticed that when Arie had touched her before. "It's just for a few weeks."

"Why can't she stay at her own place? She get evicted?"

"What? No. Did Lilly tell you that? She just got out of the hospital."

"Lilly didn't tell me that part."

"Of course she didn't. Momma, I'll have to explain later. Arie is here with me."

"She's right there?"

"Yeah, I had to bring her to work because the doctor says she shouldn't be left alone."

"Oh, that's not good. Flower didn't tell me that part either."

"She didn't stick around long enough for me to tell *her*."

"Why doesn't her family help?"

"She doesn't have anyone."

"Oh." Cees could practically hear Momma's heart melt through the phone. She would run interference with Lilly. Momma was a sucker for stray animals, the homeless, and motherless children. She would take to Arie like she had taken to Cees.

"Okay. Momma will help."

"Oh, thank you." Although Cees would still have to be careful. Lilly wouldn't dare go against Momma's wishes, at least not openly. Cees turned around to look for Arie just in time to see Miranda walk around the corner. Cees could have scripted Miranda's reaction to Arie—the wide smile, and she would use both hands to shake Arie's. Cees almost growled when she couldn't see what they were saying to each other.

"What time you have to be at work tomorrow?"

Cees almost forgot to answer the question when both women turned simultaneously to look in her direction.

"Six, same as always." Cees smiled and waved, but only Miranda waved back. Miranda had never met Arie, but it wouldn't take her long to connect the dots.

"Okay, I'll be there at five fifteen tomorrow."

"Be where?" Cees watched Miranda wave good-bye and leave Arie standing in the middle of the faux kitchen. She had her arms folded, and Cees saw her rub her arms as if for warmth. Damn, she should have known that jacket wouldn't be heavy enough.

"Your house. I stay with her until you get home from work."

"You will?" Cees mulled it over in her head, knew it was a bad idea, but couldn't figure out why. If Momma stayed with Arie, she could get some rest and Cees wouldn't have to worry that she was bored or uncomfortable around so many people. "Okay. Would you mind if I talked to her first?"

"Fine. I'll see you at five fifteen." The click in her ear told Cees that Momma had disconnected the call without saying good-bye. Cees dropped her arm, realizing how tense her shoulders had been during the call.

"Cees?" Arie's voice so close to her ear caused Cees to jump and pitch forward. Arie reached out to steady her with a hand on her waist.

"Sorry to startle you. Miranda, your producer, said Edith asked her to tell you you're due in makeup."

Cees looked at her watch. "How are you doing? You look a little pale."

"I'm fine. You were right. This place is a little chilly."

"I get working and I don't notice it as much. Be right back. I'm going to run up and get a sweatshirt for you."

Cees was already running up the stairs when Arie called out to remind her about makeup. Cees didn't stop until she reached the top. Arie was watching her with an odd look on her face. Their eyes held until Cees pulled open the heavy door that led to the offices and was forced to break eye contact.

Arie was pulling her coat out of the closet when she heard voices coming from the living room. She hadn't meant to keep Cees waiting, but she ran yesterday's events through her head while she dressed.

Watching Cees live was a much different experience than she had ever imagined. For one thing, when Cees walked back onto the set she was wearing a different outfit from the one she had been wearing when she left home. The jeans looked as if they had been made for her, the tool belt hung low on her hips, and her breasts looked—what was the word? Perky. Not that they weren't perky before, but now they drew the eye. Too many eyes, Arie thought as she watched Cees's co-host, the jerk who in one breath had said hello, his name as if it should mean something to her, and asked her out. And then there was the woman who had introduced herself as Cees's producer, but whose eyes implied that she and Cees were much more than coworkers.

The fact that Cees was seeing someone was no surprise. She was beautiful, talented, and smart. Arie was more surprised by the anger she felt at having to act like she didn't care that this woman had made no effort to hide that she had experienced what Arie couldn't remember. The aching sadness threatened to descend before Arie pushed it away. She couldn't allow herself to think about this. What was the point of missing something she might never have again?

❖

Cees had been so quiet after they'd arrived home from the studio that Arie had offered to clean up the remains of dinner so that Cees could go to bed early. The fact that Cees had practically run from the kitchen solidified her certainty that she had done something wrong. Arie had spent nearly an hour on what should have been a five-minute cleanup racking her brain for some faux pas. When she had finally retired to her room she was no closer to the answer than when she woke up that morning.

Still, she'd spent several minutes in the shower practicing her apology to Cees. Whatever mistake she had unwittingly made had upset Cees, so she needed to apologize.

Her nerves made her linger in the bedroom. The voices of the morning radio station Cees liked to listen to while she got ready for work sounded like a soft murmur. She was steeling herself for the possibility that Cees might be unhappy with her when she realized it wasn't morning radio she was listening to, but rather someone speaking with Cees. Her mind flashed to Miranda and her certainty that she and Cees had been more than coworkers. Arie stood, opened the bedroom door, and the voices stopped. An older Asian woman dressed in white pants and a salmon-colored sweater was looking at Arie with no effort to hide her curiosity. Despite at least a thirty-year age difference, Arie immediately spotted the physical resemblance to Cees's friend Lilly. Arie walked into the living room, dismayed by the look on Cees's face.

"I meant to speak with you last night, but I was a little distracted." Arie thought Cees still looked a little distracted based on the worried frown and the way she hadn't met her gaze once since they had been in each other's presence. "This is Momma

Nguyen. She's going to stay with you so you don't have to spend all day at the studio."

Arie began to protest. She didn't mind going to the studio with Cees. The memory of Cees flubbing her lines and how apologetic and flushed she looked afterward stopped her. Now she understood. Cees had, at one point, suggested she would be more comfortable watching upstairs. Arie had turned down the suggestion, preferring to watch Cees up close. Actually she was having a hard time keeping her eyes off her. Cees had finally stepped closer to her, pushing up the unfamiliar TV show glasses, and with her hand still partially covering her mouth, she'd said, "Okay, but you have to stop looking at me like that."

"I understand," Arie said, and tried to hide her hurt and embarrassment.

"Momma Nguyen, there's coffee in the kitchen."

"I don't drink coffee," Momma said, folded her arms, and looked from Cees to Arie with avid interest.

"Arie," Cees said, her voice just a little too soft to be natural, "Momma's going to stay with you while I'm at work. She'll also need to take you to your doctor's appointments. If you really want to come with me, I'm fine with it. I just thought you would be more comfortable here."

Arie tamped down her disappointment. "You're right, I would be more comfortable here."

Cees's obvious relief was almost worth being left behind. Arie looked at the still scrutinizing Momma Nguyen. "Thank you for staying with me. I hope I haven't inconvenienced you in any way."

Momma Nguyen slanted her head regally in acknowledgment of Arie's gratitude. "Yes, you are putting me out a little, but I always have to help Cees because she's a little—"

"Can I talk to you over here?" Cees pulled Momma toward the front door and lowered her voice to a whisper that carried just fine to Arie's ear. "Could you not tell her that? I *am not* stupid, and you know I'm not. She won't know that you're just teasing me when you say that."

Momma Nguyen didn't bother lowering her voice. "Oh, did I embarrass you in front of your friend?" Momma made her eyes wide and put her hand over her mouth. Arie didn't think she looked the least bit apologetic. Based on the scowl on her face, neither did Cees.

"I wouldn't worry about it." Momma turned and looked at Arie for so long that she began to feel uncomfortable. "She looks pretty stupid too."

Arie returned Cees's awkward good-bye wave from her spot across the room and watched helplessly as the door shut. She tried to meet Momma Nguyen's stern gaze but ended up looking at the floor.

"You play cards?"

"Cods?" The question was so odd that Arie forgot to be uncomfortable.

"Cards! Cards!" Momma repeated harshly, and Arie swallowed.

"I don't know, maybe. I could learn, I'm sure."

Momma looked doubtful. "You got any money?"

Arie quickly patted her front pocket and pulled out the four twenty dollar bills that the hospital staff had found shoved into her pocket when she was brought in by ambulance. Momma took the money from her hand and held the bills up to the light. "You got plastic?"

"Plastic? You mean like a bag?"

"No, I mean like Visa, MasterCard. American Express. Discover work too."

"Oh…oh, yeah, I do." Arie retrieved her wallet from the bedroom and held it out it to Momma Nguyen.

Momma Nguyen took the wallet, frowned into it, then smiled. "Good girl."

She picked up her purse and keys and stood looking at Arie expectantly. "Well, come on. You need to get more money out if you want to play cards." Arie was about to say she didn't want to play cards, but decided that making Momma Nguyen angry was not in her best interest.

"Okay, where are we going?"

"To the ATM. You don't have enough money to play cards with me."

Arie flushed. "I don't think I remember..."

"You punch in your pin number and get money. Simple."

"That's not what I mean. I know how to use the ATM, but I don't remember my pin number. I don't know that I ever knew it by heart."

Momma stopped, straightening her clothing long enough to stare at Arie as if she had just grown two horns. "Oh." Momma looked at her wristwatch. "Can't go in for another few hours. That's okay. I'll loan you money if you need it. We'll go to the grocery store. Fred Meyer is open twenty-four hours. Can't play cards without Bloody Mary."

Arie had purchased the Bloody Mary mix by swiping the credit card per Momma Nguyen's instruction. They had returned to the house and Arie had been instructed on the proper way to play poker, blackjack, and another game that she couldn't even pronounce. All of Arie's money was now neatly tucked in Momma Nguyen's bra. Despite the fact that she had taken all of her money, plus another twenty-eight dollars in the form of an IOU, Arie had to admit that she had enjoyed every moment of being teased and beat up by Momma Nguyen. She had a strange way of showing affection, but it was obvious how much she cared for Cees by how detailed her memory was of Cees and Lilly's teenage years. When Arie broached the subject of Cees's father, Momma's animated face sagged. When Arie hinted at how much Cees missed him, Momma Nguyen admitted that they worried about Cees for a long time after his death. "We thought things would get better after she met you."

Arie heard the "but we were wrong" even though it wasn't voiced. "Do you know what happened? With us, I mean."

"Cees would not want me to talk to you about this stuff."

Arie sat back and glared at the Momma Nguyen. "You don't know, do you?"

"If I did know, I wouldn't tell you."

"If you don't tell me now, I'm cutting you off. No more Bloody Marys."

"Game's not over."

"It will be. If you don't tell me what you know."

"You're a mean girl."

"And stupid too, from what I'm told." Arie smiled. Momma Nguyen's glare had lost all potency now that Arie had spent some time with her. "Tell me." Arie began stacking the cards neatly on the table.

Either the implied threat worked, or Momma wanted to tell her anyway, because she said, "All Cees told me was that you wouldn't tell her what she did. It drove her crazy for weeks afterward. She racked her brain until she made herself sick. She finally decided that you left because you didn't really want kids."

Arie frowned. "What? That can't be it."

Momma Nguyen sighed and began to speak very slowly, as if she were indeed talking to a person lacking mental capacity. "I'm just telling you what Cees told me she thought happened. Now get my Bloody Mary." Arie obediently walked into the kitchen to mix the drink. She needed to process the information she had been given. *Cees had wanted babies. So I just left her instead of trying to work it out? Instead of talking to her about it? There had to be more to it than that.*

"Olive this time. Green one," Momma Nguyen yelled from the living room.

Arie speared the olive at an angle with a toothpick and dropped it into the glass as Momma Nguyen had taught her. She was just about to lift the glass and take it into the living room when she saw her face reflected in the glass panes of the kitchen cabinets. She didn't remember herself almost two years ago, and she certainly didn't remember Cees Bannigan. She might never remember what went on between them back then. But what she did know was that when she looked at Cees now, she felt like she was scared and happy all rolled into one. She felt protective and protected. She felt whole. The thought of starting a family with a woman she barely knew but now lived with filled her with curiosity, not fear. So why would she have run from that?

Ice clinked in the glass and a drop of chilled perspiration landed on Arie's finger, pulling her from her thoughts. She carried the drink into the living room and found Momma Nguyen lying on the couch flat on her back with her mouth open.

Arie set the Bloody Mary on a coaster, turned the TV volume down, and went in search of a blanket. Momma Nguyen sighed, and murmured, "Who ate my pistachios?" as Arie put a blanket over her.

Arie folded her arms and looked around the house, bereft. Cees had left her phone number. She wondered if it would be all right to call her. A glance at the clock told her that Cees wouldn't be home for another four hours. Four hours seemed like a long time to go without hearing Cees's voice.

Chapter Ten

A rie's nightmare started the same way it had the last three times. She watched herself as if she were a character in a movie. She still looked thin, but not quite as gaunt as she was now. She saw herself reaching for a glass of wine—red, one of many she had drunk that day. She knew the doorbell would ring before it did. She knew who would be standing there, looking angry and spiteful and ready for a fight.

She always let her in, because pain was sometimes better than nothing at all, and because she deserved every damage-inducing word. Her reaction was always the same. She'd let her in, accept every verbal bullet to the chest in the pitiful hopes that, in the midst of the fury, she would get a new tidbit of information that the TV couldn't give her. At least, not until the regular season.

"She doesn't love you anymore. She's moving on with her life. She can't even stand to have your name mentioned." These words she always heard. These words she always remembered. These were the ones that woke her, and tonight was no different.

"No. Lilly, stop." The scream was new. It startled her until she realized it came from her own mouth.

She heard a loud thump and then the sound of running. Her door burst open, and she caught a glimpse of Cees's silhouette, then she felt strong hands on her body. "Arie, Arie it's Cees, you're here with me." The bed dipped and she reached out toward the voice, the one that would bring comfort. She reached for it, remembered she couldn't, shouldn't take it, but didn't understand why.

"It was just a nightmare, sweetheart. Lilly isn't here," Cees murmured into her ear rocking her in a motion that felt comfortable but unfamiliar. Cees was sitting with Arie across her lap. "Just another one of those nightmares."

Arie didn't say anything because she was starting to wonder if they really were *just* nightmares. She'd had three in the last week. For the most part they were strangely detailed at moments, yet fuzzy and hard to understand at others. Most of them had been of her and Cees. Only it wasn't her, or it didn't feel like her. She was too angry, so cold, so dispassionate, and she had hurt Cees. She had done it on purpose.

"Can you tell me what it was about? You screamed Lilly's name." Cees was speaking softly, and Arie started to tell her all the painful things her nightmare-self said to Cees, how she had made her cry, how she had erased her phone messages. But she didn't tell her because she was afraid that Cees would confirm what she already more than suspected—that the nightmares were truths of what she had been like before, and that her current life where Cees would allow her to forget how much she had hurt her was the dream. No wonder Lilly hated her guts.

"Is it starting to come back to you, Arie? Is that what's going on?"

Arie pulled away from Cees, the light from the living room just enough for her to see the wide look in Cees's eyes. How could she answer that? Her dreams felt like they were nightmarish portals to things that happened in their past, but were they really memories?

"No," she said. Her voice sounded like it had been forced out of a cone-shaped tunnel.

Cees's face changed. Closed.

"How's your head? Do you need to take anything for it?"

Arie was grateful that Cees wasn't insisting they discuss the nightmare. Arie ran her hand through her short hair. In the nightmares it had always been long; she liked it better short. She shook her head. "No headache this time."

Cees did smile then, although she still looked slightly puzzled. "Okay. Well, I might as well get ready for work. It's Friday, so I should be home at a decent hour."

Arie straightened and Cees started to rise to her feet.

"Wait." Arie reached out and grabbed Cees's hand. Cees sat back down on the bed and Arie laced her fingers through Cees's. "I'm sorry."

"Sorry? For what?"

Arie hesitated. "For waking you."

"It's okay, Arie. You just scared me. I was already awake. I wake up long before my alarm clock actually goes off."

Arie wanted to pull her close, to kiss her, to take away any pain that she might have caused in the past. But she couldn't, and she didn't know how to broach the subject without possibly reminding Cees of the pain she had caused. Besides, she didn't know if it was really a memory, did she?

"I'll make breakfast while you take a shower."

"Oh, you don't need to get up now. It's only four. Momma won't be here for another hour or so. Why don't you go back to sleep?"

"No, I don't think I'll be going back to sleep anytime soon."

Cees was standing so close Arie could smell the light scent of Cees's face wash. She fought back the urge to reach out and touch her cheek.

"You're staring," Cees said softly.

"You're not wearing your glasses."

"You scared me so bad I didn't want to take the time to find them." Cees chuckled, but she still looked puzzled when Arie left for the kitchen.

As Arie began to prepare Cees's breakfast, her thoughts were on Lilly Nguyen, or more specifically, on her nightmare about Lilly Nguyen. If the nightmare had any element of truth to it, Lilly knew a lot of what was going on.

Arie winced at the idea of having to ask Lilly for anything. Lilly had made no effort to hide that she couldn't stand to look at Arie. If there was any truth to the things Momma Nguyen said and what Lilly had hurled at her in the dream, Arie wouldn't blame either of them for wanting her back out of Cees's life.

Arie cracked an egg in a small bowl and went in search of the egg whites that she had purchased at the store with Momma Nguyen. Arie whisked the eggs and stopped. What would she do if she found out they were true? What if she wasn't a very nice person and she had purposely hurt Cees because she was tired of being in a relationship? Was that the kind of person she had been?

She heard the water in the bathroom turn off and she began whisking the eggs again. That felt as wrong as her not wanting children. Ever since Momma Nguyen had told her that, she had turned it over and over in her head. She just didn't believe it was true. It felt right that she would want a family. Cees had held her, comforted her, and yes, they had almost made love. She needed to be near Cees when she was home and she looked for Cees when she was not near. That, Arie thought, was love, and that was what made family. She knew that without much thought, so what would have made her push Cees away so ruthlessly?

Arie inhaled the scent of minerals and damp compost. She sat back with her hands on her thighs and looked at the freshly hoed soil. Cees's small house was perfect. She had made it so that all nails, screws, and beams were perfectly symmetrical. Not one beam was out of place, not one door hung out of kilter. Everything about it was as Cees had planned.

The days after her nightmare had become more strained than ever, and Arie was starting to feel like she was becoming more of a burden than a friend to Cees. She had been told she was a landscape architect, that she and Cees had met on the set of *Cees Bannigan Your Home*, but that she had left that job within a few weeks. She didn't know why, and as far as she knew, she had had no other form of employment. So how had she paid her bills? That apartment couldn't have been cheap. Arie picked up some dirt and let it run through her fingers. She stood and dusted her pants, looking with pride on her neat little rows of soil. Momma Nguyen had loaned Arie her laptop and had shown her how to Google for information about the flowers that grew best in the Pacific Northwest. As perfect as Cees's home was, it was as if she had purposely neglected the backyard.

She looked at her watch. Despite Cees's growing distance and her own worries about what was real and what wasn't in her nightmares, she still looked forward to having Cees come home.

Home? When had this house become her home? Arie shrugged. Of course it was her home. It was the only home she knew. That apartment wasn't a home. It didn't look as if it ever had been. Unlike so many things, especially those dealing with Cees Bannigan, the apartment on the riverfront brought her no memories, just a cold, stark reality of how much was blank to her.

Arie found Momma Nguyen on the phone speaking in rapid-fire Vietnamese. Arie would have continued on her way, as this was how she usually held conversation, but Momma stopped her.

"My sister hurt herself."

"Oh no, what happened?"

"Don't know. She too embarrassed to say, but I need to go over there."

"Okay, I should be fine. You go ahead."

Momma frowned. "I have to call Cees first."

"I'd rather not bother Cees at work." Arie pulled the scarf off her head and wiped it across her face. "I had very few headaches. You just go. If I start to feel one coming on I'll call her myself."

"Are you sure? If you die while I'm gone, she'll kill me."

Arie blinked. "Um, okay, I promise not to die until you get back."

Momma glared at Arie a bit longer before they grinned at each other. Arie had long since stopped being offended by anything Momma had to say, between calling her stupid and berating her about mistreating her girl. Lilly was her baby; Cees apparently was a full-fledged girl. Arie had developed a thick skin.

"Take a shower. You smell like a pig, and not a BBQ one either."

"Okay."

"And eat something."

"I will," Arie said, still grinning.

Momma picked up her bag and gave Arie one last glare.

"I promise. I still have half my sandwich from yesterday."

Momma rolled her eyes. "Half a sandwich," she muttered as she walked out the door. Arie shut the door behind her and started for the bathroom. She stopped in the middle of the living room as she noticed the quiet of the house. She had never been in it alone. Either Momma Nguyen or Cees had always been with her.

It was not a big house. In fact, all of the homes in Cees's neighborhood were small. If Arie had to guess, she would bet few had more than three bedrooms and even fewer had a second bath. But Cees's house didn't feel small; it felt cozy, like what Arie imagined a home was supposed to feel like. The only room in the house she hadn't gone into was the one where Cees slept. She had assumed it was smaller than the one she had been given and with very little closet space because she had occasionally awakened to find Cees sneaking into her bedroom during the early morning to retrieve some article of clothing from the closet. Arie hadn't been specifically forbidden, but Cees kept the door closed at all times.

Arie was opening the door before she had time to do much more than chastise herself for invading Cees's privacy. She inhaled deeply and walked in. There was very little furniture in the room, but it had been freshly painted. She remembered the faint odor of fresh paint on that first night, but it had passed and she never thought anything more of it. Now she looked at the child's room with shock. There was no cradle or crib, just a neatly made futon where Cees had obviously been sleeping. The walls were brightly colored and adorned with farm animals that had been painstakingly drawn by a patient hand. Cees's hand. Momma's words about Cees wanting a family came back to Arie as she stood in the center of the room. She walked over to the closet and opened the door. Inside was a cornucopia of items that any new parent would purchase—linens, stuffed toys, a colorful mobile—but it was the framed photos on the solitary shelf that caught Arie's eye. For some reason she knew what they would be before she turned them over, but she had to see them anyway. There were four eight-by-ten photos of her and Cees. One was taken as they sat on a log at a rural campsite, faces pressed closely together. Another was of Arie alone. Anyone looking at that photo would have no doubt that Arie was in love with the photographer. The focused eyes, the parted lips, the slight smile. Heat started at her nipples and traveled south. She was both aroused by what she guessed happened after that picture was taken and jealous of what she couldn't remember. Was it possible to be jealous of oneself? The other two photos were of them dressed up at events and smiling into the camera. They looked like they belonged together, as if they were happiest in each other's presence. But something ruined that. Arie placed the pictures back in the closet face down as she had found them. With one last look at the baby items, she closed the door. *No, not something. I ruined it.*

❖

Arie walked out of the bathroom and had to stifle a scream. Lilly didn't blink as she folded her arms and shifted her weight from one leg to the other. "Guess you didn't forget how to scream," she said straight-faced.

"You know, if your mother had said that, it would have sounded a lot less cruel," Arie said, her voice sounding as cold and unfamiliar as if a stranger standing behind her had uttered the words. Lilly dipped her head.

"How did you get in?" *The real question is why are you here?* Since her first night at Cees's she hadn't seen Lilly, and she didn't think Cees had either.

Lilly held up a small key clutched, talonlike, between bright red nails and smiled. "I have a key, remember? Oh wait, I'm sorry. Most people with memory loss also lose their short-term memory too, don't they? I looked that information up on my computer. Momma mentioned that you were quite adept at using hers the other day. Funny the things you seem to remember and the things you don't."

"Did you come over here to accuse me of something?"

"No, I could have called you for that. I came here because my auntie fell and broke her hip. Momma needed to be with her. Cees would kill us if we left you alone."

"So what you're saying is, your mother *made* you come over?" Arie smiled at Lilly's scowl. There was something about Lilly Nguyen that brought out the worst in her. Or maybe it was the truth in her.

"Nice to see the old Arie. You'll be back in your own hole in no time."

Arie blinked at the obvious attempt at cruelty. For the first time since leaving the hospital, Arie had to struggle to find the right words. "Tell me what I did to her. I know a little, but it doesn't make sense to me."

Lilly's frown deepened. "Momma said if I get in Cees's business again she would disinherit me."

Arie had hoped that Lilly's obvious dislike of her would translate into a breaking of the rules. She had forgotten the Momma Nguyen factor.

"I'm sure your mother will leave you millions. She has at least two hundred dollars in IOUs tucked in her bra from me alone."

"You played cards with her?"

Arie looked down at her feet, which must have been all the answer Lilly needed.

"You give her Bloody Mary?"

Arie looked up, startled that Lilly had guessed the truth so quickly. Lilly was grinning and then she started to chuckle, and before too long, she was in a full-blown doubled-over guffaw. "No wonder she loves coming over here. She told me that you weren't mean anymore and that car accident must have knocked some sense into you."

"She told you that?" Arie was proud that she had finally won someone over in the Nguyen family.

"Yeah, but now I know why she likes you so much. She likes taking your money. You should have seen her when she came home yesterday. Boy, she was high-stepping like a fashion model on a catwalk."

"You live with your momma?" Again the taunt came out unbidden. It stopped Lilly's laughter with the efficiency of a slap across the face. She had unwittingly found a soft spot. Or had it been unwitting?

"I promised your mother I would eat lunch." Arie started toward the kitchen. "Do you want something?"

Lilly followed Arie into the kitchen without answering. "So you remember how to cook?"

"I was only offering you a sandwich, but yes, I remember how to cook." Arie opened the refrigerator and pulled the cold cuts from a drawer. She set them on the counter and turned to face Lilly. "Look, I get that you don't believe that I have amnesia.

Unless you want to tell me why you would think I would play such an evil trick on Cees, I can't really fight that. In fact, if you want to go on home, I won't tell her you left."

"She'd find out," Lilly said grudgingly.

"Cees would? How? She won't be home until this evening. I'll tell her she just missed you. I don't need twenty-four-hour care, you know."

"No, I mean Momma."

"Oh," Arie said and went back to her sandwich preparation.

"So what do you do here all day?" Lilly asked in a tone that made Arie think she had already concluded the answer was nothing.

Arie decided on civility instead of being lured into a verbal fight. Besides, she could think of nothing biting to say. "I wake up and make breakfast for Cees."

"You do? She wakes up at the crack of ass, doesn't she?"

Arie turned to look at her, smiling at the analogy. "Crack of ass? Yeah, I suppose she does."

"What do you do after she leaves?"

"I clean up, get showered and dressed. Sometimes I watch TV with Momma. She likes watching Judge Joe."

"She told me you like him, too."

Arie cleared her throat but didn't answer. She didn't know why she was embarrassed. It's not like it was a soap opera or anything.

"Momma also said you like *One Life to Live*."

"Um, yeah, sometimes I watch it with her." Arie was unsuccessful in keeping the annoyance from her voice. "Why all the questions?"

"I just figured you might need a little help finding a J.O.B. when Cees gets tired of you free—I mean when you're ready to go back to your own place. What else do you do?"

"Momma Nguyen takes me to my doctor's appointment every other Friday. Sometimes we play cards. I just started working in Cees's garden."

Arie turned around at the sound of Lilly's chair scraping back. Lilly walked over to the door leading to Cees's small backyard and opened it as if she couldn't see it through the eight glass-paned windows.

Lilly stood with her hands on her hips for a few moments and then returned to her interrogator's seat. "Cees avoids the yard at all costs."

Arie didn't speak. It was a statement, not a question. She braced herself for what Lilly would say next.

"She didn't used to hate yard work. That's how we made our extra money when we were kids. She loved being outdoors. I think you ruined that for her too."

Arie opened her mouth to speak, and when nothing came out, she just shook her head. *Do not cry*, Arieanna, told herself, but Lilly's verbal barbs were starting to take a toll on her. Maybe it was what she had seen in that room, maybe it was the fact that Lilly was probably telling the truth—Cees was better off without her in her life. Arie took a deep, shuddering breath and tried to ignore the fact that she could feel Lilly's eyes on the side of her face.

"Looks better," Lilly said grudgingly.

Arie took a few moments to compose herself before answering. "I thought if I made it nice, she could sit and relax after work, weather permitting." Arie could have kicked herself for giving Lilly more ammunition to hurt her.

"Yeah, she could use some relaxation. She used to come dancing with me to let off steam; now she's too afraid to leave you home alone. By the way, you can cross Subway off your list of prospective employers 'cause I'd have to hurt you if you took this long to make my damn sandwich." Arie dropped the lettuce into the colander and turned around to find Lilly rooting around in her bag. She smiled and pulled out a small book of crossword puzzles. Arie realized that Lilly was pretty when she wasn't scowling, glaring, or using her words as hate daggers.

"Cees likes to dance? I didn't know that."

Lilly pulled the top off her pen with her teeth. She was frowning again, but this time in concentration. "Loves to dance. She'll dance by herself if she has to. Doesn't even need a drink."

"Really? I wonder why she didn't tell me." Maybe that's what they needed to break the tension that seemed to have developed between them since they had almost made love. She could ask Cees to go dancing with her. Arie was just warming up to the idea when she realized that she didn't know the first thing about dancing.

"What's the matter with you?"

Arie was so caught up in her disappointment that she hadn't realized that Lilly had temporarily abandoned her crossword.

"I thought maybe I could ask Cees to take me dancing. You know, to relieve some of the stress of all this, but I don't think I remember how."

Lilly stared just long enough to make Arie feel uncomfortable. "Cees told me you didn't dance." Arie must have done a bad job of hiding her disappointment because a few moments later Lilly smiled. It wasn't an unkind smile, just a little too thoughtful. "I can teach you."

"Why would you do that?" Arie asked, not bothering to hide her suspicion. She and Lilly had a very open relationship. She was very open about her dislike of Arie, and Arie was openly bewildered by it.

"Because someone needs to help her blow off some steam. She isn't going to leave you behind, and I won't be seen with you, so I think you should go with her."

Arie turned back to her food preparation. She would love to help Cees blow off some steam in a different way, but she'd be damned if she would mention that particular inadequacy to Lilly.

"We'll start after we eat."

"Seriously?" Arie looked over her shoulder at Lilly. "You don't have to if you don't want to."

"I know I don't. Just think of it as payback for the lunch you're making for me."

Arie turned back to the sink. Now *that* she understood. Repaying a debt was important to her as well. Right now she felt like she owed Cees so much she didn't even know where or how she could start to pay her back.

CHAPTER ELEVEN

Cees felt a confusing barrage of dread and anticipation descend over her as she went to unlock her front door and found that the handle moved freely in her hand. Momma Nguyen was almost fanatical about never leaving a door unlocked—leftover caution from more unpleasant times when she lived in Vietnam. She was always telling Lilly and Cees how single young women needed to be more careful.

Cees walked into the house and shut the door behind her. Lilly, not Momma, popped up from the couch and reached for her coat. Arie was standing in the center of the living room with her arms wrapped around herself. One head-to-toe glance told Cees that she was fine. No, not just fine. She looked damn good. She had changed into tight-fitting jeans and a shirt that Cees didn't remember seeing when they had packed her clothes at the apartment. Arie looked very nervous, which made Cees suspicious. "Hey, Lil, what are you doing here? Where's Momma Nguyen?"

"Auntie Mem fell down again. Momma sent me over to baby-sit."

"Oh no, is she all right?" Cees asked, her suspicion curtailed by concern for Momma Nguyen's older sister.

"She'll be fine, but you know, every time she hurts herself, Momma tries to get her to come live with us." Lilly shook her head in resignation. "Part of me hopes she listens, but I am not volunteering to look after another invalid." The annoyed look on Lilly's face changed almost instantly. "Oh hey, I was talking about her." She canted her head toward Arie. "You know I wasn't talking about—"

Cees smiled. "Yeah, I know." Lilly could be cruel, but she wasn't heartless.

Coat on and properly adjusted, Lilly ran a critical eye over Arie, seemed pleased with what she saw, and walked toward the front door.

"Thanks, Lilly." Arie's voice sounded nervous. Cees's suspicion returned.

Lilly looked back at Arie. "Momma is superstitious."

"She is?" Cees said, but Lilly ignored her and continued to look at Arie.

"Next time you play cards and she asks for a Bloody Mary with an olive, give her something else, celery or something. Sit in a different place or play out of turn. It'll throw her off."

"Okay," Arie said through her obvious surprise.

"It hurts her pride every time she loses. Just take enough that she won't want to play you anymore. Don't take all of her money."

"I won't."

Lilly finally turned her gaze toward Cees. The angelic smile that spread across her face had always signaled trouble when they were teenagers and still did.

"You girls have fun," she said, and before Cees could question her further, she was gone.

"You and Momma Nguyen have been drinking while I'm at work? And what did she mean by that 'you girls have fun' business?"

"I wasn't drinking, but Momma—Lilly thought—I thought, since it was Friday night, you might want to go out. Maybe dancing or dinner?" Weariness settled on Cees's shoulders and bore down. The hope slid from Arie's face. "Oh, but if you're too tired, I can cook something while you shower. Then you can call it a night," she said.

Cees realized that Arie had just summed up her life. For several days, all Cees had done was eat, go to work, come home, eat whatever was put in front of her, and go to bed. Seeing Arie every day was wearing her out emotionally. She vacillated between wanting to hold Arie to wanting to yell obscenities at her for how much she'd hurt her. Neither option was really available to her, and it exhausted her.

"No. Actually, dinner and dancing sounds good, although I'm not all that hungry yet, so maybe we'll reverse the two." This Arie, unlike the old one, hadn't learned how to hide her emotions. Her obvious excitement made warmth bloom in Cees's chest. "I'll take a quick shower and change."

"I only brought jeans from the apartment, so don't dress up."

"Good. I'm not in the mood for anything formal, anyway. I'll just take a quick one. Give me ten."

Cees hopped into the shower, her mind going from Arie to Lilly and back again. Something just didn't feel right about Lilly's presence in the house. She hadn't heard from her since she had found out that Arie was living in the house. She had expected a berating phone call when she found out that Cees had agreed to let Momma stay with Arie while she was at work, but there had been nothing. With Lilly, quiet was the calm before the storm. Cees got out of the shower and dressed.

She found Arie sitting on the couch, hands folded in front of her, wearing the leather jacket that had been her mainstay a year and half before. Cees felt a painful twist in her heart when she saw it. She didn't need to bury her nose in its soft leather to remember the smell.

"So was this Lilly's idea?" she asked to clear the thickness gathering in her throat.

"The dancing part was Lilly's, but I thought you might like to do something different."

Cees sighed. "I thought so. I suppose there is no harm in telling you that you always claimed to hate dancing."

Arie looked shy, and to Cees's surprise reached out and took her hand. "Yeah, but you love it, right?"

The first sob took them both by surprise. Cees wasn't sure if it was Arie's eagerness to do something she liked to do, or the fact that she was just so damn tired of keeping her feelings in check while Arie was trying the best way she knew how to get to her. She was finding it hard to defend herself against this type of sweet assault. Her Arie had been kind, even gentle, but this Arie was all those things with the protective instinct removed, and she scared the shit out of Cees.

Cees saw the look of fear on Arie's face as she pulled her into an embrace.

"I'm doing everything all wrong," Arie said softly, and Cees heard the sad consternation.

She had gotten hold of herself quickly, but she wasn't ready to face Arie's confusion, so she held on to the hug a little longer.

"What is it you're trying to do?" Cees's voice was thick with tears.

"I'm trying to get you to trust me." With a finger beneath her glasses Cees dried her eyes. "I figured dinner and dancing would be a start to getting to know each other all over again."

Again the look of concern and earnestness touched something in Cees. "You're right. I love to dance. But I always got the impression that you didn't like it because you didn't know how."

Arie looked relieved. "Oh, that's no problem. Lilly taught me."

"Lilly did what?" Cees ran over the words in her head but still couldn't make sense of them.

"She taught me how to dance. Well, she showed me a few things," Arie said with a little less surety.

What was it Lilly had said before she left? *You girls have fun?* Lilly was more than her friend. She was her sister, which meant there were times when they just plain didn't like each other. Frankly, Lilly could be a bitch. Cees had called her that on several occasions. Mind you, no one else had better call her that, or Cees would be ready with a right hook.

Lilly rarely did anything for people outside the family unless there was something in it for her. Teaching Arie to dance was one of those fine-line things that made Cees nervous.

"What did she show you?"

Whether it was in response to Cees's suspicion or to her own self doubt, Arie had begun to look nervous. "Just some stuff. Not a lot. She said I was passable and had done surprisingly well for just a few hours."

A compliment? Cees thought. *Lilly doesn't compliment.* "Show me," Cees said.

Arie looked uneasy and Cees felt bad.

"Show you what?"

"What Lilly taught you."

"You mean now? Here? There's no music." Arie was smiling, and the heaviness and tension that had caused Cees to burst into tears eased. She couldn't help but respond to that smile because there was something so carefree about it that she wished she had met Arie when they were both younger and life hadn't created so many question marks and exclamation points in both. Cees gently turned Arie around and pushed her toward the stereo.

"Well, put some on. Surely she wasn't in here beat boxing while you busted a move." Cees folded her arms in front of her and watched as Arie pushed the CD tray in without changing the CD.

"Okay, so Lilly said I would do. I'm not as good as she is or anything, but I'll practice." Now she was back to being nervous, and Cees thought she looked incredibly cute.

Cees did an imitation of her third grade teacher Ms. Austin and clapped her hands to get attention. "Less talk, please. Let's see what you got."

"Okay." Arie walked to the middle of the room and tossed

her jacket on the couch. She was looking down at the floor, obviously waiting for something. A small electronic beep, and then a song with so much bass came on that a glass of water that had been left on the dining room table began to quiver. Arie bobbed her head a few times as if counting and then she began to move her hips. Cees's eyes were drawn to the tight-fitting Henley and the hips moving in perfect unison with the bass. The CD must have been from Lilly's car, because she owned nothing like it. But if Arie liked it, she would buy more tomorrow. The music sped up and Arie suddenly turned her back to Cees and squatted down, slapping the floor in a move that made Cees's mouth drop. The gyrating had become downright sensual and Cees could imagine herself on the dance floor being used as a pole in a strip club.

Cees's finger went up as if she were calling a cab; she uttered a half word, but stopped when she realized that if she couldn't hear herself, neither could Arie. Cees dropped her hand.

Arie's eyes were closed now and she was obviously into the music, so Cees was able to look at her with open lust. She fervently wished they were on the dance floor where she could touch Arie without having to feel guilty.

Oh, Lilly, you deserve a swift kick in the ass, or that new Coach bag you've been ogling for over a year. Maybe you deserve both. The song choice was a raunchy rap song about going deep. Lilly had choreographed Arie's moves to create a warmth in Cees's underwear, and she had done her job well. Cees realized with some trepidation that the song's tempo was slowing, and she didn't know whether to feel relief or sadness that she would have to act like the dance had not pushed her beyond aroused. Apparently Lilly had taught Arie the importance of a great climax because her movements became more fluid, her arms moving with the bass in the song. Cees had thrown all caution to the wind and was now alternating between staring hungrily at Arie's chest and the arousing cyclone of her hips. The music went abruptly silent, and Arie stopped dancing, obviously winded but quite proud of herself. Cees thought about closing her mouth, but decided it was way too much effort.

"What do you think? Am I any good?" Arie asked while trying to catch her breath.

"Perfect." The word ricocheted throughout the room. "I'll just get my coat." Cees hooked her thumb toward the bedroom. Eyes wide, she scurried away before she did something stupid like offer to show Arie what the song was really referring to.

Arie and Cees had been on the dance floor since they walked into the dark club. Lilly was right. Cees loved to dance. The other dancers were a shadowy blur to Arie. All her concentration was on Cees, first on keeping up with her, then on enjoying the sensation of having her pressed against her as the dance floor became crowded. Arie felt that if it weren't for the clothing between them they would be making love. She should have been embarrassed, but she wasn't. And apparently neither was Cees, until a slow song came on and brought reality back with a vengeance.

Cees pushed up her glasses and said, "I think we're overdoing it a bit here."

It took Arie a moment to realize that Cees was referring to her recent release from the hospital and not the fact that they were making a spectacle of themselves. Arie became conscious of both her damp back and the pulse throbbing at the base of Cees's throat. Cees took her hand and navigated them slowly through the crowded club.

Arie forced herself to stop staring at the backside she had been cupping with impunity minutes before. One glance at the women still milling around the dance floor had her flushing. It was obvious from the myriad of knowing looks that they had made the assumption that she and Cees were going home to make love.

She couldn't exactly blame them. Their dancing hadn't exactly been platonic. Arie was about to revert her eyes to the floor when she saw a small woman with short hair and wearing work pants whisper something in her companion's ear. Arie didn't hear what was said, but she could tell by the way her lips moved and the quick look toward them by her companion that Cees had been recognized.

The warmth created by her sexually charged dancing with Cees faded. If her suggestion that they go dancing had somehow caused Cees grief, she would feel guiltier than Lilly had already made her feel for staying in Cees's home.

They burst through the door of the club and into the dark billowing nicotine haze of a large group of women taking a smoke break. Cees started walking toward the car, but her steps weren't as fast or as purposeful as usual. Arie wondered what that meant. Arie was thrilled and maybe a little confused that she hadn't released her hand yet. "Will that make things bad for you?"

Cees smiled. "How could dancing my stress away make things bad for me?"

Arie couldn't seem to find the right words for what she wanted to say, and it frustrated her.

Cees's face became serious and she pulled Arie to a stop. "Do you mean because it was a gay club?"

"Yeah, I think some of those women might have recognized you."

"Did I lead you to believe I was closeted? Because I'm not. I mean, the people I work for have asked that I not lop off my right breast and join the lesbian militia, but I don't let them tell me who I am."

The answer thrilled Arie for reasons she didn't understand, but she felt the need to ask some of the questions that had been dogging her about Cees.

"Momma Nguyen let me borrow her computer. She taught

me how to Google people. Said she does it for all the men she meets at the social club."

Cees grinned. "Good for her. Lilly probably taught her that."

Arie blurted, "I Googled you."

Cees did her best to look taken aback, but Arie could tell by the amused look on her face that she wasn't at all perturbed or annoyed, so she pushed on. "Did you know there was picture of you in a wet T-shirt and…"Arie couldn't finish because she saw by the embarrassed, resigned look on Cees's face that she did know.

"Um, yeah, that was not a moment of brilliance on my part. It was raining, and I was wearing a white T-shirt. I thought it would look cool if we kept working in the rain. I had no idea it would come out like that. I'm starving. Let's go get something to eat."

Arie agreed, despite the fact that she wasn't really hungry. The abrupt change of subject wasn't lost on her. Who was she to question Cees about why her breasts were showing in a picture she'd found on the Internet? She hadn't said anything until now because she had been telling herself it was none of her business and tried to push it out of mind. Unfortunately, that seemed harder to do than she anticipated.

"There isn't much open this time of night, and we look like we just ran a race. There's a place that's open twenty-four hours down the way. We could walk."

"I'm sure it'll be fine." Arie's nervousness about asking the question faded slightly. They walked to the corner and waited with a straggly-looking couple at the corner. Arie barely kept from wrinkling her nose as the scent of body odor and mildewed clothing drifted to her. The woman looked at their intertwined hands and made it a point to step closer to her dingy-looking boyfriend. After one glance in their direction, he decided to look straight ahead until the light changed again. Arie noticed that

Cees didn't bother looking at the couple or acknowledging the hostile look.

As the couple turned a corner, Cees let out an audible breath. "As if I suddenly woke up and decided I wanted to go down on a meth head." Cees's voice sounded angry. Arie didn't ever remember hearing Cees sound that angry, even when dealing with Lilly, who in Arie's opinion, could anger a saint. Not that she wasn't grateful for the dance lessons.

"I wondered if you noticed that."

"I always notice. It's just different when it's directed at you."

"We don't have to." Arie held up their clasped hands. "If it bothers you or you think someone might recognize you." They had reached Sheri's, and Cees's other hand was on the door handle.

"Hey, what's this about? The only people that I've ever had a hard time telling were my dad and the Nguyen family. That was when I was seventeen years old. It was the hardest thing I ever had to do. The rest is trivial. I hold your hand—" Cees turned away from the door and stepped right up into Arie's personal space until they were almost touching. After the closeness at the club, the hands that had gone everywhere, the lips that had brushed skin, hips grinding together on more than one occasion, this small amount of closeness shouldn't have made Arie shiver, but it did. "Because I want to, okay?"

"I just don't want the night to end," Arie said.

Cees smiled. "Something happening tomorrow that you're trying to avoid?"

Arie tried to return her smile but couldn't quite manage it. She was being bombarded with all kinds of emotions: arousal, fear, jealousy, more arousal.

"Hey, look at me. Ah, sweetie, you look exhausted. I knew dancing would be too much for you. Let's get you to bed."

Arie had to work hard not to show how much Cees's words startled her. Cees's face looked too concerned for her to have intended the double entendre. Arie told herself to stop it. "I'm fine. I'd like to get something to eat first."

"If you're sure." Cees looked dubious, but she opened the door for Arie, letting her walk in slightly ahead of her, never releasing her hand. Once they were seated, both were quiet as they contemplated the choices on the menus. Arie only pretended to study hers as she tried to think of a good way to initiate a conversation about the distance that had grown between them and her own inadequacies in the bedroom.

"I really only come here when I need comfort food. I have to keep my weight down for television."

Arie dropped her menu so she could make sure Cees wasn't joking. "But you can't weigh much more than I do, and Momma Nguyen said I look like the walking dead."

Cees's mouth dropped open, but her eyes twinkled. "You do not. I can't believe she said that."

"She said it was because I wasn't finishing my lunch like she wanted me to."

"Well then, serves you right." Cees softened the statement with a smile. "Don't you just love her?"

Arie returned Cees's smile. "Yeah, I do. She acts mean, but she's always really sweet to me. Makes me come back into the house to put on sunscreen when I forget."

"She call you stupid first?"

"Uh-huh. But she doesn't mean it."

"No, she doesn't. I'm glad you realize that. She does it to me and Lilly too. It's become her form of endearment. It can be disconcerting at first, huh? I probably should have warned you."

"It's probably…"

When the waitress appeared to offer them coffee, Cees asked for decaf while Arie requested tea. Arie waited until the waitress disappeared to continue. "It's probably no more disconcerting than having me in your home."

"It wasn't something I would have foreseen a few months ago," Cees admitted and then returned to her menu.

"Cees." Arie decided to jump right in before her nerves stopped her. "Can we talk about what happened that night when we almost…made love?"

Cees looked up from her menu. The light flush that made her face glow disappeared. "Arie, I'm so sorry. I don't know what happened. It's like I forgot that you didn't remember and I just… I just went too fast."

Arie moved closer, wanting to reach for Cees's hand, but Cees looked so upset that she contented herself with waiting until Cees looked at her. "It wasn't too fast."

"It was too soon then. You didn't know me from Eve," Cees said, the mental abuse she had been heaping on herself evident in her voice.

"Please let me finish. I told you, I was scared. I didn't know what to do."

Cees nodded, but Arie could tell she was still beating herself up over it and she didn't know what to do to make her feel better. "Is this why you've been pulling away from me, because I don't know what I'm doing? Because Lilly offered to—"

Cees had a look of utter horror on her face. "She better not!"

Arie was laughing now, and Cees's face softened.

"So you're making fun of me now? That's not very nice. If you're learning that kind of behavior, I'm going to have to make sure I keep you two apart." Cees did smile, but the worry lingered.

"I was very jealous of Lilly. I saw you hug her the night you bought me home from the hospital."

"Oh, listen, Arie, Lilly and I are like—"

"Sisters, I know. Momma Nguyen set me straight about that."

"You should have asked me. You can ask me anything, you know?"

Arie tried to digest that statement as Cees pored over the menu.

"Even the salads have deep-fried chicken in them. It's good, by the way, just fattening. I think I'm going to have myself a big huge platter of Belgian waffles with whipped cream and strawberries." Cees shut her menu. "Completely low fat and healthy," she said with a grin. "What are you thinking?"

"You said I could ask you anything, right?"

"Of course. I have nothing to hide from you."

Cees's tone was so encouraging that Arie found herself asking the question that had been plaguing her since she had visited the set of *Cees Bannigan Your Home*. "Did you sleep with Miranda?"

"Yes, but—"

Arie was up and walking away before Cees could finish her sentence. Arie thought she had murmured something about the bathroom, but there was a sob lodged in her throat and she wasn't sure if she had gotten the words out.

She knew she had no right to feel angry or jealous, but she was. Mostly because of the memory of how inept she had been when she had had the chance. Cees had been very clear about the fact that they had been apart for some time before she had been in the accident. She had no right to feel angry. No, *angry* wasn't the right word.

Arie hurried toward the curtain that divided the bathrooms from the rest of the restaurant. Once she was sure the curtain hid her from Cees's view, she sagged against the wall in an effort to catch her breath. The idea of Cees making love to someone else, someone who knew what they were doing and wasn't afraid, hurt. A slow throb began at her forehead. A normal headache, not a migraine, thank God. Arie tapped the palm of her hand between her brows.

"You all right, hon?" Arie dropped her hand and noticed for the first time that she was sharing her space with a woman sitting on a stool in front of a bank of three video poker machines. She looked toward Arie with concern but never stopped pressing the buttons of her machine.

Arie straightened, was about to tell her a lie about being fine, but was interrupted when Cees came storming through the curtain. She didn't stop until she had Arie pressed up against the poker machine and was holding her tightly. Arie held on and closed her eyes. Dancing had been a tease, close touches, erotic, but even the grinding against each other had been safely covered under the pretense of a dance. This was different. They were clinging to each other too desperately to deny their feelings now. When Cees leaned back to look at her, it seemed natural for Arie to press her lips to Cees's, to melt into the embrace, and to allow Cees and the poker machine to keep her upright.

"Guess you're just fine, then." The woman's voice was haughty, making it quite clear that she didn't appreciate the public display of affection.

Arie thought the kiss would have gone on forever if they hadn't had an audience. "You just made me feel horrible for sleeping with someone when we weren't even together," Cees said in a voice just loud enough for Arie to hear.

"I know," Arie said softly. "I don't know why I got so upset."

"I don't think I want to know about the people you slept with either." Arie wanted to tell Cees she hadn't slept with anyone, but how could she know for sure? Arie saw regret on Cees's face when she moved away from her.

"Do you really need to go the restroom?"

"No, I just needed some air."

Cees took in the smoky little enclave and the sour face of the video poker player. "Nice place for it. Why don't we go sit down? I think there are a few things we need to get out in the open."

CHAPTER TWELVE

Cees stuck her fork in the large waffle, then set down her fork. She wasn't hungry and neither was Arie, based on the fact that she made no pretense of picking up her utensils.

"Not hungry?" she asked.

"Not really."

"Me either. Listen I think it's time we talked about what's going on between us."

Arie inhaled and looked up at Cees, shocked. "Really?" she asked with such obvious pleasure that Cees had to look away, thinking how perfect she was. Beautiful or attractive just didn't cut it. If Cees were to break out a pencil and map out a blueprint for what she thought would be the perfect woman, Arieanna Simon would be the outcome.

"Why are you so surprised?"

"Because you've been avoiding me lately."

"Arie, I have a feeling you want answers that I can't give you. Only you know why you handled certain things the way you did. Anything I tell you is only guessing."

"I saw the room, Cees."

Cees sighed. "I figured you would ask about that eventually."

"I'm sorry. I've tried to respect your privacy, but it's a small house."

"And Momma Nguyen has a big mouth."

"Don't blame her. I practically forced it from her."

"What did she tell you?"

"She said you thought I left because I didn't want children." Arie scowled. "Why wouldn't I have talked to you about that?"

Cees let out a bark of laughter that sounded bitter even to her. She picked up her water glass and drank before speaking. "I asked myself that same question for weeks after you asked me to leave. I never did come up with an answer that made sense. I felt there was something bothering you, especially toward the end, but I was never sure what it was. I was guessing, but it was the only thing that made sense. I was happy with you. I thought you were happy with me. Maybe things would have been different if I could have forced you to tell me what was bothering you, but," Cees shrugged, "you're a little different from the Arie I used to know."

"How so?"

"You're softer now, I guess."

"I'm getting a gym membership tomorrow," Arie deadpanned.

Cees was caught between wanting to laugh out loud and wanting to apologize profusely.

"Arie, that's not what I meant at all. I think you look great. I mean you're a little thin, but certainly not walking-dead thin." Cees closed her eyes. *Oh, Daddy, what am I doing here?* She opened her eyes to see Arie grinning at her. "But that's exactly what I'm talking about," Cees said. Warmth bloomed in her chest in response to that grin. "You were so very serious. There were times that I wondered if I was making you happy. You always told me that you were the happiest you had ever been in your life, but then there would be times I'd catch you looking at me, and you would look so sad."

"I know we met at the studio. How long did I work there?"

Cees smiled. "Only about two weeks."

"What happened?"

"I finally got up the nerve to ask you out and you said no."

"I said no?" Arie's eyes were large with surprise.

"Yeah, that was my reaction too. You were really nice about it," Cees said as she remembered how embarrassed she had felt. "You said you wouldn't date me because we worked together."

"That seems like sound reasoning." Arie suddenly remembered that Cees had been seeing her producer, Miranda. "Oh, I didn't mean anything by that."

"I hear what you're saying. It's not as unheard of in our industry as you might think. We were working long hours back then. A lot longer than we are now, and if I didn't meet people on set, more than likely I just didn't meet them. But I don't want you to think it was like that with us. I was really surprised when you turned me down, because the minute I saw you, I felt a connection. It was like my body always knew where you were."

"I think I know what you mean. I find myself..." Arie seemed to search for the words and looked down at her untouched plate of food. She only looked up when Cees covered her hand with her own. Arie opened her fingers so that Cees could curl hers under.

"I lean toward doors when I expect you to come through them. When you kissed me in there, it's like my whole body was saying *finally*." She paused. "I'm not saying this right."

"You are," Cees said, and Arie looked down again, but this time from shyness. This too was new. The Arie she had known in the past was anything but shy. She was nowhere near as open about her feelings as the Arie sitting before her now.

As if reading her thoughts, Arie asked. "Am I very different? From the person you..."

"Loved?" Cees finished for her. "Yes and no. The stuff I loved about you is still there."

"The stuff you didn't love isn't?" Arie looked so hopeful that Cees laughed, and Arie joined her, though Cees was sure that she had no idea why she was laughing.

"No, I just mean stuff like that. You were always so serious,

Arie. When you told me you wouldn't date me I thought I had imagined the connection between us. I had a hard time looking at you for days after that. Doing scenes together was excruciating."

"We did scenes together? Do you have tapes?"

"I could probably get them. We did an entire series on outdoor bedrooms. That's why you were hired."

"So what happened?"

"You quit. You walked into Al Sandoval's office—he was the producer then—and said you wouldn't be staying on after the series. You left his office and made a beeline for me."

Arie was riveted by the story. "What did I say when I found you?"

Cees smiled as she remembered that moment as clearly as if it were yesterday. "You said, 'I've tried to ignore this thing between us, and I've decided a job isn't worth the possibility of losing something extraordinary.'"

"I said that?" Arie said softly.

"You did."

"I walked right up to you and that's what I said?"

Cees felt tears come to her eyes. Happy tears, because Arie had said exactly that, and sad tears because Arie had forgotten such a special moment.

"I was pretty serious, huh?"

Cees reclaimed Arie's hand across the table. "That's what I mean. You were always like that. You had to have a purpose. Even when we were just lying in bed, your purpose was to relax. You had a hard time just 'being,' and now you…you're different. Whatever it is that weighed you down, is gone."

Arie looked serious for a moment, and Cees's stomach churned in protest. She didn't miss that look. "I'm certain it's not gone, Cees. I've temporarily forgotten it, but I'll remember." The silence after Arie's proclamation was long and thick. Cees realized that her second deepest fear, besides Arie remembering what had made her fall so quickly out of love with her, was that Arie would remember what made her build that invisible protective shell around her heart.

"Tell me about Momma Nguyen," Arie said. "What was it like growing up with her?"

Cees grinned. "Where do I start? I always went to the Nguyen house after school so that I wouldn't be home alone all the time. My father worked long hours and lots of weekends. Momma Nguyen became my surrogate mother, and in return, I tried to keep Lilly in line. Mostly she led me astray, but I was more likely to draw the line than she ever was, so everything worked out.

"When my father died, Momma and Lilly took care of me. I was a mess for a long time. Just going through the motions. I probably would have checked out completely if they hadn't insisted that I keep dealing with the world. One day I woke up and things weren't so gray."

"Momma Nguyen goes on and on about what a fine man he was."

Cees grinned. "I think she had a crush on him." Cees saw the unasked question in Arie's eyes and wondered if it would ever get easier. She had told the story to Arie before, but this time she wanted to keep it brief. "He had lung cancer. He was in so much pain they kept him medicated, and toward the end—"

"He didn't remember you," Arie said before Cees could.

Cees wondered if the tight-lipped pronouncement was a guess or a memory. "He didn't remember anything. I had to do everything for him."

"I am so sorry you had to go through that alone, and now here I am with—this."

"Arie, I wasn't sorry. I never knew my mother. She died when I was two. He took care of me all by himself. I was honored to do the same for him. It tore me up that he couldn't remember me, but he was my daddy."

"I wish I could have been there for you," Arie said.

"We didn't meet until years later. Lilly and Momma Nguyen did what they could." Cees deliberately lightened her tone and

Arie tried following suit, though Cees could tell that she was still having trouble processing the information she had just been given.

"Lilly can't stand the sight of me."

"Oh, I don't know about that. She taught you to dance, didn't she?" Cees tried for levity. She would have to decide how she felt about Arie's dancing. On the one hand, she really liked it; on the other, it would be next to impossible not to get turned on any time they took to the dance floor.

"It's because things didn't work out between us?"

"Yeah, pretty much."

"You aren't going to tell me what happened, are you?"

"I can't tell you what I don't know."

"It's just, I don't want to feel like the rest of my life hinges on the fact that I can't remember anything past the last few weeks. I want…"

"What is it? Tell me what's on your mind." Arie's agitation was starting to spread to Cees.

"I want to make love to you, and I don't remember how. I don't remember what you like and dislike. I don't know anything, and it's frustrating."

The honesty was what got her. She hadn't expected such an honest admission, and she was speechless. The waitress misconstrued their body language and thought it was the perfect time for her to gravitate over to top off their already full coffee cups.

"Something wrong with the food? Neither of you have touched a bite."

Cees looked down at her waffle and said, "Uh, no. Thank you." The waitress frowned at her, looked as if she decided she had been drinking, and walked away.

"Sorry, I know I'm supposed to say that better, but…"

"No, I appreciate your honesty."

"So?"

"So, we can't," Cees said into Arie's crestfallen face. "I'm sorry, Arie. I just can't. Not until you remember everything else that happened between us."

Arie looked as if she was going to protest. Instead, she picked up her fork and began eating the eggs that must have been cold. Cees wanted to soothe Arie, to wipe away the hurt she had glimpsed briefly in her eyes. But she had yet to figure out how to heal her own hurt. How could she possibly help heal the person who had caused it?

Cees wondered if Arie noticed how slowly she drove home. Despite the discomfort in the restaurant, she didn't want the evening to end. More importantly, she was afraid of losing her resolve. She kept the music as low as possible in case Arie wanted to talk more, but neither of them had uttered a word since leaving Sheri's.

The problem was, Arie wasn't the only one who was forgetting. Cees also had to have some form of selective amnesia in order for her to allow the woman who had hurt her so badly into her home and even close enough to kiss her. *No, scratch that, Cees Bannigan. You kissed her. You did more than kiss her.* Cees tightened her grip on the steering wheel. It was the dancing. It was that damned Lilly's fault. It would serve Lilly right if she did sleep with Arieanna. *What the hell am I thinking?*

Cees grinned. She kept trying and failing to be mad at Lilly. Arie had had every eye in the place on her. People would have assumed that the two of them, who couldn't keep their hands and other body parts off each other, would be in bed within minutes of leaving the club. Instead they'd ended up in an all-night café with one of them in tears. Cees almost wished it was as simple as sleeping with Arie instead of this thick-headed feeling of being on a train headed toward disaster.

As if following her line of thinking, Arie sighed. Cees glanced at her profile and wished she could see her expression.

"Tired?" Cees asked and could have kicked herself for her tone. The one word probably telegraphed her feelings as clearly as if she had written it on a piece of paper.

Arie's smile, illuminated by the glow of the console, was a more honest answer than her simple "a little."

She is so confused, Cees thought and then tried to harden her resolve with a thought of "well, she should join the club," but couldn't quite get there. She pulled into her driveway and Arie opened the door and jumped nimbly down from the monster. Cees noted with some satisfaction that she was moving well despite exerting herself on the dance floor.

"May I make you a cup of tea before you go to bed?" The proper use of the word "may" was what got Cees. Arie's sadness and confusion were palpable, and Cees's own yearning returned full force.

"Come here." Arie's only move was to cross her right arm over herself and grab her left bicep. Cees put a hand on Arie's hip and Arie moved into her embrace. Cees pressed her forehead against Arie's and they stared solemnly at each other. "Don't look at me like that," Cees said.

"I can't help it. You're confusing the hell out of me," Arie said, her breath smelling of the grape jelly from the one bite of toast she had attempted to eat.

"I'm confusing me too." Cees straightened, but kept their bodies tight against each other. She wondered if she could do her show like this: Arie glued to her front and a stupid grin on her face. She heard Miranda's voice intone, "Ratings would go through the roof."

"What's the smile for?" Arie asked with an answering smile of her own.

"Nothing, I'm just thinking silly thoughts."

"Share?" Arie asked, and Cees wondered if Lilly had given Arie classes on how to give a tummy quivers with the sound of her voice. She pushed aside thoughts of Lilly and how she owed her a good ass kicking.

"I'll share mine if you share yours," Cees answered. It was a natural response. It wasn't as if she expected Arie to share everything on her mind.

"Okay," Arie said with little to no hesitation. "Right now, I want to lay you on the floor, take off all your clothes, and taste you everywhere for as long as you let me, and then I'd like to watch you sleep."

Cees turned her head so she could let out a choking cough without doing it in Arie's face. When she faced Arie again, she said, "Um, you're supposed to, you know, hold back because we're afraid of being hurt."

"Oh, okay. Let me try this again. I'd rather we went into the bedroom and lay on the bed. I'll take your clothes off slowly. Shoes first." Arie smiled. "Then I'd kiss—"

"Um, yeah, that's about the same as before," Cees said as her stomach somersaulted, stuck the landing, and waited in anticipation for her score.

Arie's brow rose. "No, it's not. I put a bed in this time because the floor might be a little hard. Unless hard is good, because we could—"

"Arie, please just kiss me."

Arie smiled triumphantly and Cees pulled her forward by the back of the head. She barely kept herself from moaning. God help her, this part of Arie had not changed. Her kisses could always set Cees on fire. She felt as if all pride, all pretense of coyness had slipped from her and she was willing to beg Arie to do all those things she spoke of.

First the floor, and then the bed. Hard, then soft. She wanted it all, she always had. Her hands were at Arie's stomach, unbuttoning her shirt and tugging it out of her jeans. Arie was wrestling with her own belt. Cees reluctantly let go of Arie's swollen lips long enough to find the fastener on Arie's pants. Her heart slammed against her chest and she tried to calm it, but gave up when Arie rested her head on her shoulder. Arie's pants unfastened, she closed her eyes and paused.

"I hate how much I want you." Cees didn't realize she had actually spoken the words out loud until Arie's body stiffened. Her hands were on Cees's shoulders and she pushed her back.

Arie had a completely shocked look on her face. "It'll never go away, will it?"

"I didn't mean that," Cees said, but Arie wasn't listening. She was righting her clothes, and Cees realized with a sinking heart that the moment had passed. She might not have meant to utter the words, but there was truth in them. Now Arie realized it, too.

"I don't think I can keep doing this with you," Arie said, and Cees felt her confusion and pain as if it were her own because it had been her in this same position almost two years ago. She remembered what it felt like to be loved passionately, only to have that passion ripped away moments later. She remembered, and she still dealt with the scars daily.

Cees reached for Arie, but she stepped back shaking her head. "No more," she said. But Cees knew all she had to do was step forward and take her in her arms and whatever resolve Arie had come to would fade. It had always been that way with her, hadn't it?

The tone of the doorbell froze both of them. Seconds passed where they both just looked at each other.

Cees broke the silence by stating the obvious. "It's midnight."

"Maybe it's your neighbors?"

"I doubt it." Cees walked to the door and looked out the spyglass. "Damn it, Lilly, your timing is impeccable." Cees unlocked the door quickly and swung it open. She was actually grateful that Lilly had come by. She needed something or someone to light into.

"Lilly, what the hell are you doing here at—" She stopped speaking because from the looks of her, Lilly had just come back from the club, only she wasn't alone. Lilly's companion was maybe five-foot-one and handsome, if you overlooked the fact that his forehead glistened with the remnants of whatever products he had used to spike his short dark hair out in all directions. His biceps looked as if they were about to burst the seam of his pristine white long-sleeved shirt. His shirttails hung wrinkled and loose outside of the waistband of his tight leather pants. From his features, Cees figured he wouldn't be meeting Momma Nguyen. If he wasn't Vietnamese, Momma didn't want to meet him.

"This is Chuck," Lilly said as she pushed past Cees and stepped into the room.

"Charles. You can call me Charlie if you like," the little muscle man corrected. Cees stepped aside so that Charlie could follow his hell-on-heels date.

Lilly turned her back on Arie, who was starting to look a little pale and was holding her arm again. "How was dancing?" she asked Cees.

"Dancing was great. Why are you here, Lilly? It's after midnight."

Lilly smiled. "We were on our way to Chuck's house."

"Of course you were," Cees said sarcastically. Arie looked as if she needed to sit down. Cees wanted to get Lilly out of her house so that she could talk to Arie.

"Chuck was telling me about his job, and I came up with a fantastic idea."

Cees waited for Lilly to finish her story and when she didn't, she finally stopped looking at Arie long enough to say, "Okay, Lil, I'll bite. What is this fantastic idea?"

"I think we should hypnotize her ass."

CHAPTER THIRTEEN

Cees fought the urge to laugh as the room became still. The only person who seemed comfortable showing emotion was Chuck, and it was obvious he was already mapping out an escape route.

"Chuck here—"

"Um, it's Charlie, actually. Nobody really calls me Chuck." Chuck unwittingly made mistake number one—of his allotted three—when he corrected Lilly.

"Chuck here is a hypnotist," Lilly continued unperturbed.

"I'm a clinical psychologist who uses—"

"He hypnotizes people to make them—"

"I help them to—"

"Chuck, if this relationship is going to be successful, you are going to have to stop interrupting me." Lilly ran her bright red nails through her hair as if showing off fine fabric to a prospective buyer.

"Sorry," Chuck said.

Lilly must have accepted his apology because she turned back to Cees. "Anyway, I think we should make her remember the crap she put you through."

"Lilly, you are really starting to piss me off," Cees said between clenched teeth.

Arie's hand on her arm was the only thing that kept her from saying something she would regret later. "Cees, maybe we should try it."

Cees lowered her voice, despite the fact that Lilly had perfected her eavesdropping skills long ago and would probably pick up on everything anyway. "Arie, this isn't about you. This is about Lilly proving her point. If you want to try hypnosis, fine, but not with some guy Lilly picked up at a bar." She hated the disappointment she could read clearly in Arie's face, but Cees was determined to assert some control over the situation. "That's it. Lilly, it's time for you to go. We'll discuss this when we're calm, but you overstepped this time. Chuck, it was nice meeting you."

"Overstepped?" Lilly said as if surprised, but her face was far from surprised. "How am I overstepping? By asking her questions that you should be asking? Because I want to find out why she left you and if she's likely to do it again?"

"You two need to leave, now."

"I want to do it," Arie said without taking her eyes from Cees's, making it clear that she was only speaking to her. Cees's heart plummeted at seeing distress and frustration on Arie's face. She wanted to go to her, but Lilly's words rang in her ears as if they had been spoken in a deep, cavernous hall. *Why she left you and if she's likely to do it again?*

"You don't have to. It may not work," Cees said.

"She's right. It might not work if—" Charlie chimed in, his tone much different than the one he had used to apologize to Lilly.

"Don't butt in, Chuck," Cees said, the sharp ring in her tone caused by her distress instead of any real anger with Chuck.

"Sorry," he said, in that same whining, contrite voice he had used with Lilly.

"Where did you find *him*?" Cees asked Lilly.

"At the leather bar," Lilly said with unabashed honesty.

Cees broke contact with Arie and turned to him. "What are your qualifications?" Chuck quickly snapped back into his professional mode and rattled off his alma mater and his internships, his years of practice, and the fact that Palo Cantiones, one of the foremost specialists in his field, was his friend on MySpace.

"Arie, can I speak with you for a moment?" Cees didn't wait for an answer; she walked into the kitchen and shut the door behind them. "Why are you doing this?"

"Because I need to know and so do you."

"I don't know anything about this. Don't you think that Dr. Parrantt would have suggested it if he felt it would help you?"

"Dr. Parrantt is telling us that he doesn't know when or how. Hell, he doesn't even know why I can't remember, Cees. He's not telling us anything. You need to be able to trust me. I need to be able to trust myself."

"I do trust you."

"No, you don't, and the worst part is, I don't remember why." Arie cradled Cees's face in her hands. "We have something that's so strong. I don't remember a whole lot, but I know that this is real and it doesn't happen often. And despite the fact that I hurt you, you can't stop yourself from feeling it either. I need to know, so I don't make the same mistake twice."

Arie's words thrilled Cees. But then reality set in. This Arie couldn't possibly make such a promise. How could she? What Arie couldn't know was what Cees couldn't bring herself to tell her: That even if she had the answers for Arie, she might not be able to bring herself to tell her. Not if it meant Arie could disappear from her life again.

"Then I'd like to try this."

"You finished in there?" Lilly called from the front room and Cees rolled her eyes.

"She must have been a holy terror when she was thirteen," Arie said.

"She was exactly that, plus some. She's also a genius. An evil one. She means well, Arie. She doesn't want me to get hurt."

"Well, we shouldn't keep her waiting, then. She might decide to use that genius to plot my demise. Chuck probably has a degree in dismantling bodies."

Cees was taken aback for a moment. "You been watching those true crime shows with Momma Nguyen?"

"Yeah."

Cees shook her head. No wonder Arie had nightmares.

When they walked back into the living room, Lilly had already moved the table back and had placed two chairs in front of each other.

"If this gets weird, you're both out of here," Cees said sternly and stood with her arms folded as Arie reluctantly sat down. "You comfortable?"

Before Arie could answer, Lilly interrupted. "Want me to get you a pocket watch? Cees probably has one."

"Now, why would you think I would have a pocket watch lying around?"

"You have all that old stuff in your shed."

"Those are antique tools my dad collected."

"Ladies, please, would you step into another room?" Chuck's professional voice left no room for compromise.

Lilly sighed loudly. "I need a cigarette anyway." Cees watched Lilly slam out the front door and made a mental note to apologize to her neighbors.

"I'll be outside, okay? You need me, you just yell. You have thirty minutes." She directed the last sentence to Chuck, who canted his head almost regally and returned his gaze to Arie.

"Tell me what you know," Cees heard him say just as she closed the front door.

Cees turned around in time to see Lilly drop a half-smoked cigarette into her front lawn and step on it.

"Lilly!" Cees said, and Lilly squatted down and picked up

the butt. "I thought you quit?" Lilly had promised she would quit smoking after Cees's father's death.

"I did. I just need something every so often to help with my nerves. I only smoke half, though."

"What the hell were you thinking bringing that weirdo here?"

"He's not a weirdo. He's a doctor."

"Fine, that weirdo doctor. Hypnosis is not a real science."

"How do you know? Who died and made you hypnosis expert?"

That caught Cees off guard. The truth was, she didn't know if hypnosis was an acceptable form of psychotherapy. So she came back with the only line that was sure to get her one up on Lilly. "I'm telling Momma Nguyen."

"Her idea," Lilly returned.

Cees went silent before common sense prevailed. "Liar! You just met that guy at the club. You were on your way to his house to do whatever freaky things you do when he let slip that he can hypnotize people. You then decided it would be great fun to come over here and make our lives hell."

"Since when did it become *our* lives? I was trying to help you get *your* life back."

"I have a life."

"You *had* a life. One me and Momma helped you rebuild. Twice."

"Are you're referring to when my father died?"

Lilly's voice softened. "Cees, I'm not trying to hurt you, but I think you were looking for someone to love when Arie popped into your life."

"My dad had been gone years before I met Arie."

"So what's that got to do with anything? I don't know what I'll do when Momma…"

"Momma Nguyen will never die," Cees said.

Lilly smiled, but to Cees's surprise the smile was sad and

retrospective. "I think Auntie Mem is going to need to come live with us. She's not getting around so well, and Momma is afraid she's not eating like she should."

"Lil, why didn't you tell me?"

Lilly shrugged. "I just found out myself. Doctor said she fainted because her electrolytes are off. She's not doing so well, Cees, and Momma gets real sad. They only two years apart." Lilly's accent thickened, signaling how distressed she was by the situation, and Cees realized that she had been so tied up in her own worries, she had no idea what was going on with her friend. *Family,* she corrected. *They are my family, and deserving of just as much of my attention as Arie is.*

"You know I'll be there for Auntie Mem."

"I know. And you know me and Momma will be there when, you know..." Lilly looked down at Cees's stomach, her expression thoroughly mystified. She had made it very clear to Cees that she didn't get why anyone would go to so much trouble to become a mother.

Cees laughed, "Yeah, I know, but you keep being so mean and I'm not going to have you around."

Lilly rolled her eyes. "Yeah, right. So does she know what you intend to do?"

Cees looked back at the house. "No, I haven't had a chance to talk to her about it yet."

"She's been living with you for weeks."

"Yeah, I know, but the subject hasn't come up."

"Just promise me you won't fall in love with her again, okay?"

Cees was saved from having to answer because the front door opened and Chuck stepped out with his hands shoved into the front of his tight leather pants. Anxiety kept Cees from asking the question, but no such compunction afflicted Lilly.

"How'd it go?"

"I can't really discuss the details."

"I didn't ask for details, I asked how it went," Lilly said sharply, and Cees had to admit she was about ready to knock poor Chuck's block off too.

"Did her doctor suggest she see a psychotherapist? She's a classic example of someone who would benefit from treatment with hypnosis."

"He said we could explore other forms of treatment when she felt up to it. Arie goes back to see him next week."

"Give him my card. I'll need more sessions with her."

"So you're saying you got nothing?" Leave it to Lilly to get right to the meat of the matter.

Chuck looked very serious, and for the first time he ignored Lilly and spoke directly to Cees. "When people have hard to reach memories, and I've never seen anyone as conflicted as your Arie, it's usually for a fairly complicated reason. She doesn't want to remember. You can't just expect her mind to release whatever it is that's causing her pain in one thirty-minute session."

"See, I told you, Cees. She doesn't want to remember."

"That's not what I'm saying. She's not doing this on purpose. Her mind has blocked her memories until it senses she can handle whatever it is she's avoiding."

"The doctor at the hospital pretty much said the same thing. So what can we do about it?"

"Like I said, we can try more sessions, but it hasn't been that long since she got out of the hospital, has it?"

"A few weeks."

"I'm afraid that if we pry, she'll just wall herself off more."

"Wait, you just said she's not doing it on purpose. Why would she wall herself off if we pry?" Lilly asked.

Looking exasperated, Chuck turned to Lilly. "We all have different people inside us. Arie doesn't remember hers, but she's there. And no, I'm not saying she's got split personality." Chuck answered the question he saw in Lilly's face before she could voice it. "What I'm saying is that part of her wants to remember, because she knows that it causes you pain, but there is a reason she shut down in the first place, and part of her remembers that reason too."

Cees thought about that. She had been dealing with the same struggle herself.

"Just give her time," he said, and again, Dr. Parrantt's words were thrown back in Cees's face. Again, she felt helpless in the face of the unknown.

Lilly yawned elaborately.

"Make sure you get her home before sunup, or she'll turn to dust." Cees's words lacked bite, as evidenced by Lilly's second yawn.

Chuck pulled out a business card and handed it to Cees. "I gave her one already. If she wants to continue the sessions, I think I can help."

Lilly was surprisingly quiet as they walked toward her car, barely giving Cees a wave before she drove away.

Arie was still sitting in the same chair that she had been in when Cees left, but now her hands were buried in her hair and Cees rushed to her, kneeling in front of her. She sniffed and sat up, and Cees saw the reddened eyes and the tired look on her face.

"He tell you?"

"He just said he would need more time with you."

"I mean about the fact that I don't want to remember."

"Yes, he told me that, but Dr. Parrantt said as much."

Arie looked at her. "I can't see how that would be true. I want to remember with everything I am and I can't. It's just blank."

"What about the nightmares you've been having?"

Arie stiffened. "What about them?"

"Why do you get so upset when I try to talk to you about them?"

"I don't, do I?"

"Yes," Cees said gently, "You do."

Arie frowned. "I don't remember them, so I don't know why I would."

"Do you think you'd benefit from having more sessions with Chuck? If not him, maybe someone else?" Cees was careful to keep her own emotions in check.

Arie shrugged, "I don't know, maybe."

Cees noticed that Arie's brow was furrowed and the sides of her mouth were drawn down in pain. "Your head hurt?"

"A little."

"I'll get your meds." Cees waited for Arie to respond with a nod or an acknowledgment. When none came, she hurried into the bathroom, grabbed the nearly full prescription bottle, and then to the kitchen to get a glass of water.

When she returned to the living room, Cees found Arie had abandoned the couch for the comfort of her bed. Cees entered the room quietly and set the glass and medication on the nightstand. Arie lay fully clothed and on her side. Her head was supported by her arm, and her eyes were squeezed shut.

"Arie, I have water and your pain medication. Do you think you should take them before you fall asleep?" With a wince that made Cees sick to see, Arie lifted her head as if it weighed a ton, and accepted the meds. Cees kept a hand on the glass as Arie took a few sips from it. "Should you drink more of the water? The bottle says half a glass." Without a word, Arie took a few more sips, paled, and lay back down.

Cees put the glass on the nightstand and would have left had Arie's eyes not opened, freezing her in place.

"Stay. Please," Arie said in a voice ripe with pain.

"Rest. I'll be here when you wake up," Cees whispered, and the moment the words were out of her mouth, her stomach roiled. She had spoken similar words to her father in his final days.

Arie looked at Cees for a few moments longer, sighed, and closed her eyes.

Cees quickly shut off all the lights in the house and checked the doors. She kicked her shoes off and grabbed the blanket from the back of the couch. Once in the bedroom, she listened for the sound of even breathing in the hopes that Arie had fallen asleep. When none came, she walked around the bed and tried not to jostle as she lay down and pulled the blanket over both of them. She scooted as close as she could to Arie and was surprised when Arie immediately scooted back, tucking herself into Cees as she often did when she had that right. When Cees didn't have to feel guilty about the fact that there was nowhere else she would rather be than right there in that bed comforting Arie. Lilly's warning about not falling in love with Arie was both too late and unnecessary. The truth was, she had never fallen *out* of love. She had simply learned to live without Arieanna in her life. Once she admitted that fact, it was natural to admit that having Arie in her home, seeing her every day, allowing so many intimate moments had been a mistake. She and Arie could never go back, not while they still had the mystery of what went wrong hanging over their heads.

CHAPTER FOURTEEN

A rie clutched the cloth bags to her chest and stared at the droplets of water as they streamed down the cab's window. Either the driver had left it cracked to give her fresh air or didn't realize that it was open. Every few seconds a small droplet of cold moisture would hit her forehead or cheek. One flew into her eye, and she blinked it away sluggishly. The driver pushed a button and spoke into a radio in quick bursts of a foreign language.

The cab pulled into the circular driveway of the apartments and the driver hopped out. "Do you need a receipt?" he asked gruffly. Arie shook her head. She moved away from the cab, unaware of how much money she had given the driver, nor did she care. Arie turned her face up to the sky. The rain had stopped temporarily, but the clouds had turned the world gray and dingy. She remembered Cees coercing her from the incredibly uncomfortable couch, but she didn't remember Cees joining her in the bed. She'd left Cees curled into a ball on the right side of the bed. It had taken everything she had not to wake her, but she had left her a note—a note she had started and stopped several times, only to decide that Cees didn't need to be burdened with the truth. The note she'd left read simply, but it had taken all the energy she had left to write it.

Arie found the key ring in the bottom of her bag and ran the fob in front of the door. She pushed the button to call the elevator. She jumped as a man, her neighbor, slammed his mailbox shut and stood next to her to wait for the elevator. Arie wondered if they knew each other, if she should say hello or if they had been on a first-name basis.

"It's going to get worse before it gets better," he said as the doors slid open.

"Sorry?" Arie thought her voice sounded as if she hadn't used it in a year.

"The weather? I noticed you got caught out in it." He looked embarrassed as he pushed the button for her floor and his own. "Sorry. I just meant the weather report said the rain is going to get worse before it gets better." The man got off without a good-bye, and the elevator continued its slow ascent to her floor. Arie had to try two keys before she found the one to her apartment. If not for her driver's license, she wouldn't have known the number because the doors all looked the same. She stepped inside and shut the door. She left the bags at the front door and flipped a light switch. She walked to the window and watched the cars drive over the steel bridge. The storm clouds had rendered it more night than evening, and drivers had already turned on their lights. Arie felt hot and achy. She turned around and looked at the sparsely furnished apartment. It didn't feel warm or welcoming like the inside of Cees's home. It felt like a hotel, as if all unnecessary furniture had been removed.

She remembered a writing desk in the bedroom from when she and Cees had come to get her clothes when she got out of the hospital, and she went right to it. It sat in front of a window with a view of the bridge as well. Arie paused long enough to watch the cars go across that bridge and wondered what it would feel like to have simply worked a hard day and to be looking forward to returning home to a family. She closed her eyes. *Don't even think about it. It won't do any good.* But despair had already started creeping up around her chest, a despair that had been kept at bay by Cees's presence. Arie close her eyes, burning the memory of Cees's sleeping face into her brain. *I won't forget her again.*

Inside the first desk drawer were two envelopes and some photographs of bridges and scenery around Portland. She took them out of the drawer, sure that they had some significance. One of the envelopes caught her eye because the name scrawled on the front was Cees's. The one to Cees was sealed, but the one with her name on it wasn't. She pulled out the two sheets of paper and opened them slowly with trembling hands.

Darling, by the time you are old enough to read this I will either be dead or past caring. I want you to know that you were brought into this world because of love. Your mother and I loved each other enough to hope, perhaps foolishly, that love would keep us safe from life's unfairness. We were wrong. There are things that you must know to keep yourself safe. Things I do not trust my father to tell you, and therefore, I have instructed my attorneys to give you this letter on your eighteenth birthday. I hope that my father has been straightforward with you, as he never was with me. However, I cannot be sure and I would like you to have the ability to make your decision without his influence. Your mother was never strong. Please don't blame her if she cannot be there for you. As you know by now, he is not an easy man to defy. He will no doubt use his money to make it difficult for you to make a decision on your own. I want you to make your own life. I want you to love as I have, with no fear of being left destitute. Between my life insurance and what I received from my mother, compounded by eighteen years of interest, I hope to leave you with enough money to make your own way.

Now, my dearest Arieanna, is the part that I find

most difficult to write. I have suffered for many years with falling down and forgetfulness, with headaches so debilitating I nearly pass out from the pain. My mother had the same issues, but my father led me to believe she had an alcohol problem. I have no doubt that she did drink. However, the doctor has confirmed that she died of the same disease that will eventually relegate me to an invalid, no longer capable of remembering my own name, let alone yours. The idea of it horrifies me, but what horrifies me more is that I may have passed on the gene for Huntington's to you. My father knew of the possibility of my carrying the genes from my mother and did not give me the choice of taking a test. In doing so, he allowed me to ignorantly bring you into the world. As much as I hate that I may have cursed you, I cannot help but be grateful for having had the few years I have had with you.

So, dear Arieanna, you have a choice. You can live life as I have, not knowing if you carry the gene, or you may take the test. I hope I have not unwittingly passed this legacy on to you, but please know this. I have had a short but full life. My only regret is that I will not live long enough to see you become an adult. No matter what, do not let my father stop you from doing anything you desire. Do not let him tell you who you can love. Live your life, Arieanna.

A sob escaped, relieving some of the pressure in her throat. The letter had been dated two days after her third birthday. A memory flashed before her eyes: voices raised, light spilled from a room where women in white uniforms hovered over a bed doing something to a small figure. She wasn't allowed in this room, so she stood outside watching, wishing they would move so she could see. Grandfather stood against the far wall, his hair and eyebrows stood out all over his head in a way that scared her. Slowly, the two nurses straightened and looked at Grandfather. He turned away and saw her standing outside the door. She didn't understand. She hadn't come in.

He walked toward her and she froze, unable to run away, though she wanted to. He grabbed her by her arm and pushed her out into the hall. "You are not supposed to be in here," his voice boomed. The skin around her bicep began to sting. She began to cry, but before she could tell him she had not been inside, the door slammed in her face.

Arie jumped, let her breath out in a gasp, and reached for her right arm. She held it tightly against herself, trying to find comfort. That small, debilitated old man in the bed had been her father. Her father. He couldn't have been more than thirty-two years old. Arie covered her eyes with the heels of her hands. The slow, steady throb began at the base of her neck, and she felt nauseous. She forced herself to stand. Her hair was damp from the rain and she was cold, but she didn't have the energy to find dry clothes, let alone pull back the comforter on the bed. She lay across the bed wondering what Cees was doing, if she had found her note, and if she would ever be able to forgive her.

The migraine struck with the force of a sledgehammer. She put her hand over the top of her head and curled into herself. But neither her hand nor her body could prevent the painful daggers of memory as they sliced her apart with the cruelty she had dished out to Cees. *No, no, no,* she thought, but the memories kept coming. Relentless, spiteful, tearing her apart with clarity and truth until finally they left her filled with utter hopelessness.

❖

Cees turned onto her back and opened her eyes. She smiled as she remembered the evening with Arie and then blushed as she remembered how bold her hands had become in the dim light of the club. It had felt good to hold her and it had felt good to get things out into the open, even if she had hurt Arie by admitting to sleeping with Miranda.

Cees sat up and reached for her watch. Her hand stopped in midair. The house was too quiet. Cees struggled out of the bed, opened the door, and walked into the living room. She half expected to find Arie asleep on the couch in a misguided effort not to wake her, but the throw blanket that Momma Nguyen had bought her as a housewarming gift was still on the back of the couch and the house was quiet with the exception of the sound of heavy rain hitting the roof and windows.

"Arie?" Cees called, but didn't wait for a response. She walked into her second room, the one she had been using since Arie had come to stay with her, but found it empty. She quickly left the bedroom and looked for a note. When she spotted it next to the phone, dread swept over her even before she had taken a step toward the piece of paper. She picked it up as if afraid to get her fingerprints on incriminating evidence.

Cees, I think it might help me to remember if I spend time by myself. I'll call you. Please don't worry.
Love, Arie.

Cees reread the note twice. *Why wouldn't you talk to me first, Arie?*

"Love, Arie," Cees said out loud. First she felt disconcerted, and then she felt angry. *How could she just leave without talking to me first? How could she...* Cees closed her eyes. What had she expected? Lilly and Momma were right. She was stupid, as dumb as they came. She had lain on the ground like a doormat and now she was shocked that Arie had wiped her feet on her for the second time. Cees sat down, felt the bile rise up in her stomach, and forced it down again. She would not cry, she would not... The phone rang and Cees rushed toward it.

"Hello," she said, desperately hoping it was Arie, despite her anger of a few moments before.

"Hey, so when is Arie going to call Chuck?"

"Lilly, I can't talk right now. I need…" She couldn't think of anything to tell Lilly, so she fell silent.

"What's wrong? What happened?"

"Nothing, I'm just tired. I was up all night thanks to you and Chuck."

"You two fighting?" Cees bit her bottom lip to keep from telling Lilly to buzz the hell off. "Well, put her on the phone. I'll straighten her—"

Cees dropped the phone softly back in the cradle. Lilly had her on speed dial, so the phone began ringing again almost instantly. She sat down with the note in her hands. She read it once, then read it again, then balled it up and threw it at the stereo. The phone rang several more times before it stopped. Her tears started a few minutes after. She told herself she was crying because she was tired, and then she told herself the truth. She was crying because she felt like a fool. Despite all her intentions, despite Lilly's warnings, despite everything. If Arie would have come to her instead of leaving, she would have gladly made love to her. She would have opened herself even more for another assault on her heart.

Headlights passed in front of the living room window. A car door opened and closed. Shit. Cees jumped up and ran into the bathroom to throw water on her face. She should have known Lilly would come over when she didn't answer the phone. She should have just talked to her.

Cees grabbed a towel, dried her face and hands, and hurried toward the door when she heard the doorbell ring. What was she going to tell her? That Arie and she had had a fight? That she had finally gotten some sense and told Arie that she couldn't handle it? Or the truth: that she had offered herself to Arie and Arie had not only refused, but had moved out while she was sleeping. Cees closed her eyes, counted to three, and yanked the door open.

"What the hell did you think you were doing?" Cees hated how thick her words sounded, how her stomach twisted at the sight of Arie's pained, shell-shocked eyes. Cees dropped her arm from the door. Arie's hair was plastered to her head as if she had been walking for hours. She had no coat, nothing in her hands.

"Arie, what happened to you? Why—"

"Cees, I know what happened," she said, her voice raspy from crying.

Cees knew instantly what Arie was referring to.

"You remember?" she asked, so afraid of Arie's answer that she had to brace herself against the open door in order to hear it. Arie was staring at her as if she had never seen her before, and fear tugged at Cees. "Arie?"

"I remember," Arie said and she sounded so lost, so hopeless, that Cees wanted to take her into her arms. But that thought faded as she realized that it meant Arie remembered everything—the reason she had left, the way Cees had begged her not to.

"I was so cruel." Arie's voice was emotionless. She had to be freezing standing in her wet clothes, but her body was rigid, and she seemed incapable of taking her eyes off Cees. *She's in shock.* Cees realized.

"You need to come inside. Get out of those clothes."

"I need to tell you everything."

"Okay, but you have to come inside to do that." Cees moved out of the doorway to allow her in. Arie walked by, finally breaking eye contact. Cees saw the tremor that went through Arie as she stepped into the warm house.

"How did you get so wet?" Cees went to the closet to get a towel.

"The phone at the apartment was disconnected so I had to walk a couple of blocks to a main street to get a cab." Arie took the towel, held it in both hands, but didn't dry off.

"I was raised by my grandfather."

Cees handed Arie a towel. "You told me he passed away shortly before you moved to Portland."

Arie looked at the towel in her hands. "He did. I went to his funeral but…we were never close. His idea of raising me was sending me to boarding schools. I managed to get kicked out of so many that he decided to allow me to go to public schools just to avoid the embarrassment. I spent most of my teen years doing things that would piss him off."

Arie swayed and Cees put her hand out to steady her. "Here, sit down."

Arie looked like she was going to protest but must have changed her mind because she finally sat down. Arie frowned. "Why would you take this couch? I'd rather sit on the floor."

Cees momentarily blanked on the answer. "Lilly's idea; she said it would piss you off."

If Arie found fault with the explanation she didn't voice it out loud. "I had been avoiding my grandfather's lawyers for almost a year when you and I met. I didn't want anything to do with his money. The only reason I finally agreed to meet with them was because they said they had a letter from my father."

"Your father? I thought he died just after you were born."

"I always thought he did, too. After I read his letter, I remembered something that happened to me when I was young. There was a commotion coming from the side of the house that I wasn't supposed to go to. The door was open, so I looked inside. I saw him. He looked—I thought he was an old man. Older than my grandfather. He was curled in a fetal position. He looked so small. I was too young to think much of it, and then, as I got older, I guess I forgot." She smiled wanly at Cees. "I seem to be adept at forgetting things I don't want to deal with."

Cees wanted to pull Arie into her arms, to tell her she didn't need to go through this now. But she couldn't do it. Not yet. Arie wasn't the only one who needed answers. "Why would your grandfather hide this from you?"

"Have you ever heard of Evander Simons?"

"The software guy?"

"My grandfather. He ran his family like a business. The things he didn't understand he tried to control. Unfortunately, he didn't understand me at all. When I was young I'd rebel in small ways. I did things like get a navel ring and announce to his dinner guests that I was a lesbian. Once I became an adult, I realized that if I wanted a life of my own, I would have to make sure he wasn't a part of it. I hadn't seen him in years when I got word that he had passed away. I avoided his lawyers, moved to Portland, met you, and tried to forget. When I heard about the letter from my father, I couldn't ignore it anymore."

"Those two days I couldn't get a hold of you?"

Arie nodded. "I was catatonic in a hotel in Seattle."

"What did the letter say?"

A muscle in Arie's jaw twitched and she pulled two envelopes out of her pocket and looked at them. "The sealed one is for you. I wrote it when I thought I would never see you again. I wanted you to know…I wanted you to know that I lied. I never stopped loving you."

There they were. The words she had wanted to hear since the day Arie had pushed her out of her life. She should feel happy, triumphant even. Instead, all she felt was anger at being robbed of precious time.

"The other is the letter from my father. It says a lot of things, the most important of which was that my father knew he was dying of Huntington's disease and that my grandmother died of the same disease. She was only forty-eight years old. My father was thirty-two."

Cees sat down next to Arie, took her hands, and rubbed them between her own because they were ice cold. "Huntington's disease." Cees's hands stilled. "What does that mean?" Cees's body grew as cold as Arie's hands. Somewhere she must have read or heard about the disease, because the moment Arie named it, the word *incurable* blasted her mind.

"It's a hereditary disease. It affects the brain—cognitive skills, motor skills, everything. Some of the symptoms are irritability, trouble walking, forgetfulness." Arie recited the information as if she were reading it.

A sinking feeling started in the back of Cees's mind and settled in her chest. She tried to shirk from it, but the feeling persisted. "Your grandfather never told you? Why would he hide something so important?"

"I can only guess that he thought it best that I not know."

"Why would he think that? You had every right to know how your father and grandmother died."

"I left my grandfather's house two days before my eighteenth birthday because I was tired of him making every decision for me. I wanted to live my own life. Maybe…maybe he thought by not telling me he was giving me that chance. I'm not saying he was right, but once I found out…I felt like my life was over. My father's letter suggests that my grandfather didn't tell him until he was already exhibiting symptoms. My father was afraid the same thing would happen to me. If I had gotten that letter on my eighteenth birthday as my father had intended…"

"You would have never entered into a relationship with me," Cees said.

"How could I have?" A tear dropped down Arie's cheek, and Cees wanted to reach out and hug her to take away the sadness, but she didn't because she needed to hear it all.

Cees couldn't answer her question. She didn't want to think about a life without Arie, even with the pain that was threatening to become a permanent part of her life. "The thing I'm still having a hard time with is that you broke things off before you made sure."

"I'm not asking you to forgive me for that. I just…I just wanted you to know why I thought what I did was the right thing at the time. You'd told me about your father. About how you had to watch him die and how he didn't remember. I still remember how devastated you looked when you told me he didn't remember your name."

Anger flared so hot that it was all Cees could do to keep from shaking Arie. "Do you realize that you did to me exactly what you accused your grandfather of doing to you? You took away my ability to make my own decision, Arie."

"It wasn't just your decision, damn it. I had every right not to want to put you through that. I didn't want you to have to watch me die. I didn't want you to…" The sob racked Arie's body so hard that Cees's hands went up to steady her, but she stopped short of touching her. "I couldn't bear the thought of you knowing I had forgotten you. Can you understand that?"

"You forgot me anyway." It was a cruel thing to say. Cees knew it even before she saw Arie's face pale, but she said it anyway. "What you've been doing for the last year and a half isn't living. So explain it to me so that I understand. Explain it so that I can stop being so damn angry with you for wasting time that we could have spent together. Why couldn't you have had the test with me still in your life? Why did you have to end things?"

"I was working up the nerve to get the test done, but things just kept moving so fast, and I could feel myself falling deeper every minute we stayed together and I just…I just needed a moment to take a breath. I was trying to put on the brakes, and you were pedaling faster and I was so damn scared."

Some of the fear that Arie must have struggled against began to pierce the wall of anger Cees was using to keep herself from flying apart.

"When you asked me if I would carry the child and—"

"Arie? Oh my God, Arie, I was just talking. I wouldn't have insisted that we have children if you didn't want them."

"You don't understand. I wanted a family with you, Cees. I wanted it more than you'll ever know. But all I could think about was how my grandfather had to watch his wife, then his son die. I kept remembering how you had to take care of your father when he was…"

Cees inhaled and turned away from Arie. "He was my father. I loved him. I was honored to take care of him for a few years. He took care of me for twenty."

"But it just about killed you."

"No, it didn't. It made me stronger. I won't lie to you and say that a piece of me wasn't buried with him, and I won't lie to you and say that it didn't hurt when I finally had to admit that my dad really had no idea who I was toward the end. But, Arie, I don't regret one minute of being there for him."

"I don't want to do that to you again. I don't want to put our family through what my grandfather must have had to go through. I don't want you to hurt."

"So you think I'm better off if you leave my life?" Anger flared and was quickly doused by the tortured look in Arie's eyes. "Why not just have the test? Why put us through this if you don't know for sure?"

"I'm fifty percent likely to have this disease."

"Then you're also fifty percent likely not to have it."

"If I had told you, would you have changed your mind about starting a family with me?" Arie asked, despite the fact that she had to have known the answer.

"Of course not."

"Why would you do something like that?" Arie's voice broke from stress. "Why would you risk the possibility of raising a child alone?"

"Because I loved you."

Arie held her gaze for a long moment. Some of the turmoil in her eyes quieted. "I loved you too. I…never stopped. I thought I was doing the right thing. I know it's hard for you to believe that, but it's the truth. I just needed time to get the test. If the test came back negative, I intended on coming back to you and throwing myself at your mercy."

"And if you weren't, you were just going to sit in that cold-ass apartment and die a martyr? It's been over a year and a half, Arie. You still haven't had the test."

Arie closed her eyes. "Lilly came to see me a few months after we broke up. She…told me that you had moved on and that you were over me and that…she said so many things. I had already lost everything. What was the point of having the test?"

"Lilly had no right."

"She was trying to protect you."

"By keeping you out of my life?" Cees could feel her voice

rising to hysterical levels. She wasn't angry at Lilly; she was angry at the universe and Arie's grandfather and whoever else was responsible for putting them through this.

"Lilly didn't keep me out of your life. That's my cross to bear. Lilly loves you," Arie said softly. "She begged me to talk to you. When she realized that nothing she said would work, she lashed out. She told me you had moved on and were better off without me, and something came loose in me."

There was a long moment of silence while Cees tried to digest what Arie had just said. As angry as it made her, she did believe that Arie had loved her. She had always believed it. That's why the end of their relationship had been so devastating.

"Cees, please believe me. I thought I was doing the right thing. But after Lilly came to see me I realized that I had made a mistake, and I just shut down. Up until that point it never even occurred to me that I had ruined something special. I just couldn't think past what if I had it, to what if I didn't have it. Once Lilly came by my apartment, once she told me you had moved on, I realized that it didn't matter. If I had the disease, I had pushed you out of my life before I needed to. If I didn't have it, I would live the rest of my life knowing that I had lost you because I was too afraid to know the truth. A year and half isn't long enough to admit that you're a coward."

"You're not a coward."

Arie smiled. "I am. But I loved… I love you with everything that I have. I hope one day you are able to believe that again."

"Then I guess we both are. Arie, I knew there was something wrong, but I was too afraid to confront you if it was something I couldn't fix."

"Like Huntington's disease?"

Cees paused. "Yeah."

"And now? You aren't afraid anymore?"

"No, I'm still afraid. But I'm here. And this time I'm not going anywhere."

Arie's tears were coursing down her cheeks now. "How did you become so strong?"

Cees smiled sadly. "My father built me that way." Cees reached out and wiped the tears from her eyes. "Did you get any sleep?"

Arie sighed. "A little. Did you?"

"Not enough. Come on, I'll read the letters later. You look like you need more sleep, and I need to be close to you," Cees said. She stood up and held out her hand. Arie took it and allowed herself to be pulled to her feet. Cees took the envelopes still clutched in her hand and drew her close, wet clothes be damned. "I'll take whatever time we have. No more running away. No more wasting time. Understood?"

"Yes," Arie said and Cees heard the conviction in that one word. She led Arie to the bedroom, helped her undress, and held her tight until the shaking eased and Arie fell into an exhausted sleep. Cees loosened her grip on Arie and retrieved the envelope with her name on it from the nightstand. It took her several minutes to open the letter and several more to read it in the dim light. After she had read it twice, she eased out of the bed and sneaked quietly into the living room where Arie wouldn't be awakened by the sobs that racked her body.

CHAPTER FIFTEEN

A rie was glad when they both stopped pretending that they were sleeping. Cees was trembling from the effort of keeping her tears at bay, and Arie hated herself for causing Cees's distress. That feeling, hating herself, was familiar. Hate had been her constant companion since she had pushed Cees from her life. Hate, and the question—did she have it?

Even though her intent in leaving had been to spare Cees pain, it didn't make her certain that she had done the right thing. She had believed she was saving Cees a lifetime of sadness by making her hate her. The problem was, Cees could no more hate her than she could hate Cees.

"I am such a fool," she said. Cees didn't answer. Arie kissed the back of Cees's hand, her open palm, and then placed it over her heart so that she could feel it beat. She breathed in Cees's scent, remembered it, pulled it inside herself so that she would not, could not, forget it again. She wanted to turn over so that she could hold Cees, but fear of rejection won out over need. She tried to content herself with the feel of Cees's breasts pressed against her back, her bottom nestled into the curve of Cees's hips—puzzle perfect. Cees's hand settled on Arie's hip, her thumb just above the soft triangle of hair. Chills formed on Arie's arms, despite the heat their bodies created.

In the past, she hadn't needed to see Cees's expression to know if she wanted her. She always knew by the way Cees touched her, as if asking permission despite knowing she needed none. Now she needed to hear the words. She didn't want to risk an assumption, not when they had both been through so much emotionally.

"Cees? I need to know what you want." Arie turned until she was flat on her back looking up into Cees's face, looking up into desire meant for her.

"I want you to make love to me," Cees said. Arie translated that request into "Make me forget." Arie wanted more than anything to make Cees forget, even for an instant, the dread she had been living with all of her adult life.

Arie sat up and kissed her, opening her lips only slightly, giving Cees the chance to change her mind. When she didn't, Arie deepened the kiss, easing Cees onto her back and settling on top of her.

Arie expected the kiss to be gentle, hesitant. It wasn't. Cees held the back of her neck, deepening the kiss and forcing them both past tentative. Arie inhaled as she felt herself tighten, constrict. She was perched on the edge of a small orgasm. This too was familiar.

Arie covered Cees's breasts with both hands, delighting in the familiar weight and feel of them. Cees caught her breath. "Cold?" she asked.

"A little," Cees whispered. Arie could feel the gooseflesh as it welled up over Cees's skin, and she sought out Cees's lips again. Then she slid her lips over Cees's cheek, her neck, and down to her breast. She trailed her nipple with her tongue and then took it into her mouth. She knew Cees would arch, but the hiss followed by the whimper was new, and Arie immediately gentled her touch.

She was rewarded with the feel of Cees against her hips. She could feel Cees's eyes on her and she realized that she was perhaps moving too fast. She closed her eyes and willed herself to calm down. Cees's hand circled her wrist and pulled her down. Her fingers ran along Arie's back, up to her breast and down her sides. Their kiss was slow and seeking, and if Arie knew what strength or weakness made her able to break away from Cees in the first place, she forgot it in that moment.

Arie laced her fingers through Cees's and pinned them on the pillow above her head. Arie opened her legs wide, easing Cees's apart, and was rewarded by Cees's hips lifting off the bed and into her. Now it was Arie's turn to moan. She released Cees's hands, but they stayed on the pillow and hers went to cup Cees's ass, to pull her close as she lost herself in the movement and the friction for a few torturously slow moments. When she felt that they were too close to continue, she lifted off Cees and immediately felt the protesting hand on the back of her neck. She ignored it and kissed her way between Cees's breasts and down her rapidly rising and falling stomach. The pressure disappeared from the back of her neck and Arie imagined that Cees put her hand back where she had left it; open and palm up on the pillow. She kissed the line of hair, saw it in her mind's eye, and then pushed the vision away. As her heart rate increased, she settled between Cees's legs, lifting her leg around her shoulder. With her hands beneath Cees's ass, she kissed her with the gentleness that she knew drove Cees beyond crazy. Parting her lips and kissing her as if it were their first time together.

Arie could hear her own heart pounding in her ears as she captured Cees's clitoris and ran her tongue down its shaft. Cees's soft cry was Arie's cue to begin a steady suction. She tried to ignore the flush of heat that bloomed between her own legs and concentrated instead on the increasing moisture between Cees's. Soon both of Cees's hands were on Arie's head, not pressuring, not really directing, just there while she loved her. When Cees was close, Arie entered her with her with trembling fingers, and Cees immediately embraced her as she knew she would. Cees's hips lifted high and Arie tried to support her, but she was already lost in the feel of Cees holding her inside as she held her inside her mouth, and lost in the sound of Cees calling out her name as her orgasm came hard and with so much force that she was left dumbstruck for a few seconds afterward. Arie was struck with acute awareness of all she had missed. She could never ever make up for those lost nineteen months, and it tore her apart.

"Arie, come up here," Cees said and Arie complied though she was completely drained. The moment her head struck the pillow, Cees was covering her, looking at her with those eyes that had always been able to see through her. Those eyes were responsible for Arie's decision to force Cees out of her life. Those eyes would have found out eventually.

"Why are you looking at me like that?"

"I don't know."

"Yes, you do," Cees said softly.

"I was just thinking how you had my number." Cees was moving against her and Arie was having a hard time thinking, which she figured was Cees's plan.

"Funny, I was thinking the same thing about you."

"Cees, would you…" Arie took Cees's hand and moved it down near her hip.

"What is it, sweetheart?"

At first, Arie couldn't tell if Cees was teasing her or if she honestly didn't know what she was about to ask. Could she tell her what she wanted? Could she admit that she wanted Cees to— "Finish what you started a few weeks ago." The thought had turned into a verbal order. Cees went still and then moved to the side.

"I thought…"

"I was scared. I didn't know what to do with all that…"

"Passion?" Cees finished for her.

"Pleasure, but yes, passion too." Cees's hands were already playing with the hair between her legs, and Arie eagerly opened her legs. Arie didn't have to open her eyes to know that Cees would be smiling. She arched her hips, sought out Cees's hands, and guided her to where she needed her. She opened her eyes just in time to see Cees's smile fade as she felt the need that had been building from the moment Arie realized Cees was going to let her make love to her.

"I don't want to wait anymore," Arie said. Cees held her gaze as she entered her. Arie arched to give her access. She turned her head, and Cees was there kissing her, helping her to climb the ladder to pleasure. Once again, Arie's heart rate was escalating and she listened to it as she increased her hip movement. When the time came, she called out Cees's name. She had been such a fool.

❖

Arie was lying on her back; her pulse throbbed visibly at the base of her throat as she slept. Cees kept perfectly still because she knew that any movement would wake Arie.

The first few nights after Arie's return, Cees seemed to have reveled in having her there. The fourth and fifth nights were spent differently. Even with everything that Arie had told her, even the fear of losing her hadn't dissipated the anger.

Arie's lips parted, and Cees noticed a piece of lint on Arie's bottom lip. She removed it without touching skin, but even that small bit of movement caused Arie to stir. Cees waited with her hand poised above Arie's face and smiled at the thought of Arie waking to see her like this. She would probably roll out of bed in horror.

Cees winced. That third night, she had hardly spoken to Arie at all when she came home. Arie had been happy to see her but accepted her quietness and didn't question it until Cees had burst into tears when Arie asked her how her sea bass tasted. Then when Arie touched her, Cees had been so angry that she had been tempted to physically push Arie away.

But she hadn't, Cees reminded herself.

Instead, the tears came. She had cried out her anger and Arie had let her. Not shushing her. Just letting her cry. It wasn't until later that Cees realized that Arie was crying too. Even after their lovemaking became less of an apology, but a rejoicing at finding each other again. The anger and the fear of losing her were still there.

If and when the nightmares began, she would turn over and brush a hand against Arie in the pretense of accidentally touching her in her sleep. Anything to stop the thought of being without her again.

Cees was so deep in thought that she hadn't noticed Arie was awake until she turned to her and smiled. Arie's eyes traveled her face slowly as if imprinting Cees's face on her memory.

"How long?" Arie asked. Cees understood the question. How long did they have? How long before she had to leave to go to work? How long before they would be forced apart?

"Two hours, maybe a few minutes more. Did I wake you?" Cees asked, strangely made shy by the intense look on Arie's face.

"You touched my lips."

"No, I was careful not to touch you."

"I felt you just the same." Arie rolled over on top of her, and Cees put her arms around Arie's shoulders, loving the perfect weight of her.

The lovemaking was slow and exploratory, but the apologies had all but disappeared. They were just exploring each other. *She's savoring me,* Cees thought, right before she arched her back off the bed and grabbed her pillow for an anchor. She pushed the thought away and rushed toward her pleasure.

The first few days after Arie regained her memory, they had tried to pretend that Arie was still sleeping in the other bedroom, but Momma Nguyen had seen through that by the second day. Cees and Arie had an appointment with Dr. Parrantt to discuss the fact that Arie's headaches had all but disappeared. Momma Nguyen would be able to focus her attention on her sister. Arie had voiced how much she would miss the curmudgeonly woman, and Cees had admitted that she, too, would miss seeing Momma on a daily basis. The fear and insecurities were still there, but life didn't seem to care and was returning to some semblance of normalcy. That is, if not hearing from Lilly constituted normal.

Lilly, it seemed, was still angry with her. This was the first time in years that things had gotten so bad that Lilly refused her calls. Arie had suggested that they visit Lilly together, but Cees had flat-out refused. She had her pride too. As much as Cees loved Lilly, Arie was her main concern now. If anything, the return of her memories was taking more of a toll on Arie physically than her amnesia had. She wasn't sleeping as soundly as she had been, and Cees often caught her watching her.

The apologizing and self-deprecation had stopped, but the fear was still there, and she knew the only way to make it go away was for Arie to take the test for Huntington's disease. That was the only way they would ever move forward on whatever path they had to travel. Arie had said she wanted to live life with Cees like every day was going to be their last. But what they were doing was cocooning themselves in the house, making love to each other, and releasing old hurts. Cees didn't think either of them was living.

Cees pulled herself from her melancholy thoughts, got out of the truck, and was hurrying inside when she noticed Miranda's car. She wasn't expecting her back for another day or so. She jogged up the stairs to her office and found her on the phone. Miranda waved her in, and Cees walked into the room and sat down.

Miranda finished her call looking both frazzled and excited. "Wow, you look great."

Cees raised a brow. "I do?" Despite the worry over Arie's health, she did feel energized, ready to take on the world if need be.

"Maybe a little sad, but still nice and glowy. What's going on?"

"I just saw your car and wondered why you were back so early."

"I got some good news in New York. I've been promoted."

"Wow, that's great! I guess I should have seen that coming. I can't lie and say that I'm happy you're leaving, but I am happy for you."

Miranda's smile was made up of equal parts excitement and nervousness. "This is exactly the opportunity I've been waiting for."

"I know." Cees returned her smile because she was genuinely pleased for Miranda. "I need to get downstairs. Philly will be looking for me. Let's get together and talk soon."

"I noticed you didn't answer me when I asked what was going on, and you do look a little sad. I'm not conceited enough to think it's because of my pending departure."

Miranda looked genuinely concerned, and Cees really wanted to sit down and tell her how she was both the happiest and the saddest she had ever been in her life. But Miranda was not Lilly. And despite Lilly's rough exterior, they had a lifetime of sharing fears and triumphs together. She and Miranda could never have that.

"I'm fine. Just a little tired."

"Well, after next Friday, you should have a full six weeks off. Any special plans?"

Cees smiled. "Yeah, I do." She turned to leave.

"Oh, and don't worry, I'm still going to be heading up the cabin project. I'll hire the new producer and oversee everything, so make sure you keep out of trouble." Miranda winked.

Cees winked back, barely stifling a laugh. She had every intention of getting herself into some big trouble very soon.

Vance met her halfway down the stairs. He had such a somber look on his face that Cees was tempted to ask him what was wrong. Tempted, but not stupid. She kept walking. "Uh, Cees? I think you should know…there are rumors among the crew that you're not into men."

Cees studied him seriously. "It's good you told me. I hate having people trying to guess things about me." Vance's relief was palpable. "The truth is, I saw how badly you were doing with women, so I thought I would give it a shot. To be honest, I don't get why you get shot down so much. I have no trouble finding attractive women to spend time with."

Miranda chose that moment to leave her office carrying a large box and wearing the same frazzled expression she'd worn when she had ended her phone call. Cees moved to the side to let Miranda by, but she stopped, shifting the box to the rail. Miranda had always been the peacekeeper between Cees and Vance, alternating between placating Cees and catering to Vance's ego in order to keep the show going. Now she ignored him completely.

"Hey, I almost forgot to ask, would you mind telling Arieanna that I'm sorry if I upset her when she was here? I was probably a little more jealous of your relationship than I had any right to be. I hope there are no hard feelings? I really do wish you two the best."

"Of course, there aren't. I'll make sure to tell her," Cees said as Miranda passed her. She was about to follow her, but couldn't resist the wink she gave Vance. His mouth clamped shut audibly, and Cees went in search of Philly. The moment was tempered by the fact that the one person who would have enjoyed hearing about the exchange was not accepting her calls.

CHAPTER SIXTEEN

Cees felt the tumult of fear and anger that always came over her when she walked into a medical facility. She reached for Arie's hand and held it tight. Arie squeezed, and Cees tried to make the corners of her mouth turn up, but failed.

This was the right thing to do. *Most importantly, this is what Arie said she wanted to do.* Today she and Arie stood at their fork in the road. They would learn which direction the rest of their lives would follow.

The show was on hiatus, and the producers were happy with her because the ratings were good. They weren't exactly happy that she planned on being pregnant next season, until Miranda pointed out that more and more women were making the choice to become single parents.

Voices had become excited over the prospect, but Cees had tuned out. To them, portraying her as a single parent meant she would appeal to yet another group: single mothers. To her, it meant Arie wasn't by her side.

"Are you all right, sweetheart?" Arie grasped her wrist gently, pulling her hand down from her glasses. This was a new side of Arie that had returned after her memory. Cees loved how attentive Arie was but hated the undercurrent of apology that was always between them. She felt sure that they would get past this someday. Given time.

"I just need a minute." The irony that she was having a harder time than Arie seemed to be having didn't escape her notice.

Arie's face appeared passive, cold and unreadable. *No*, Cees corrected herself. Arie was just more adept at hiding; she had always been adept at concealing her fears. But now that Cees knew what to look for, she could see it clearly. She had been awakened when Arie put her key in the lock. But the truth was, Arie was as afraid as she was of spending even a single minute apart if they didn't have to.

The two thoughts she had forbidden herself to think about before Arie told her about the possibility of her carrying the trait for Huntington's disease came to mind. *Can I live without her again? Can I love her and let her go when the time comes?*

The nurse smiled at them and raised a hand. Cees told herself that it was a good sign. No look of compassion, but a smile, a wave. She remembered the two of them. She cupped her hand over the phone. "Dr. Parrantt is getting your file now. Why don't you two head on into his office?"

Cees realized the doctor hadn't yet seen the results, which meant that the nurse's smile meant nothing. Cees's hopes plummeted again and she stood up. Arie was much slower, and Cees noticed how pale her face was. Cees wrapped her arm around her waist. She didn't release her when they sat in the two visitor chairs in Dr. Parrantt's office. She put her mouth near Arie's ear. "No matter what, we said we'd live like there's no tomorrow. Remember?"

"I remember," Arie said in a voice that sounded as old as time itself. And Cees felt a strange calm settle over herself.

"Good, what do you want for dinner?"

Arie grew still and turned to look at Cees. "Are you serious?"

"Yeah, completely. Part of living like there's no tomorrow means we eat whatever we want." Cees patted her belly. "I have an excuse to get all chunk and sassy, so I'm going to do a bang-up job of it."

"You're not pregnant yet."

Arie was smiling now and Cees winked at her. "Nobody has to know that." Cees wanted to get pregnant as soon as possible, and although she could see Arie was excited by the idea, there was still that little bit of turmoil that growing up without her parents had left with her. Cees had pointed out gently that she would make sure that their child was loved, and Arie been forced to relent. "I'm thinking I want one of those brownie fudge sundaes."

"For dinner?" Cees heard the smile in Arie's voice.

"Of course. It's a little late for breakfast. What will you be having?"

Arie did laugh now. "We can't split the brownie sundae?"

"No," Cees said. Arie laughed again, and Cees tried to join in, but it sounded hollow and sad. *I love your mouth, your skin, your nose, and your sensitive neck...*

"Don't do that," Arie said; all that was left of her smile was a memory.

"What did I do?"

"You're trying to imprint me on your brain. I used to do that every time you came to visit me in the hospital because I figured you weren't going to show up the next day."

Cees shook her head, but Arie reached out to stop her with a hand on her cheek. "I'm still here. No matter what he says, I'm not ready to say good-bye to you yet. You understand?"

Cees cupped the back of Arie's hand and kissed her palm. She would have apologized for her slip, but the doctor walked in with a thin manila folder in his hand.

"Ladies," he said, as he had the last two times they had visited with him.

Cees felt Arie pull into herself and attempt to remove her hand, but Cees held fast. She was unable to rip her eyes from the manila folder. The contents of that slim folder would tell her whether she would have to watch someone she loved die. How could something so thin hold the blueprint for the rest of their lives?

Dr. Parrantt opened the file and said simply, "Arie, we are ninety-five percent certain that you do not carry the gene for Huntington's disease."

The stark quiet in the room went unbroken for so long that Cees ran the doctor's words through her mind three times. Arie was ninety-five percent certain not to develop Huntington's disease. Arie's hand had gone limp in hers and Cees couldn't take her eyes off Dr. Parrantt. Finally, he smiled, and that drove it home for both of them.

The smile was what did it for Cees. She felt something come loose inside. Arie pulled her onto her lap.

"Take as long as you need." Dr. Parrantt closed the door softly as he left.

Soul-wrenching sobs ripped from the deepest parts of Cees's body. Arie held on to her, telling her to let it out, telling her that they were going to be fine and that she loved her. Cees wanted to tell her that she knew all that, but Arie began to cry too, and at some point they started to rock each other to ease the pain and the fear.

Eventually the hold they had on each other gentled, and Cees worried about her weight bearing down on Arie's legs. She wiped beneath Arie's wet eyes with her thumbs, then kissed her swollen lips. Arie's arms tightened to support her as she reached across Dr. Parrantt's desk for a tissue.

She dried her eyes and cleaned her glasses on her shirt. She sighed and asked, "Should we let the good doctor have his office back?"

"Probably a good idea," Arie said and Cees reluctantly extricated herself from Arie's lap.

"You up for that dinner?" Cees asked.

Arie smiled. "I'd much rather we went home. I need to be close to you."

It was Cees who said the proper thank-yous to Dr. Parrantt, and it was Cees who put the paperwork in front of Arie to sign. She led Arie to the car and gently reminded her to put on her seat belt. Cees pulled the truck to a stop at the end of the parking lot. Arie's head had fallen to the side. She was asleep. Cees closed her eyes briefly and saw a twenty-year-old memory of her father running down the sidewalk as he tried to help her fly a kite. He had been tall, strong, and happy then. She sent him a silent thank-you and pulled the monster onto the street. She drove five miles below the speed limit, careful to avoid potholes and streetlights that could jar Arie from a much-needed sleep.

EPILOGUE

Two Months Later

A rie knew how Lilly would react when she saw her sitting at the table alone. She held her breath as Lilly slowed her step, shifted a purse almost half her size, and looked over her large glasses at Arie. She stopped in front of the table, looking at Arie as if she were something of interest that had been discarded on the sidewalk. Finally, she closed her phone with a flip of the wrist and a snap that made Arie jump.

"Where's Cees?"

"She's on her way," Arie said, and disappointment settled heavily on her shoulders as Lilly flipped open her cell and began to dial.

"I'll see what's holding her up."

"No, wait. Don't call her yet."

Lilly closed her phone and set it carefully on the table. She then removed her sunglasses and set them next to the phone. Arie wouldn't have been surprised if she pulled boxing gloves out of her gigantic bag and started whaling on her.

"What are we doing here?"

"I sent you the text message asking you to lunch, not Cees. I told her that you called while she was in the shower and asked that she meet you here." Now that Arie could see Lilly's eyes, she wished that she hadn't removed the sunglasses. Lilly Nguyen made her feel like the creepiest bug on earth.

"I remember everything," Arie said.

"So Momma told me. You want an award?"

"No, I mean, I remember you coming to see me a few weeks after Cees and I broke up."

Lilly's expression didn't change and Arie couldn't help but think how unalike Cees and Lilly were, but how close they were and how she was the cause of the rift between them.

"So what about it?"

"You told me I was making the biggest mistake of my life."

Lilly said nothing. The wind picked up and several strands of her long dark hair blew across her face. She didn't move them and her gaze never wavered. Arie stilled herself, forced herself not to back down.

"You were right. Look, I know you can't stand me because of what I did to Cees. I know she's like a sister to you, but…"

Lilly leaned forward, her expression finally changed, and Arie got a glimpse of the depths of her anger. "She is my sister." The words were hissed through thinned lips. "And you broke her heart. You broke *her*. Cees gave you everything and you threw it back in her face. I don't know how she could ever forgive you, let alone forget what you did."

Arie inhaled and said the only word that she could get out of her tightening throat. "Don't—" Arie stopped herself. She wanted to defend herself against Lilly's wrath, but how could she? Why had she asked Lilly here? What had she expected? Lilly was doing what Cees had every right to do. What Arie would have done if anyone had hurt her family. "Cees forgave me because she loves me."

Lilly let out a very unfeminine snort, but Arie went on as if she hadn't heard it. "Please let me finish. She loves me, but every time she looks at me there is this little bit of pain that she can't hide. No matter how tightly I hold her and how long I make love to her, I can't make it go away. I don't need *you* to punish me, Lilly." Arie tried to hold on to Lilly's gaze, tried to make her understand that she was sincere in her desire to heal the hurts she had caused.

"Why did you text me from Cees's phone?"

"Because I knew you wouldn't agree to come if I asked you myself. I told Cees you phoned while she was in the shower. She'll be here in fifteen minutes, I wanted us to have time to talk first."

"What do we have to talk about? I told you how I felt about what you did that day I came to see you."

"You never told Cees about that."

Lilly shrugged. "Why would I? I should have kept my nose out of it anyway."

"When my brain shut off everything else, I remembered you yelling at me. I remembered how painful it was watching you leave, how I gave up on everything after that." Lilly's eyes narrowed but she didn't speak. "I asked you here because I want to tell you the truth." Arie wiped a tear from the corner of her eye, sighed. "God, I've been doing that too much lately. Okay. When I was very small, my father died of a genetic disorder called Huntington's disease."

Lilly went very still. Arie took advantage of her stillness and told her everything she had told Cees about her grandmother and her father's deaths. "My grandfather thought it best that I not be told, and for a while I hated him for it. Now I'm not so sure he was wrong. I don't know what I would have done with that possibility hanging over my head."

"I do. You would cut yourself off from the rest of the world and disassociate yourself from all relationships."

Arie raised a brow and Lilly shrugged. "I couldn't sleep, so I read some of Chuck's journals."

Arie picked up her tea cup, more to steady her quivering lip than for a need to drink. "It took me two hours to fall in love with Cees. I thought she was the most beautiful human being I had ever met."

Lilly wrinkled her nose. "She's not all that."

Arie laughed. "She's pretty great." Lilly conceded her point with a nod.

"She has forgiven me, Lilly. But she doesn't understand how I could make that sacrifice for her. You were there when her father died. I only see the remnants of that pain, but can you understand why I did what I did? I'm not asking you to agree, but just understand that I thought I was doing the right thing."

"It doesn't matter what I understand."

"It does. It matters. You're her family. She cares what you and Momma Nguyen think, and you've been avoiding her for weeks now. She misses you. I can tell by the way she answers the phone when it rings that she's hoping it's you, and it never is."

Lilly shrugged, but she did look guilty. "She could have called me, you know?"

"Come on, Lilly. She tried at first. You refused to take her calls." Lilly didn't deny it, and they both grew silent. Arie watched as a streetcar packed with people headed toward the waterfront. Her lease on the apartment ended on Monday, but most of her things had already been moved to Cees's small home. Another wind blew and Arie closed her eyes and leaned back. "Cees is here. She's early." Arie opened her eyes and smiled.

Lilly looked behind Arie and then back, incredulity on her face. "She just turned the corner. How did you know?"

Arie stood up to embrace Cees.

Cees kissed her. "What are you doing here? I thought you were going to your place to pick up the rest of your stuff."

Arie filled Cees in on her plot to bring her and Lilly together. When she was done, Cees sat down in the chair that Arie pulled out for her. "Um, Lil, you know I had nothing to do with this?"

"Yeah, I know. You're not devious enough," Lilly said into her teacup.

Cees kept staring at Lilly until Lilly finally looked at her. Arie picked up her water glass and drank so that Lilly wouldn't catch her grinning. It was hard for her to ignore Cees when she did that too.

"I missed you, Lilly. I missed you a lot and I don't want to fight anymore." Cees pulled her into a hug and Arie looked away to give them privacy, but not before she saw a tear spill down Lilly's cheek.

The waiter was approaching and Arie shook her head. He immediately turned away, and Arie mentally reminded herself to leave a big tip. Eventually, Cees and Lilly straightened and Lilly picked up her purse and pulled out a compact. Arie picked up her menu and studied it, giving Cees and Lilly time to get over their discomfort.

"You gonna make it?" Lilly asked. Arie looked up when Cees hadn't responded. Two sets of eyes were looking at her, and she realized that Lilly was speaking to her.

Arie set her menu down. "Oh yeah, I had the test and I'm ninety-five percent unlikely to get the disease."

"That mean you're going to go through with it?" Lilly looked down at the table, indicating Cees's stomach. At least that's what Arie hoped she was indicating.

"Yeah, we're going to try. It might take a while, though." Cees asked gently, "Momma Nguyen didn't tell you?"

"Nah, she's mad at me because I'm mad at you."

Cees smiled and looked at Arie. "See, Momma Nguyen is on our side."

"Always is." Lilly's voice was grumpy, but Arie noticed that she didn't move away from Cees, nor did her annoyed tone reach her eyes. Lilly picked up her menu just as her cell phone began blaring Momma Nguyen's theme song. "Yeah," she said and began speaking in rapid-fire Vietnamese.

Cees turned to Arie. "I can't believe you did all this," she said and bumped her nose gently to Arie's.

"I just want you to be happy."

"I am happy."

"You're happier now," Arie said, and despite the people milling around them, kissed those smiling lips until they were soft and suppliant.

Lilly's Vietnamese was interrupted by a clear bout of English. "They're right here being gross at the table." Lilly returned to Vietnamese and the kiss ended because both Arie and Cees were grinning too hard. Lilly snapped the phone shut and looked at them seriously.

"Momma said two stupid people make genius baby."

Cees turned to Arie, her eyes wide. "You hear that, sweetheart? We're going to have us a genius in the family!" Cees stuck both hands in the air, and Arie high-fived her and offered Cees an idiotic grin of her own.

"Come on, Lilly. Give me some love. People are going to start looking pretty soon. What if one of your friends drives by and sees you sitting here with a nutter with her hand stuck in the air for no apparent reason?"

"They'll think I'm helping the homeless or doing community service."

Arie had never seen anyone look as happy as Cees did at being insulted.

"Oh, Lilly," Cees said with a smile, "no one who knows you would ever believe you would do community service."

Lilly glared and Cees's grin grew wider. Arie got it now. They were playing with each other, the way family does. Bending under the pressure of blackmail, or perhaps it was that grin, Lilly slapped the proffered hand, albeit reluctantly. Cees dropped her hand into her lap and looked pleased with herself.

"A little Cees, huh?" Lilly grumbled.

"Actually, we are thinking about having at least four," Cees said happily.

"Four?" Lilly looked from Cees to Arie. "How the hell are you going to do the show if you spend the rest of your life knocked up?"

"Cees wouldn't have to carry all of them. My not having the gene means I can carry our children, too. I didn't have any siblings growing up. I spent a lot of time alone. I don't want that for our children." Arie felt very vulnerable for having admitted that to Lilly, but if she wanted Lilly to trust her, she would have to do the same.

"Four little Ceeses and Aries? Lord help us all," Lilly said, but she couldn't keep her face straight and soon they were all laughing. As the waiter walked hesitantly toward them, Arie looked over at Cees and Lilly. Light head pressed against dark over a shared menu. She saw them as they were when they were younger and understood their closeness. Cees looked up and caught her gaze.

What she had told Lilly was the truth. The remembered pain was there in Cees's eyes, but so was the newfound happiness, so was the joy, and so was the eagerness for what would come tomorrow.

About the Author

Gabrielle Goldsby is the author of *The Caretaker's Daughter*, *Never Wake*, *Such a Pretty Face*, and the 2007 Lambda Literary Award–winning mystery, *Wall of Silence* 2nd edition.

When not writing, reading, or in the gym, Gabrielle enjoys exploring the trails near her home in Portland Oregon, camping—the kind that requires a tent—and watching movies in her home theater with her partner of nine years.

Gabrielle's works in progress are *Paybacks* (Bold Strokes Books, 2009) and *The Burning Cypress*.

For information about these and other works, please visit www.boldstrokesbooks.com.

Books Available From Bold Strokes Books

A Guarded Heart by Jennifer Fulton. The last place FBI Special Agent Pat Roussel expects to find herself is assigned to an illicit private security gig baby-sitting a celebrity. (Ebook) (978-1-60282-067-8)

Saving Grace by Jennifer Fulton. Champion swimmer Dawn Beaumont, injured in a car crash she caused, flees to Moon Island, where scientist Grace Ramsay welcomes her. (Ebook) (978-1-60282-066-1)

The Sacred Shore by Jennifer Fulton. Successful tech industry survivor Merris Randall does not believe in love at first sight until she meets Olivia Pearce. (Ebook) (978-1-60282-065-4)

Passion Bay by Jennifer Fulton. Two women from different ends of the earth meet in paradise. Author's expanded edition. (Ebook) (978-1-60282-064-7)

Never Wake by Gabrielle Goldsby. After a brutal attack, Emma Webster becomes a self-sentenced prisoner inside her condo—until the world outside her window goes silent. (Ebook) (978-1-60282-063-0)

The Caretaker's Daughter by Gabrielle Goldsby. Against the backdrop of a nineteenth-century English country estate, two women struggle to find love. (Ebook) (978-1-60282-062-3)

Simple Justice by John Morgan Wilson. When a pretty-boy cokehead is murdered, former LA reporter Benjamin Justice and his reluctant new partner, Alexandra Templeton, must unveil the real killer. (978-1-60282-057-9)

Remember Tomorrow by Gabrielle Goldsby. Cees Bannigan and Arieanna Simon find that a successful relationship rests in remembering the mistakes of the past. (978-1-60282-026-5)

Put Away Wet by Susan Smith. Jocelyn "Joey" Fellows has just been savagely dumped—when she posts an online personal ad, she discovers more than just the great sex she expected. (978-1-60282-025-8)

Homecoming by Nell Stark. Sarah Storm loses everything that matters—family, future dreams, and love—will her new "straight" roommate cause Sarah to take a chance at happiness? (978-1-60282-024-1)

The Three by Meghan O'Brien. A daring, provocative exploration of love and sexuality. Two lovers, Elin and Kael, struggle to survive in a postapocalyptic world. (Ebook) (978-1-60282-056-2)

Falling Star by Gill McKnight. Solley Rayner hopes a few weeks with her family will help heal her shattered dreams, but she hasn't counted on meeting a woman who stirs her heart. (978-1-60282-023-4)

Lethal Affairs by Kim Baldwin and Xenia Alexiou. Elite operative Domino is no stranger to peril, but her investigation of journalist Hayley Ward will test more than her skills. (978-1-60282-022-7)

A Place to Rest by Erin Dutton. Sawyer Drake doesn't know what she wants from life until she meets Jori Diamantina—only trouble is, Jori doesn't seem to share her desire. (978-1-60282-021-0)

Warrior's Valor by Gun Brooke. Dwyn Izsontro and Emeron D'Artansis must put aside personal animosity and unwelcome attraction to defeat an enemy of the Protector of the Realm. (978-1-60282-020-3)

Finding Home by Georgia Beers. Take two polar-opposite women with an attraction for one another they're trying desperately to ignore, throw in a far-too-observant dog, and then sit back and enjoy the romance. (978-1-60282-019-7)

Word of Honor by Radclyffe. All Secret Service Agent Cameron Roberts and First Daughter Blair Powell want is a small intimate wedding, but the paparazzi and a domestic terrorist have other plans. (978-1-60282-018-0)

Hotel Liaison by JLee Meyer. Two women searching through a secret past discover that their brief hotel liaison is only the beginning. Will they risk their careers—and their hearts—to follow through on their desires? (978-1-60282-017-3)

Love on Location by Lisa Girolami. Hollywood film producer Kate Nyland and artist Dawn Brock discover that love doesn't always follow the script. (978-1-60282-016-6)

Edge of Darkness by Jove Belle. Investigator Diana Collins charges at life with an irreverent comment and a right hook, but even those may not protect her heart from a charming villain. (978-1-60282-015-9)

Thirteen Hours by Meghan O'Brien. Workaholic Dana Watts's life takes a sudden turn when an unexpected interruption arrives in the form of the most beautiful breasts she has ever seen—stripper Laurel Stanley's. (978-1-60282-014-2)

In Deep Waters 2 by Radclyffe and Karin Kallmaker. All bets are off when two award-winning authors deal the cards of love and passion… and every hand is a winner. (978-1-60282-013-5)

Pink by Jennifer Harris. An irrepressible heroine frolics, frets, and navigates through the "what ifs" of her life: all the unexpected turns of fortune, fame, and karma. (978-1-60282-043-2)

Deal with the Devil by Ali Vali. New Orleans crime boss Cain Casey brings her fury down on the men who threatened her family, and blood and bullets fly. (978-1-60282-012-8)

Naked Heart by Jennifer Fulton. When a sexy ex-CIA agent sets out to seduce and entrap a powerful CEO, there's more to this plan than meets the eye…or the flogger. (978-1-60282-011-1)

Heart of the Matter by KI Thompson. TV newscaster Kate Foster is Professor Ellen Webster's dream girl, but Kate doesn't know Ellen exists…until an accident changes everything. (978-1-60282-010-4)

Heartland by Julie Cannon. When political strategist Rachel Stanton and dude ranch owner Shivley McCoy collide on an empty country road, fate intervenes. (978-1-60282-009-8)

Shadow of the Knife by Jane Fletcher. Militia Rookie Ellen Mittal has no idea just how complex and dangerous her life is about to become. A Celaeno series adventure romance. (978-1-60282-008-1)

To Protect and Serve by VK Powell. Lieutenant Alex Troy is caught in the paradox of her life—to hold steadfast to her professional oath or to protect the woman she loves. (978-1-60282-007-4)

Deeper by Ronica Black. Former homicide detective Erin McKenzie and her fiancée Elizabeth Adams couldn't be happier—until the not-so-distant past comes knocking at the door. (978-1-60282-006-7)

The Lonely Hearts Club by Radclyffe. Take three friends, add two ex-lovers and several new ones, and the result is a recipe for explosive rivalries and incendiary romance. (978-1-60282-005-0)

Venus Besieged by Andrews & Austin. Teague Richfield heads for Sedona and the sensual arms of psychic astrologer Callie Rivers for a much-needed romantic reunion. (978-1-60282-004-3)

Branded Ann by Merry Shannon. Pirate Branded Ann raids a merchant vessel to obtain a treasure map and gets more than she bargained for with the widow Violet. (978-1-60282-003-6)

American Goth by JD Glass. Trapped by an unsuspected inheritance and guided only by the guardian who holds the secret to her future, Samantha Cray fights to fulfill her destiny. (978-1-60282-002-9)

Learning Curve by Rachel Spangler. Ashton Clarke is perfectly content with her life until she meets the intriguing Professor Carrie Fletcher, who isn't looking for a relationship with anyone. (978-1-60282-001-2)

Place of Exile by Rose Beecham. Sheriff's detective Jude Devine struggles with ghosts of her past and an ex-lover who still haunts her dreams. (978-1-933110-98-1)

Fully Involved by Erin Dutton. A love that has smoldered for years ignites when two women and one little boy come together in the aftermath of tragedy. (978-1-933110-99-8)

Heart 2 Heart by Julie Cannon. Suffering from a devastating personal loss, Kyle Bain meets Lane Connor, and the chance for happiness suddenly seems possible. (978-1-60282-000-5)

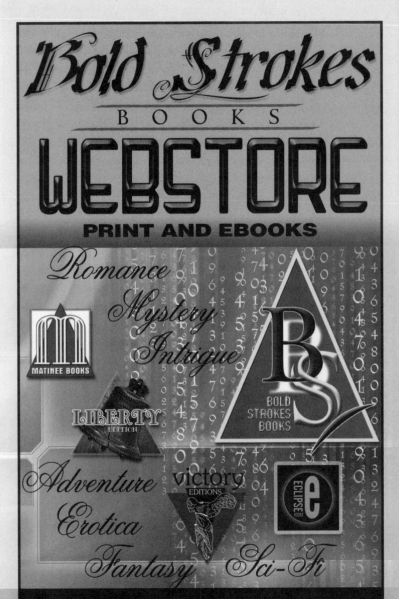